FROM RUST

THE FALL

FROM RUST

THE FALL

DANIEL JAMES CLARK

Published by Vulpine Press in the United Kingdom in 2024

ISBN: 978-1-83919-577-8

www.vulpine-press.com

To my parents, who managed the delicate balance of encouragement and pressure that made me who I am.

AUTHOR'S NOTE

From Rust: The Fall is unlike most second books in a trilogy. This is a parallel novel, taking place at the same time as *From Rust: The Forge.* While the two books share many characters and scenes, they provide vastly different perspectives on the story. To everyone who has decided to stick with this story through another telling, I am sincerely grateful. It's a lot to ask for someone to indulge a story once, and to ask you to do it again seems unthinkable. It's what this story called for, however, and I am so glad you've come along to see what more there is to discover.

Delta Sieve Information Transfer Request Number: 000421984

Origin Search Parameter: Harbingers of the Fall, Creeds, Tenets, Beliefs, Doctrine

File: HTF_IndoctrinationSample_CoreTenets

Request Status: Approved

Method: Manual Type Transfer

Delivery Location: Internal GovNET System at Station Taycher_07

Requested Text:

We, the Harbingers of the Fall, hold true that the system of governance known as Human Civilization no longer serves a purpose other than Systemic Survival. Any systems of governance that survived the Decline did so only as a direct result of an evolutionary struggle to maintain existence. Systems, both organic and systemic, grow and change according to a set of rules larger than any one individual.

We, the Harbingers of the Fall, hold true that Human Civilization has incorporated human suffering into its core structure. Despite, and even making use of, human suffering, Human Civilization operates independently of any moral structure that values human life.

We, the Harbingers of the Fall, hold true that Human Civilization must be dissolved and reconstituted. What shape the reconstitution of Human Civilization should take is not the concern of the Harbingers of the Fall.

We, the Harbingers of the Fall, believe that a Systemic Extinction should be brought forth to clear the way for any and all systems that may develop after the Fall.

We, the Harbingers of the Fall, hold true that any measures necessary to bring about the Fall are justified.

We, the Harbingers of the Fall, are willing to destroy even ourselves in this cause.

Someday, we will all fall. Fall with grace.

CHAPTER 1

Sergeant Major John Phillips sat alone at a desk facing his floor-to-ceiling window. He sipped from a glass of whiskey, now nearly empty. It had been poured from a bottle that now rested in the trash bin next to his desk. He picked up a small red plastic data chip from beside the glass and turned it over in his fingers. The metal contacts that allowed for data transfer glinted in the low light. He tapped it on the desk, and then with a swift gesture, tucked it into a breast pocket on his uniform. The uniform itself had the look of a garment that had already seen its best days. Once a deep teal with rich crimson accents, it was now the color of faded grey and rust. The same could be said for John. He was a decade past retirement age, and while he preferred to remain quiet in important rooms, he could still command attention when he needed to.

From his living quarters on one of the top floors of the United Entities Mechanized Warfare Academy's central tower, he looked out toward the ridge that surrounded the base. Diverting his gaze, he could see the cadet barracks buildings below. No doubt there were a few cadets still running around, hiding in the darker corners to get in a bit of extracurricular activity before bed. Others were probably roaming the base, looking to start some trouble to help them establish an identity. The new semester was just beginning, and the students would be feeling adventurous.

John tilted his glass back, draining the watery remnants within, and stood up. His quarters were spacious, but sparsely furnished. Along one wall were outdated framed commendations, certificates, and photographs. Mementos from a career spent in domestic counterinsurgency operations, and later helping to found mechanized warfare as its own military discipline. Along another wall were three much more modern projected screens. Information was still displayed from the last time he'd used them. On one was a tactical scenario he'd been working on for use in the introductory mech piloting class he taught at the Academy. The scenario involved a large command mech being surrounded by enemy forces, but he hadn't worked out most of the details yet.

The glow from the screens was the only light source in the room. It was just enough for John to find his coat and the front door. As he put on the coat, his back cracked unpleasantly, and he left for the elevator down the hall.

Once inside it, he pressed on the screen for the ground floor and waited to see if the sudden lurch of the elevator would bring any of his liquid dinner back for dessert. He was lucky and was greeted only by a rumbling belch. Once at the ground floor, he turned and headed toward the cadet barracks buildings, intending to clear his mind a bit before heading out on his errand with the red plastic chip in his pocket.

While not specifically within his role at the school, he often took it upon himself to patrol the grounds after curfew when he felt up to it. Besides, the night air was good for him, and it allowed him to collect his thoughts. The habit also provided excellent cover for when he needed to leave the base occasionally.

John worked his way past each barracks, looking into the deeper shadows for any movement. If he did see any, he tended to ignore it and continue walking. His mere presence in the area was usually enough for amorous cadets to zip up and head home for the night. If they were still there on a second pass, he usually stopped and flushed them out with a few gruff shouts.

Tonight, the shadows were still. He made his way toward the main parade yard, where the cadets lined up every morning for a company uniform inspection before being dismissed to their courses or assignments. Standing in the center of the meticulously manicured lawn, Phillips patted his pockets in search of cigarettes. He drew out a package and tapped one into his hand. He lit it by flicking the tip sharply, causing a customary crackle as a small charge ignited the tip. He drew in deeply, allowing the smoke to fill him completely for a moment. When he released, he envisioned his anxiety escaping with it. It was a modification on another, less toxic, method proposed to him during an annual mental health evaluation many years ago. It was surprising to him how often the practice actually worked. There was always the chance, however, that it was the nicotine and not the visualization that was doing the trick.

When he finished his cigarette, he continued his walk through the darkened school grounds. Taycher Mechanized Armor Base, or simply Taycher as the whole compound was known, trained pilots and support crew on the Academy side of the base and manufactured mechs on the other. The goal was to synchronize the process so that personnel and hardware could be joined and shipped off as efficiently and frequently as possible.

When he reached the vehicle garage, he loitered outside for a few moments, mentally preparing. The garage was set into one of the high base walls, allowing for trucks to be taken into town, or for cadets to go on approved excursions in the desert. While he wasn't technically violating any regulations by going out at night, he always had a fear that someone would ask him what he was really up to with these trips outside the base.

John made his way inside and used his officer codes to unlock one of the trucks. As he climbed into the seat, he knew his entry would still set off a security alert with whoever was on duty. When he turned the ignition, a voice came through the communications panel.

"Is that you, John?" a voice asked. He sounded tired, like the alarm had roused him from an unscheduled nap. "Another drive tonight?"

"Yeah, it's me, Adams." John keyed in his authorization code again. "Go back to bed. I'll lock her up tight when I get outside, I promise."

"I wasn't sleeping," Adams said unconvincingly. "You know my watchful eyes are always open."

"Sure thing," John said. "Just wake up when I get back and let me back in."

The radio stayed silent this time, and the broad bay door in front of him rolled open. John pulled out into the desert night. He stepped out of the truck and as he closed the door behind him, it slowly blocked out the pool of light spilling onto the sand. With the door secured, he drove off in no particular direction at first. John was eventually headed to a point on the high ridge a few miles away, but the route he took needed to be different each time he went out. If he was ever asked about these occasional drives, he would say they were a lot like his strolls through the Academy grounds. He was looking for anyone where they weren't supposed to be. But he'd never been asked. No one cared about a drunk instructor surely nearing retirement who liked to go out for an occasional drive. Indeed, Adams had probably already alerted a number of cadets that the coast was clear inside the base walls.

The sky tonight was clear, with a nearly full moon hanging high and cold above him. He drove aimlessly for a while but eventually made his way to a spot on the ridge that overlooked a low desert valley to the north. The ridge made a nearly complete circle around the base, and behind him, he could still see the central spire of the tower he lived in, its glass glittering in the starlight. He killed the engine and leaned back into the well-worn leather chair of the truck. The moonlight made the landscape out in front of him look almost alien, a distant and cold world. A world with no Academy, no United Entities, and no revolutionary cells operating across the globe. It was a wonderful place to live for a moment, an untouched desert with endless stars in the sky above. It was a place where his guilt had no reason to exist. This particular exercise wasn't covered in his yearly shrink visit, but he liked to think it was effective.

John waited in the truck at the edge of the ridge for a while. After he determined he hadn't been followed, he cracked the door a few inches. He dropped the small red data chip onto the pool of light that spilled out from inside the cab, then closed the door and turned on the engine. His trip back to the Academy was much like his trip out to the ridge. He meandered around and over the tops of dunes, but eventually ended his journey in front of the same door he'd left through. After he sent a customary coded radio burst, it opened just as slowly as it had closed before, and he drove the truck inside.

"Welcome back John," Adams said over the radio. "Leave the truck in there. I'll fill it back up. It's not like I've got much else going on tonight."

"Thanks," John said. "I should turn in. You keep those eyes open."

As John made his way back to the central tower, he ignored a few rustling shadows. As he rode the elevator back up to his room, a conflict of ideals thrummed in his head. He took off his coat and laid it over a chair, allowing the soft sound of fabric in the stillness to calm him. He turned the illuminated screens on his display wall off one by one until the room was only lit by what moonlight streamed through the broad window. He walked to his desk and picked up the empty glass, remembering that he'd finished off a bottle before he left. He set the glass back down, vowing not to open another.

He had a shiny new class of cadets coming in for their first Live Piloting course the following morning, no doubt full of hope, wonder, and potential. It would be better to avoid having a substantial hangover when he greeted them. He thought about it again, about what that potential would someday become, and sat down at the desk. The wooden chair, an antique he'd been gifted by some dignitary years before, creaked under his weight.

The cadets he taught at the school all eventually left to become new cogs in a machine he'd lost faith a long time ago. He opened the lowest drawer of the desk and removed one of the bottles from the shadows within.

~

John was standing in front of a huge, rusted piece of junk the techs at the salvage yard had told him was beyond repair. In the light of day, he'd been able to push his doubts aside and get himself out to the Live Piloting training fields early. He'd even managed to smile when he saw the broken-down mech sulking in the morning sun.

No matter how many times he did this, he always enjoyed it. According to the requisitions office, this mech had sat in mud for months awaiting extraction from a swamp on the southern coast. It now looked more like an excavated relic than anything that had once strode nimbly across the landscape. He stood outside with it, in front of a large rolling garage bay door, waiting for the cadets inside to receive their new uniforms. When the door opened, he would be the first person to see their faces when they realized what "Live Piloting" was actually going to be: repairing this dilapidated and broken piece of machinery. When John had first started teaching this course, each class had been given a newly minted mech, fresh off the line. More often than not, by the end of the course the mech was battered and in need of major repairs.

One year, though, he had decided to change that practice. He'd pulled a mech from the scrap yard, and made the cadets work on getting it to function again. He had found that the cadets who actually worked to get their mech to function tended to have a greater respect for the machine at the end of it all. From then on, the practice had become a tradition for the Academy.

It was also a tradition that the cadets further along in their coursework made up wild and extravagant stories about their first day of Live Piloting. Senior cadets often talked about how amazing seeing their mech was for the first time. John had done nothing to discourage the behavior, all for this moment, and the long process that would follow.

At last, the garage door began to roll open. The early morning sun would be blinding the cadets inside, obscuring their view of him and the mech behind him. No doubt some of them believed they could see a regal and beautiful mech through the glare. And then came the part he was waiting for. He had to work at not allowing himself to smirk as all of their eyes adjusted to the bright light.

Their crestfallen and devastated looks were priceless. It was a moment of transition easy to watch, knowing how fulfilled they would be once their mech was eventually fully repaired. These cadets were at the beginning of a journey, and he would be their guide. This moment often let him forget completely about what their training was actually for, what the mech behind him had been doing before it had fallen into disrepair. What these cadets would go on to do once they graduated. It was surprisingly easy to simply focus on teaching the skills and push aside the future.

He could feel the cadets' eyes shift from the dilapidated mech and onto him. John must come as a surprise to them as well.

Most of the instructors at the Academy were in the prime of their careers, or perhaps just outside of it.

Attempting to mask his limp, earned on a painful day many years ago, John walked toward the cadets, knowing that anyone looking hard enough would likely notice it anyway. His eyes landed on each of the new cadets as he approached. Some still seemed to hold onto some hope that this was a joke.

"I'm not going to bother taking roll," he said. "It's safe to assume that every last one of you is here. Is that right?"

"Sir! Yes sir!" The cadets rang out in a nearly simultaneous effort that crashed through his head.

"Quiet down!" He reached beneath his hat and rubbed at his scalp. Whatever age had done to him, he'd managed to retain most of his hair, even if it was all grey. That had happened before he was even thirty, though. It had helped him to look more wizened and respectable early on in his career. Now, past his prime and past most people's retirement age, it fit him. "I've got a hangover and I don't need any of that.

"Now that we have that rule out of the way, I'll go on. You will call me Sergeant Major Phillips or Sir. That, or Screwdriver if I become drunk enough in rec time."

He paused and looked at a cadet who was staring at the rusting bulk outside with an amused expression. He consulted his roster, with his internal optical display, and was alarmed to see that the cadet's name was Zakary Lockwood. John found himself staring at the cadet for longer than he should, thinking that the name must be a mistake. He broke his gaze and then launched back into his customary speech.

“This mech is a piece of shit,” John said, swinging his arm out toward the mechanized combat armor unit behind him. “I know that. Whatever it can do, you’re allowed to do with it. If it walks you can walk it. If it jumps, you can jump. Whatever you get to do with it will be as a direct result of your ability to make it work.”

“You, the short one.” He pointed at Lockwood. The boy’s face was too familiar. “What were you expecting from today?”

“Just what I’ve been told, sir,” the cadet said and clenched his jaw. “That we would be piloting a mid-to-high-level mech with the most advanced controls and abilities, sir. To prepare us for the units we’ll eventually pilot in the field.”

“Thank you, Lockwood,” John said, still searching the cadet’s face. “Now, I’m pleased to be the first to tell you that everything you’ve been told about Live Piloting is bullshit. It’s a little joke you get to be in on now. Yes, it’s a scrap heap. But now it’s yours.

“This is an early model Jotun class Orion, used in the later years of the Decline, so it’s old.” He walked back and forth in front of the line of cadets. “Please be sure to note the line on the hull that shows how far it was submerged in mud before it was recovered from some farmer rebellion in the deep southern regions. Please also note the missing equipment. When a similar mech needed a replacement set of armor for its right arm, this one gave an offering. This mech has been slowly pieced out, baked in sunlight, and soaked in rain until yesterday’s reassignment to Educational Service by yours truly.”

John spread his arms in a mock show of benevolence. “Eventually you’ll name the goddamn thing.” He paused to let the information sink in. "Just don't call it the Phoenix. It's not original."

He followed this speech with instructions on how to boot up the mech, then asked each cadet to start it themselves.

"You'll each go, one by one, into the cockpit and attempt to boot the mech yourselves. While each cadet cycles through, everyone else will walk around the unit creating a log of whatever you think is important. A loose bolt, rodent damage, rust, missing pieces, whatever."

He pointed at Lockwood again, aware that it must have looked like he was picking on him, but he had to know if it was the same kid. "Lockwood, you're up first. I hope you were paying attention."

"Yes sir," the cadet said, and walked to the rear of the mech.

John followed behind him and watched as he pulled at the cockpit door fruitlessly for a moment before finally getting it open. Zakary stepped inside the mech and was taking in his surroundings when John stepped into the doorway. The cadet turned around, and in the shaft of light from the open door, John could see his eyes. It was him. No longer a child, but unmistakably him. Somehow, fate or bad luck had brought them together again.

"Good luck, Lockwood," John said as tears began to well up from deep within him. Afraid the cadet would see, he slammed the door shut and then leaned against it to compose himself.

After a moment, he walked out to where the rest of the group was examining the outer components of the mech. When Lockwood finally got the mechanized combat armor fired up from inside the cockpit, the class immediately took a step back. As it rose from the ground, long dormant pistons and joints cracked away years of mud and sediment. A cloud of dust drifted away from the unit as it equalized and asserted its own space. The audible gasp from the cadets allowed him to snap back into the present moment.

"Some life in her yet," John said to the group, "Who's next?"

~

Alison took in a deep breath of dry desert air and she welcomed the harsh gleam of the midday sun. She'd been away from this landscape for too long. Her work had carried her away from the mountains she'd grown up surrounded by, and even just being this close made her homesick. All that would have to wait, however. She had one more assignment before some long overdue rest time. Time with her family. Time with her daughter. Time with Eva.

She returned to her small single-seat all-terrain vehicle. It had four large wheels, was open to the elements and had handlebars like a motorcycle. It was good for the rough, uneven roads of the west, and could overcome obstacles even a fully equipped tank might have trouble with. This one was like many of the vehicles the Harbingers had scattered across the western region to aid in courier assignments. She was but one of the many such couriers moving information across the landscape at any given time, but this vehicle was a bit more special to her. She'd inherited it from her father when she'd left her home to join the cause. It featured modifications she'd engineered herself over the years to make it more suited to her driving style, and it came with the added benefit of knowing it was well maintained. On more than one occasion she'd resorted to using one of the general-use vehicles marked on her maps and had found that they either had no fuel or were simply inoperable.

Removing a pair of old sunglasses, she'd also taken from her father, she pulled off her hat, pushed her hair back away from her face and donned a helmet. Innumerable nicks and scratches on its presumably once glossy surface belied a lifetime of use. She'd found it during her first trek across the desert near the wreckage of a less fortunate traveler and had kept it with her ever since. She tied the strap underneath her chin, the plastic clip having been broken off long ago.

Her most recent string of assignments had kept her out for months and had taken her further north than she'd ever been. And, while she liked to think of herself as a valuable asset to her cause, the high volume and nature of the information she had been moving lately indicated another level of trust had been imparted on her. Most of the information she'd transferred had been completely indecipherable to her. There was still at least a day of travel ahead before her final pickup, but she was making good time. Thinking about her rapidly approaching leave time, she fired up her ATV, relishing the guttural sound of the gasoline powered engine. It contained a secondary electric engine of course, but when she was this far out, it often made sense to use up the combustible fuel first and rely on the quieter electric engine once she was closer to civilization.

As she raced across the desert, she pulled up a trail of dust behind her. All she needed to do was pick up a small intelligence drop from a regular informant and then ferry it to her regional commander. After that, she'd be able to rest.

CHAPTER 2

At the end of his Live Piloting class, John had the cadets move their new mech into the training hangar. It lumbered slowly across the wide-open training fields, but it eventually made it to the massive hangar. Inside, there were a number of mechs they would use throughout the course to run simulated battle scenarios.

After John dismissed the cadets he went upstairs. No one would be coming out to the hangar for a while, and he needed some time alone. Once he was safely inside one of the upper classrooms, he looked out the window. Below, the class was headed back toward the huge grey walls of the base. Zakary Lockwood stood out to him, a smaller cadet with an even stride that seemed to somehow reflect his intelligence. John allowed himself to wonder how Lockwood could even be there. The last time John had checked in on the boy, he'd still been so small. He had just begun his coursework with a state education facility. Had it really been that long?

John watched as the cadets made it to the large rolling door to the base. One by one, they headed inside, and then they were gone. He let out a deep sigh and felt a little lightheaded. With Lockwood out of sight, he was able to relax and turn his mind to other tasks. Right now, the only thing he needed to do was get back to his room.

~

John kept his head down as he walked, trying his best to avoid the gaze of anyone that might want to strike up some conversation. He managed to make it across the campus and back to the bottom of the central tower when he felt a tap on his shoulder. He closed his eyes, sighed, and turned around. To his surprise, he found the Academy Director, Vice Admiral Katherine Scholl, in front of him. His heart raced, thinking of his drive to the ridge the night before.

She was the epitome of a well-pressed military leader, all edges and flat, even tones. The deep burgundy uniform she wore should have been the same as his, but somehow it felt brighter the way she wore it. When he thought clearly enough to read her face, he found a smile, and so he relaxed. She wasn't there to ask him about his late-night drives.

"How do our new pilots look, John?" she asked. "I heard they actually got their mech to fire up."

"Yes, sir." He always felt strange when senior officers tried to speak to him as if there wasn't a power structure in place. When it happened, he reverted instinctively to strict protocol in hopes that they would follow suit. "The cadets were able to perform well, considering the tradition of surprise we've upheld."

"A 'tradition of surprise,' huh?" She smiled, clearly an advocate of the tradition. "That's a good one. Giving them a piece of junk, you mean. Also, how many times do I have to ask you to call me Katherine unless we're court-martialing you?"

"Sure, Katherine." He put on a smile. "I'll try to remember that. Is that the only reason you wanted to talk?"

"No, actually." Her smile faded, and he felt something unpleasant was coming. "I was wondering if you'd be able to pick up another course. We're pretty thin right now and we need someone on urban tactics. You spent some time in an urban police force, is that right?"

"Yes, sir. Katherine," he corrected himself. "I did twelve years under whoever was holding down Columbus at the time. I think it was Sisko?"

"That's great." Her face brightened a bit. "That's the sort of experience we need to be teaching these kids. It's a morning assignment. Urban Tactical Response and Operations. They've been basically teaching themselves for a week now, and that's no way to work with first-year cadets. I'll send you the details."

"Alright." John couldn't remember actually agreeing to teach the course, but there didn't seem to be any turning back now. "I'll be sure to catch them up as fast as I can."

"Thank you, John," Katherine said. "I'll have to owe you for this one."

He nodded and turned back to the elevator to punch in the code for his floor. When he turned back around, Katherine was already walking away toward the administration offices at the other end of the compound. It was probably good that she hadn't asked him to join her for some perfunctory round of drinks. The less he interacted with her the better. The last thing he needed were personal relationships inside this place.

He stepped into the elevator when it arrived and, with a customary lurch, it began to ascend the tower toward his room. As the Academy portion of Taycher Mechanized Armor Base receded below, he began to see over the looming outer walls. The mountains in the distance were already catching the warm hues of a sunset that promised to spread across the sky at any moment. With any luck, he would be able to shut his blinds before that happened. He was feeling lost, and a beautiful sunset would only cloud his thoughts further.

As he stepped into his room, he saw that it was too late. The window at the end of his room had already become a floor-to-ceiling watercolor. The sight should have soothed him, but instead he felt a familiar place inside him grow cold.

"This world is not that beautiful," he said quietly to the room. "You're a fucking lie."

John reached over and pressed a button that adjusted the opacity of the glass until it blotted the scene almost completely. He took off his coat and walked to his desk, a familiar routine. On the desk was a new bottle of whiskey, another familiar routine. He had a deal worked out with the woman that cleaned his room to bring a replacement whenever she found an empty one in the trash. John did this to avoid any uncomfortable conversations at the common store on base.

He sat down and pulled up a display on the screen at his desk. After sorting through correspondence, he added the Urban Tactics course to his schedule. He grimaced at the start time, earlier than any course he'd led for years. Once done with that, he opened a copy of his Live Piloting course roster. For a long time, he simply stared at the name Zakary Lockwood on the list. The cadet's eyes should have been proof enough, but John still wanted to be sure. He tapped on the name, and a file began to load in the background.

While he waited for the information to be passed through the maze of wires and security filters into his display, John poured a glass of whiskey from the fresh bottle on his desk. Digital file transfers had been easier in the early days of his career. He used to have everything he wanted basically instantly. But the lessons of the Decline had been taught harshly. Information had become a lethal weapon before anyone had understood the scope of the problem. Networks that were once used to maintain the vast and spreading global digital world had either gone offline or actively worked against the users when the Decline had reached its peak. Some of the costliest battles of the Decline had been fought over wireless networks. The kinds of skirmishes fought with conventional bullets and bombs had only accounted for a third of known casualties.

Now hard-wired systems, with daily inspections of the physical connections, were the only way information travelled in a network. One of the only ways information could theoretically be taken from a network these days was through a complicated manual transfer involving authorization from a number of independent points in the network. Of course, this hadn't stopped the practice of network terrorism. It just made the process a bit harder. Malicious agents needed to be physically connected to any network to alter or access it.

John glanced down at the mess of wires underneath his desk. He spotted the familiar boxy addition immediately. It was a contraband access port spliced into his network cables. He'd installed it himself to get information off the network easily. That was another part of his agreement with the maintenance woman. She turned a blind eye toward what was a blatant disregard of digital security policy. John wasn't alone in this transgression of course. There were probably a dozen or more of these unauthorized splices in the network throughout the base installed by other people. Sometimes it was just faster and easier to siphon information onto a portable device than to wait for the proper authorization from the network. While the use of a splice like this was typically for efficiency, the potential hazards were immense.

His display emitted a pleasant tone that let him know his file had been approved and was ready to be viewed. The file consisted of a dense set of tables filled with information alongside a photo of Lockwood staring forward without expression. John reached out and opened one of the subfolders from the table of information, a section titled Enlistment Parameters.

This portion of the file detailed the specifics of Lockwood's testing, vetting, and any notable recommendations for service. These things were notoriously dry and hard to read, but this was unmistakably the same Lockwood. The file informed him that the cadet had been in state custody since childhood. The beginning of the file said he'd been placed into care after an "unspecified incident" where he was left without a guardian. These two words, buried deep in a personnel file, were the only record of an event that had altered the courses of both their lives.

John focused in on those two words, "unspecified incident." He and his Urban Response Unit had made sure to scrub the official record of any specifics after they'd sorted through the aftermath of the incident. They hadn't met any resistance from their superiors. After all, civilian casualties were a known variable in their line of work. They did tend to undercut their apprehension metrics, and any way they could pump their numbers was good in the long run. It meant heavier budgets and more substantial bonuses.

Still, no amount of scrubbing records had been able to erase John's memory. It was still clear enough to him that he began to feel himself drifting back.

He felt his heart stutter uncomfortably in his chest just like it had when he had prepared to kick in the door all those years ago. He'd been on point, and two of his men were flanking either side of the door. It was an unassuming apartment door, a dark shade of red if he remembered correctly. He kicked at the door and felt the frame splinter in under his boot. The enemy terror cell must have reinforced the wall there because the door held. Precious moments ticked by as he kicked at the door again, this time sending it flying open.

John wasn't sure who fired first. There had been times in his life when he remembered clearly firing off the first short burst of shots into the apartment. There had also been times when he remembered the sound of bullets passing very near his ears before he even stepped into the room. Each time he allowed himself to remember the event, he felt it lacking in specific details that would help him answer the question of fault.

There were a number of people living there, terrorists working to undermine Stability and the authority of the United Entities. This part of his memory could have been lifted directly from an Urban Tactics textbook. They'd moved through the apartment, dodging bullets and clearing each room of hostile occupants with pinpoint precision. After the haze from gun smoke and debris in the apartment had begun to settle, the reports from his team came back.

"All hostiles neutralized."

Then, in the relative calm that had followed, he'd heard crying. It was muffled and terrified. John looked around for the source, but the cries couldn't have been from inside the unit. They'd already cleared it. His mind clouded as he realized the cries were from a child.

Along one wall, peppered with blood and bullet holes, he could see light coming in from the apartment next door. The cries had become impossible to ignore, and John found himself disregarding his team's calls to stay where he was. He walked back out into the hall and forced his way into the apartment next door. A child was sitting at a fold-up card table, a shattered bowl of cereal in front of him with the milk still dripping onto the cement floor. Against one wall was the crumpled form of a woman.

The child began screaming and tried to get up from his chair. His legs didn't reach the ground, and he slipped in the milk as he tried to scramble over to his mother. John tossed his rifle to the side and rushed forward before the child could reach her. John held onto the boy as he shook with grief and terror in his arms. There were no words in this moment, only the terrified screams Lockwood had continued to make. All John could think to do was increase the pressure of his embrace and rock back and forth in an attempt to quiet the child.

John snapped quickly back into his room inside the Academy tower. The memory of Zakary crying in his arms had threatened to bring on another memory, and John refused to look back there now. Shakily standing up from his desk, he was breathing in big gulps and wiping tears away furiously.

That day had forever altered the shape of his life. He'd used what little influence he had to make sure the boy had been selected for government protection. If that meant forging a few test scores, so what? The child had been through enough, and there was no way the scores were even going to be accurate after a traumatic event.

After that, John had requested a transfer out of Urban Enforcement and into the National Service. The Mechanized Armor Corps, then a relatively new branch, had been a creative place for him. The wing of the military that had been handling the new clunky machines was led by a number of young, inexperienced officers, and it was thought that Phillips could bring some sense of order to the program. He had poured himself into the task, eager to build something new.

Most of his own training had occurred during real-world operations on battlefields across the globe. The more formal Taycher Mechanized Warfare Academy hadn't been constructed yet. Indeed, it had been John and the other first-generation pilots and officers that staffed the school when it opened. Now John was one of the few remaining pilots from early days still clinging to their post. When asked about his reasons for remaining in service, as was increasingly happening, he told people that quitting would be surrender. Appealing to a sense of patriotism and duty was usually effective, and it was easy enough to fake.

His real reasons, the reasons he drove out to a spot on the ridge at the edge of the base perimeter, he kept to himself.

John thought for a moment and then decided to take another drive. He didn't have another drop scheduled for another two weeks, but he drained his glass and put on his coat anyway. He took the elevator and went directly to the vehicle garage without so much as a glance into the shadows along the way. Once he was inside the vehicle, a familiar voice came through the radio.

"Two drives in one week?" Adams asked. "You joining the kiddos for their party in the desert? Or is something wrong?"

His tone was vaguely patronizing, but underneath it was a sincerity that John didn't like. No one here mattered, and he needed to remember that. This school, and the base attached to it didn't matter.

"I'm fine Adams," John said. "Open the damn door."

"Whatever you say," Adams said.

The door opened, and the radio remained silent as John pulled out into the night. He drove directly to the ridge, fending off memories and conflicting thoughts about his allegiances the entire way. He remembered the concerned looks in his co-workers eyes all those years ago when word began to spread through the precinct about what had happened to his own family. He distinctly remembered the way the clouds had hung low and oppressive in the sky, almost suffocating the city beneath it by sealing in the smog as he'd driven home.

"Stop it," he said to himself, and he allowed tears to flow unabated from his eyes as he neared the ridge.

Seeing the boy, now a man, really, in his class had stirred up a whirlwind of dust he'd long neglected to sweep away. The thoughts continued to come at him, fast and harsh. He pulled up to his customary spot on the ridge and shut the engine off. He flashed the headlights into the distance three times, paused, and then flashed them once more. He got out of the truck and tried to clear his head. Bending down to the dirt, he retrieved the small red chip he'd dropped there the night before and put it in his front coat pocket. The wind raced up and over the ridge, whipping away his breath as soon as he released it. He'd left his hat in the car, and the wind tugged at the thick grey hair he refused to cut more than twice a year. Let them reprimand him for it. He'd like to see what that could bring.

After a few minutes of waiting, he drew out a cigarette and flicked the tip. It began to smolder. Smoking in high wind was often a disappointing endeavor, but it was something to keep his mind centered. Below him he saw a shadow move, finally. In the light of the moon, he could see that it was his usual contact.

"You're not supposed to be here Phillips." Her voice was young, but full of authority.

"I'm tired," he said simply.

"Fuck you man." She climbed the loose gravel at the top of the ridge and took a moment to catch her breath. "I just drove god knows how many miles to get here, and now I have to put up with your pampered ass telling me you're tired. At least give me one of those."

She covered the last few yards to him and held out a hand for a cigarette. The woman's name was Alison, and she'd been his main point of contact for drops that required an actual conversation. Most of the time, however, they didn't see each other.

He would drop one night, and she would pick it up the next day.

She shrugged off a tattered backpack and let it fall to the dirt. It was hard to tell through the layers of gear and clothing, but John knew she was of a strong but thin build, like a long-distance runner or similar. She kept her dusty brown hair pulled back through a brimmed cap more faded than his own. The skin that showed on her face and hands was deeply tanned by the sun. Everything about her appearance spoke of an efficient and lean existence in the desert.

"These things are poison for someone young like you," he said as he handed over the red chip and a cigarette.

"They're poison for everyone." She took the offered items, pocketing the chip. "Also, fuck you. You're not my dad."

She smirked and leaned against the truck. They smoked together in silence for a few minutes, the wind ripping at their clothes. John wanted to talk to someone. He needed to bounce his thoughts off a real human being and not some therapist in a tower he could only tell half of the truth.

"I'm tired of being in there and pretending," he said, waving one hand back toward the Academy.

"Just enjoy your posh suite and shut up, Phillips," she said turning to look back at the school in the distance.

"It's harder than you know," he said. "Hating them is hard sometimes. Most of them have no idea how bad it is outside. Some do, I suppose. The kids who tested high and were conscripted from the general population probably still remember a bit of what it's like outside the Enclaves. But it's hard to hate people who just think they're keeping the world stable."

"You have to be joking." She tossed her cigarette into the wind. It landed a few yards away in a shower of sparks. "Stability is a fucking joke to everyone outside the Enclaves and military bases. A lottery for access to healthcare? Forced labor postings, food rationing? They sponsor our schools, but just long enough to determine who's good enough to skim off the top. They take anyone who might be able to help and pull them into their Enclaves." There was a bitter sadness in her voice. "You of all people shouldn't need a goddamn list."

"I know, I know," John said. His paternal reflex was to reach out and hug her, but she was right that he wasn't her father. It wasn't his job to fix her. And, he realized, it wasn't her job to fix him either. "It's just hard to be inside and know everything that's going on outside. I feel like there are no right choices left."

"John." Alison looked at him, seeming to question whether or not she should continue. "Stability is the lie the powerful have manipulated to control the lower class. They used it to save themselves during the Decline. The massive tower…" She broke off and waved her hand back at the central tower of the school where John's room awaited his return on one of the top floors. "The massive, rotten, towers of the world governments and corporations nearly fell under their own weight when the Decline began. They told us, as they still do, that through hard work and partnership, the governments and corporations were able to save the world from a complete collapse. They drill it into us from every billboard, classroom, and piece of media. 'Stability Before Self.' We're meant to believe that the United Entities are holding the world back from the brink of collapse, and that it is our duty to maintain that Stability."

It sounded like she was reading from a script. In a way, John thought, she was. He'd written most of what she was saying.

"But you know the truth." She was breathing heavily now. John saw in her eyes that as hard as they had drilled the Stability narrative into her all her life, she'd been pushing back just as hard. "You know this and so do I. The mangled towers of wealth and greed continue to rest on the backs of the people. Stability is not for the common people; it is for the masters."

Alison looked up at the sky for a moment and shook her head, and John fought off another urge to comfort her.

"I don't know why I'm even saying all of this to you," she said. "Don't they call you the Voice of the Fall? Thanks for the intel, John. You've done a great service to the Harbingers of the Fall." She rolled her eyes at him and headed back for the ridge.

"I want to see him," John called out before she could pretend she hadn't heard. "Next week. I'll make another drop, but I want to speak with him directly."

Her only responses were the continued shifting, sliding steps she took down to the bottom of the ridge. John let out a breath and realized his cigarette had burned down completely. He tossed the filter into the brush and got into his vehicle. The conversation, while not completely satisfying, had helped. Being able to speak plainly, however briefly, had calmed the dust storm inside him for long enough that he started to see the shape of a solution.

He made his way back to the base and waited for Adams to call over the radio. When he didn't, John sighed and got out of his truck. He went over to a panel beside the heavy rolling garage door. He used his credentials to access the terminal and sent a command override to the door. An audible click signified that the lock had disengaged on the other side. He didn't bother trying to open the door, knowing that an alarm would be blaring inside the security booth.

"I was just about to open the door," Adams finally said over the radio. "Just have a little patience."

It was possible that Adams had been busy with another task, but John was reasonably sure he'd been asleep. When the door rolled open in front of him, he pulled into the garage and turned off the engine.

"Don't worry about the door," Adams said. "I'll be down in a bit to re-engage the lock."

John turned off the power to the communications panel and stepped out of the truck. He wanted to think about what he'd say to Jim when he had his meeting next week, but his mind kept slipping off the topic. He'd been riding an uneasy sense of calm the entire drive away from the ridge. Any effort to force some concrete thought through that bubble was being met with resistance. He wanted to enjoy the moment of peace, he realized, and so he embraced it.

As he walked, he ignored a number of possible cadets around him. He wanted to get to his room before the feeling he was holding dissipated. He made it halfway to the tower when he saw a larger group than normal moving away from one of the cadet barracks.

"Well, shit," he said under his breath. There were at least six of them. Six cadets wandering the base this late at night was never a good sign, so he followed.

He watched as they made their way toward the central tower and main mech hangar. He could have stopped them then, but something he noticed kept him back. Lockwood was among the group. When they got to the tower, they all piled into the elevator at once. He watched it as it climbed the outside of the tower and stopped on the training deck. Maybe they were trying to catch up on their training hours with some late-night simulator use. More likely they had some prank or other mischief in mind. John pressed the button and another elevator on the outside of the tower opened up.

He didn't press the button for the training deck. Instead, he pressed the button for the security floor near the top of the tower where Adams was stationed. As the elevator climbed, he hoped he could get there in time. When the doors slid open, he realized his fears were misplaced. Adams was already back asleep.

On one of the video screens, John could see that Lockwood and the others were at one end of the long catwalk in the main hangar. They had placed all of the training pods there so that the cadets could look down at the fleet of mechs they'd one day be piloting. There was no direct access to the ground floor, but it looked like they were improvising. Lockwood had one of the pneumatic hoses that the techs used to power their tools in his hands.

"Wake up soldier," John said with authority. Adams jumped to attention and turned around. "Relax, Adams, I'm not here to reprimand you. But I did want to make sure you went down to re-engage that lock."

"Yes, of course sir." Adams saluted him stiffly.

“I said relax,” he stepped to one side and gestured at the open doors of the elevator. “Just go get it done.”

Adams got into the elevator and once the doors were closed, John turned to the security screens. Lockwood was preparing to jump down to the floor of the hangar and the others were eagerly encouraging him.

John didn’t need to know what they were up to. In fact, the longer he watched, the more tape he’d have to erase from the system. He used the camera controls to move the view of any camera that could see the group of cadets clearly just enough so that they were out of frame. Then he spent a few minutes deleting the footage of the cadets that existed. Luckily, he didn’t need to do much work. Only two cameras had captured any of the action, and even those had been barely in frame to begin with.

He waited in the security suite to make sure that Lockwood and his friends made it back out of the building. When he was sure that they were clear, he took the elevator to his floor and found his room. He’d have to report the incident to Katherine, but he’d make sure to do it in a way that protected the cadets. The report would be more to let Lockwood know he hadn’t gotten away with the stunt completely. John wouldn’t be in a position to protect him the next time.

CHAPTER 3

Alison walked away from the ridge, still brooding over John's newfound apathy for the cause. She drifted for twenty minutes through the desert sagebrush, attempting to shake any unseen tail that may have followed her from the unscheduled meeting with Phillips. The high brush was good for that. It was almost impossible to move through it without making a lot of noise. When she was satisfied no one had followed her, she stopped and shrugged off her backpack. She pulled out a small notebook and opened to a carefully drawn map of the area that spanned two pages. Various details had been copied from numerous road maps and atlases she'd come across in her travels through her years of service to the Harbingers of the Fall.

The ridge surrounding the base was sketched in the lower right of the page. To the northwest the city of Tonopah was drawn in with some detail. The city had grown exponentially when the United Entities had made it a hub for the western region's GovNET Core Utility. It existed near the center of the city, with an enclaved zone around it. Expanding from that orderly center was a sprawling city, now nearly deserted. Further out were the government housing camps, little more than boxes in neat rows. Out beyond even those, Alison knew there were illegal homesteads where people lived if they could manage it. Alison didn't have any of these communities on her map, for fear of the map being discovered and the homes being put at risk. Plus, she didn't need a map for those, she'd grown up out there.

A number of mountain ranges and major roadways were also laid in with care. Along with all of these details were a number of doodles denoting various caches of supplies or other points of interest. She had a dozen or so older versions of this map in her book. The act of mapping her environment allowed her to understand the landscape better than anyone she'd yet come across. It also helped to pass the time when she was between waypoints.

Though she didn't really need to, she used the map to orient herself toward her next destination: a symbol of a campfire and a bottle marked a few miles outside the city. There were a series of dates written next to it as well, indicating that there was a party happening there tonight. She located her ATV, hidden in the shadow of a particularly dense group of Joshua trees. She travelled with the electric engine now to minimize the noise she made. Once she got closer, she'd dismount and continue on foot. At some point, she would be able to find her way simply by following the sounds of the drunks. It was still a few hours out, so she packed away her map, put on her helmet, and began driving.

After some time, she crested a hill and heard the first drunken howl as it swept across the desert. Something big must have been happening at the party. With interest that she'd deny if asked, she left the ATV in another dense area of dry vegetation and pressed on. The laughter and screams came to a crescendo; they were the unmistakable sounds of a crowd cheering on some act of violence or other.

Before she was able to make it into the firelight, the cheering stopped and faded into more commonplace laughter. When she crested a final hill, the scene below her brought to the front of her mind the anger she had felt while talking to Phillips on the ridge. Some of the cadets from the Academy had crashed the bonfire party again. They were strolling from vehicle to vehicle, mingling with the Tonopah locals as if there were no gulf of disparity between them.

She spotted Jim helping a local man toward a truck. She didn't know the other man, but it looked like he'd received the worst of whatever violence she'd missed while fighting off sagebrush in the darkness.

"Jim," she called out as she entered the circle of vehicles. "I've got that fancy beer you like in my bag."

"Buck up, Herm," Jim said to the man he'd been helping. "Grab some ice from my cooler and put it on your face. While you're in there, you might want to get a drink too. You'll thank me later." When he'd successfully detached himself from the man, Jim walked over to where Alison was standing.

"The fuck kind of name is Herm?" she asked. "Sounds like something you'd say to cough something up."

"That sounds about right," Jim said. He walked with Alison back out of the light and into the shadows. "You get the data chip?"

"Yeah, I got the chip." She pulled the small red piece of plastic from her pocket and handed it over, a bit more forcefully than she'd intended. "Had a nice chat with Phillips, too."

"What the hell?" Jim's eyes flashed with alarm. "He's not supposed to be on the ridge tonight. That was supposed to be last night. I'm sorry he fucked it up."

"He didn't fuck it up, Jim. He wants to talk to you directly. Seems like he's losing it, being locked up with all those privvies. Sounds like he's second-guessing a lot of shit."

"I'll fix it." Jim squeezed her shoulder in a way Alison found vaguely patronizing. "We still need him inside. Shake it off and grab a drink, join the party. You're always so serious after one of these long courier gigs."

"I'm not staying around here while those fucking people are around," she said, pointing back at a drunk cadet. "Why the hell are they even here?"

"You know the saying, Alison," Jim said. "Enemies closer and all that shit. It keeps us in good with the students there, and anything that cracks the walls of that place is good. You know all this."

It's true, she did. Anything that could be exploited should be cultivated, and drunk cadets were potentially easy to exploit. They were certainly easy enough to cultivate.

"Yeah, I get it, but it just bothers me," Alison said. "Listen, I'll see you around. I need to get moving anyway."

"Sure." He seemed to be about to say something to try and convince her to stay, but evidently changed his mind. "I'll go see Phillips during his next scheduled drop. I'll get him straightened out. He's only got to stay there another few months, anyway."

Alison had already turned to walk away when she picked up on the last thing Jim said.

"What do you mean he's only got to stay a few more months?" She closed the distance back toward him in large strides. "Is something finally happening?"

"I don't know. I really don't." Jim held up his hands, apparently trying to think fast. She watched as he struggled to find a version of the truth he could tell her. "John's information is pretty much tapped out. We won't need him much longer. Listen, you don't need to make the new drop Phillips scheduled. Just start your break, and when you get back, I'll fill you in on what happens."

She nodded. He hadn't answered her question, but she knew when to stop pushing. "Have a good party, Jim." As she left, she reached down and opened Jim's cooler. She took out a beer, homemade of course, and took it with her as she made her way out into the cool desert night.

~

Alison crested a hill while riding her ATV down a disused power line road. Every few hundred yards or so, massive metal power line towers jutted from the desert and reached out toward the sky. Each steel beam frame was an exact copy of the next, stretching off into the hazy morning horizon. They imposed an unnatural order on the dry and undulating terrain. Occasionally, thick wires remained hanging between two or three of the towers, but most of the structures were barren. Power grids as vast as the ones seen before the Decline had become obsolete once alternative forms of energy production had become available. Now, across the landscape these outdated relics stood as perplexing monuments to a time that was quickly fading from public awareness.

Alison herself had never lived in a home powered by a traditional electric grid. Her family kept highly efficient solar panels on the roof, facing south. In turn these charged batteries that had only run dry once in her memory. Her small family had spent those two days huddled together in the living room when she was young. And although she'd been nervous, it had been exciting to spend uninterrupted time with her parents. She would be back there soon.

As she let the ATV coast down the hill, she spotted something up ahead. On the side of the road was an abandoned bus, stripped of anything worthwhile and blackened by smoke on the rear portion. Beyond it, she could see a cluster of abandoned structures; the remains of a once flourishing mining town. She turned away from the power line road and entered what was left of the town proper.

The seemingly ancient structures stood hollow in the calm morning air. These were older than any other ruins she would pass as she made her way to her family. The crumbling stone edifices and structures were from a time even before the repeating metal towers. She slowed her ATV and proceeded slowly, obeying some natural instinct to take her time here.

When she reached a tall brick structure near the center of town, she turned off her ATV and stepped down from it. The sudden drop in sound was jarring. The wind whistled as it flowed through the empty sockets of the stone buildings around her. The material used to build most of the town's structures had been quarried from nearby sandstone cliffs over a hundred years before.

Seeing these manmade structures wearing away from simple wind, rain, and time was always reassuring for Alison in a way. Their endurance was a testament to the power of mankind to create. More importantly for her, however, was how little of them now remained. It affirmed the overwhelming power of the Earth to reclaim anything humanity made.

As she stepped into the old bank building, she thought to herself that the slow process of time sometimes wasn't enough. That's why she had joined the Harbingers of the Fall, to aid nature in reclaiming those grand mistakes of mankind. Her parents had always adhered, albeit with some necessary deviation, to the law as she was growing up. Alison had fallen out of that routine as soon as she understood how her life was predetermined. She understood, on some level, that the Doctrine of the Harbingers of the Fall was just a new set of laws. But she liked to think that the fact that it was always growing and changing made it inherently different.

She stopped for a moment to decide if that was true. Government at its core was subject to change as well; it was once even integral to the whole idea in some places. The difference, she decided, was that the Harbingers of the Fall were dedicated to bringing it all down. It wasn't trying to assert power like every movement before it. Satisfied, she headed further into the building. The ground floor was open to the elements, its roof having long since collapsed. The floor below, however, had retained most of its structure. She took the stairs near the back of the building and headed down into the basement.

The basement floor was one large room interspersed with support columns at regular intervals. The ceiling here had only one hole large enough to note. A pillar of light fell in through it and pooled at the center of the empty room. There, two stunted Joshua trees and a creosote bush had grown through the disintegrating wooden floor. As she walked toward the illuminated oasis encased in this sandstone tomb, she remembered when she'd first found it.

It had been her first trip smuggling a parcel between two cells for the Harbingers. She'd found this town by accident while making her way across the desert. At first, she'd set up camp upstairs, taking comfort in what little security the crumbling walls provided. Then, as she spread out her gear, her compass had fallen through a crack in the wooden floor. After locating the stairs, she entered the basement, laid down near the trees, and rested for hours as the sun passed overhead. Then, once it cooled down outside, she moved on. This sandstone building had become a welcome way station for her on almost every trip since.

Now she approached the trees and looked for her cache of supplies she kept well stocked. She found the spot easily, having been here many times before. Beneath a loose board, she withdrew a small metal ammunition box with a hinged lid. She opened it and found everything was in the same place. A handful of energy bars, a few odds and ends for first aid, and a small notebook she used to log her travels were tucked inside. She withdrew an energy bar and the notebook. Opening to the next available page in the book, she sat down just outside the area of light coming in through the roof. She noted her direction of travel, and the date.

When she reached the column she used to notate her reason for travel, she hesitated. Above this empty space were a number of other entries: Information Transfer, Supply Transfer, Unknown Parcel Transfer, and many others. The most common one listed was a standard Information Transfer. The log served no official purpose for the Harbingers, and its sole reader was also its writer.

As she sat on the cool ground, Alison picked at the splintered wood of the floor and tried to think up a short explanation for her travel. While the log wasn't important to anyone but her, she'd always felt the need to be precise in her work. Perhaps that precision was something the government had managed to instill in her. If it was, she thought, she'd use it against them.

She could write in that she was traveling through here on leave. That felt too formal for how important this extra time was for her, though. She breathed in deeply and wrote down what she often couldn't face herself. Alison wrote down the real reason she was using her limited time away from the cause to see her family, instead of getting belligerently drunk somewhere. She wasn't going home in order to see her mother and father, not entirely anyway. No, she was going to see Eva. Alison wrote the three letters of her daughter's name into the reason column of the book and put it back inside the metal box. Just a few hours of rest in the cool basement and she'd be back on the road.

A handful of cadets stood at attention beside their desks as John entered the classroom. He was late, and as disheveled as he normally was. The cadets looked at him with well restrained contempt, but he felt it nonetheless. As he looked over their faces, he noticed just how young they all looked. Years of teaching Live Piloting to the older cadets had made him forget that the school brought in what were essentially children and formed them into soldiers. Over a period of four years, cadets learned all the skills necessary for deployment. It was amazing the difference two years made. By the time these cadets took his Live Piloting course, they would have been through two years of harsh conditioning and an almost impossible slate of technical courses.

The class he was teaching today, the Urban Tactics course Katherine had volunteered him for, was a sort of hybrid course. Some days would be spent in the classroom, while others were spent doing live exercises on the skills they'd need to move into the higher courses.

"Sit down and stop staring at me like that," John said. The class sat down immediately and in unison. "My remarks today are going to be very short because I don't really want to be here."

A couple of the students frowned at this but remained largely composed.

"I served twelve years in a tactical police unit," John said. "I understand your previous instructor left a couple of weeks ago on a deployment. I see that you've been able to keep to the structure of the course in his absence, but your live training metrics have begun to drop. That's what I'll be focusing on. From what

I've gathered, everyone here seems to have a grasp of the mechanics on paper. I'll let whichever of you was leading those lessons continue to do so."

A number of the cadets turned their heads to a girl in the front row. John looked at her as well and saw that she looked tired. Her dark eyes were locked forward, giving no indication that she'd suddenly become the center of attention. Though her youthful round face made her look even younger than her classmates, she still managed to hold her composure in a way that spoke of dedication beyond her peers.

"Listen." He consulted his roster and found the girl's name. "Listen, Vesnina, you don't rise into a position of authority by sitting on your ass. You stepped up to lead the course and you'll see that through. Consider it a lesson in leadership. For now, I'm going to go over some things that aren't in your texts.

"First of all, the diagrams you study are good to know, but they assume that things will go certain ways. What you need to be prepared for are the things that fuck up your diagrams. When you enter a home to clear a group of terrorists and find that they've completely remodeled the inside of it, you need to know how to adjust and continue on.

"And to address a concern I'm sure you've all either voiced before or wanted to, yes, this does all eventually apply to piloting mechanized armor. Sure, mechanized armor units don't engage in the same kinds of missions, but the same principles will apply. When you're moving as a team on foot, in the air, or inside a billion-dollar mech, you're faced with the same kinds of tactics and consequences. My goal with you will be to turn you into a cog that can be placed into any team and function well.

Consider yourselves lucky. I teach Live Pilot training, and I'm far too lazy to create two lesson plans from scratch. What you'll be getting on your live training days will be modified mech scenarios. Consider that your reward for keeping up on your studies without an instructor.

"Now, I'm pretty tired, so I'm going to nap in the corner while Vesnina here leads you in whatever it is you're supposed to be doing this morning."

John didn't wait for any questions. He walked to the back of the classroom where he intended to nap. Instead, he found himself listening as Vesnina led the class in a discussion on the proper formation for a room breach. The class went smoothly enough. Vesnina must have had a teaching credential somewhere in her elective history. She showed a talent for keeping her fellow cadets on task. In order to keep herself ready to educate them, she was probably working a day or two ahead of her classmates.

When they'd finished the day's work, the class filed out, leaving Vesnina alone at the front of the classroom. John stood from his chair at the back of the room and approached her as she was packing away her materials. A bit on the small side for a cadet, she had her dark hair cut short. John couldn't shake the image of her as a child who shouldn't be there. That she should be somewhere else, not worrying about the best way to shoot her way through an office building.

"You've got a real talent for instruction," John said. "How are you faring in your other courses?"

"You're asking if I can maintain this and not let it affect my other responsibilities," Vesnina said, her tone dry and calm. "It's already biting into my other work, but I've managed it so far."

"I can take over next week," John said, surprising himself. The tired look in her eyes made him want to help. "Just keep it up until then and I'll make sure that you receive an additional credit for the work."

"I didn't do it for credit," she said, turning back to continue packing up her things. She didn't say it, but he could tell by the shift in her posture that she was relieved.

"You didn't, but I'll make sure you get it. You did it because you didn't want this to set you and your classmates back. The administration here wouldn't care if this pushed you all back another year."

"I've worked too hard to get this far and end up held back by some staffing error." A brief flash of anger crossed her face.

"That's not all, is it?" he asked. Her determination was too sharp, something other than typical exceptionalism was driving her. "You're more committed than most of the cadets here. Something has you motivated to get out of here and into service as fast as possible."

"My sister," Vesnina said. "She was on New Wall Street during that recent attack. The media reported no casualties, but you know how these things work. The whole incident only made the main feed because it would have been impossible to ignore the CorNET outages it caused. I need to get out of here and stop them from doing it again."

"I'm sorry." John felt rebel counterarguments begin to pulse through him. His sympathy for the girl underwent an internal assault. “I’ll see to it you’re able to move forward at the pace you deserve,” John said after a pause.

Vesnina said nothing, only finished loading her bag. John stepped away while a battle of ideals continued to burn within him. He imagined it as a flame slowly crawling across a piece of paper. He closed his eyes and pressed his fingers into the bridge of his nose. Vesnina, and countless others, were on the glowing edge of this paper, caught in the place between paper and ash.

Even if the conflicts were to end tomorrow, those caught in the ember line would still be lost. Vesnina’s sister, Lockwood’s family, and so many others drifted behind, in the flurry of ashes on the wind. In his mind, he imagined himself trying to pluck the ashes from the air. Each time they darted away, just out of reach, and faded into the darkness. When he opened his eyes again, Vesnina was gone.

Alison woke late in the afternoon and found that the sun was already headed down for the night. Golden light filled the room from the hole in the ceiling. She swore under her breath and stood up. She’d missed almost a full day of travel. Closing the metal box tightly, she returned it to its hiding place and headed back upstairs.

By holding her hand up to the sky, she was able to use her fingers to measure how much daylight she had left. At least another hour. If she was careful, she could still make some progress toward Tonopah. Making camp in the ruins would have been the smart thing to do, but she was anxious to be on the road.

The last thing she needed was to drive off a cliff, but her need to close the distance was overpowering.

She mounted her ATV, made sure to turn the headlights on, and left the abandoned town. By sticking to the more established trails, she hoped to avoid any unfortunate accidents. Her headlights quickly became her only means of seeing the path ahead as the sun dipped behind the distant mountains. She slowed the ATV from her normal daytime speed to compensate for her limited vision.

After two hours of travel, the cold air began to sting her eyes. She was blinking them away as best she could, but she'd have to stop soon. While she wasn't going to make it there by morning, anything she could do to hasten that time helped. She decided to press on just a little while longer.

Far behind her on the ridge near the Academy, Jim would be meeting with Phillips in a week. She wondered about what Phillips might have to say. He would probably repeat some or all of what he had told Alison. He would say he's tired of living a double life, of living in his posh school, of ferreting information to the Harbingers whenever he felt like making himself feel better. Fuck him, she thought. What sacrifices had he made for the Harbingers? What gave him the right to give up?

She was aware that her anger didn't come from seeing just anyone leave the cause. She was angry that Phillips, specifically, was thinking of leaving. His voice made up a large part of the living document that was known collectively as the Doctrine. What did it say about the cause if that voice wanted to leave it all behind?

She ran over a large rock in the road and was startled from her train of thought. Fuck him. Just because he couldn't live up to his own words didn't make them untrue. His uncertainty couldn't invalidate her own sacrifices. What she was doing had to count for something. She refocused on the road ahead and put Phillips out of her mind. What mattered right now was getting home.

~

In the morning, Alison finally saw Tonopah from a high point on the trail. It was merely a smudge on the landscape she recognized, not because it looked like anything in particular, but because she'd seen it many times before. The final stretch of this trek was always maddening, with the city never seeming to get any closer. But, at the end of her travels was the promise of Eva's embrace, and that had gotten her stiff body moving in the predawn light.

There were at least another four hours ahead of her to get into Tonopah. She would also still need to cross through the city, which would add another hour or so. Of course, there were safer routes that went around the city, but those would have added even more time.

She revved the engine of her ATV, pouring on speed until she felt control slipping away. She held that line, right at the point where she could still maneuver the vehicle racing across the desert. She felt the machine below her slide along the dirt road and countered with her own weight to correct it. It was exhilarating, pushing the boundaries of what she felt she could handle. The rush was enough to take her mind off the trip itself for a while.

Then, remembering how isolated she was, Alison slowed the ATV down to a more reasonable speed. No one would take this dirt road for days, maybe weeks. If she lost control out here, she'd be left to make her way into town on her own, assuming she could even move. No, that wouldn't do, she thought to herself. Instead, she looked on ahead and watched as the city creeped toward her, more slowly now than ever.

~

The house was exactly as she'd left it. Every time she returned, the familiarity of the scene brought her immediate peace. It sat quietly in the center of a clearing, surrounded by a grove of thin old aspen trees. A single broad-branched cottonwood, older than the house itself swayed in the gentle wind nearby. It was close enough to the house that her father had needed to cut it back every year for fear of the windy months sending one of the branches through an upstairs window. A long wooden bench swing hung on old, frayed ropes from one of the lower branches.

She pressed on, stepping away from the tree line and into the warm midday sun. The screen door was still split open near the peephole, to allow someone inside an unobstructed view of the front porch. Even the ground felt the same as she remembered it, though the seasons must have made and unmade the grass many times since her childhood. The paint on the house was definitely the same shade of pale green it had always been. Any time she saw that color on another home, or on some faded billboard advertisement, she was transported back home momentarily. It was the color of her earliest memories. Now, it was peeling near the ground, where the elements had begun the slow erasure of time.

Alison wondered what she would say when someone opened the door. It had been so long since she'd last been here. As she reached out to pull open the screen door, she felt the sudden urge to run. She'd spent the last few days thinking about her eventual return, had played the moments over in her mind a hundred times. Now that it was happening, she wasn't sure she should go through with it. Maybe it would be better if she did find some dark room somewhere to drink and wait for her next assignment. What right did she have to show up in Eva's life so intermittently, just to disappear again each time?

As she pulled the screen door open, it felt like her body was moving by itself. She reached out to knock on the door and began to tremble. With each knock, she felt like melting into the wooden porch. No one answered for one agonizing moment, and then she heard a voice call from inside, clear and sharp.

"Mommy! Somebody's at the door!" Eva. It could only be her.

How long had it actually been since Alison had heard her voice? Months. No that diminished it too much. It had been nearly a year. Alison couldn't control herself as she began to weep openly on the steps. Before anyone could open the door, she retreated down the porch and into the patchy lawn. She faced out toward the wall of aspens, their leaves dancing idly in the breeze, and squeezed her eyes shut in an attempt to push back her tears.

"Allie!" Eva yelled from the doorway. "You're home! Can you stay?"

Alison took a deep breath and allowed a smile to come to her before she turned around. It was a true smile. She was happy to be there and she couldn't hide that even if she tried. What she did hide was her sorrow. That was her burden to bear, and no one else's.

"Eva!" Alison called out as she turned around. She opened her arms wide and accepted the weight of a child running at full force.

As she hugged Eva, Alison looked up at her mother, who was now standing in the doorway. She was smiling too. Even if Sandy didn't completely understand why Alison had left, she must have understood how Alison was feeling in that moment. Whatever disappointment or resentment that existed between them wasn't relevant now. Two mothers were being reunited with their children, and everything else would wait.

Eventually they all made their way inside. Alison saw her father through the back door, working on some piece of machinery or other in the backyard.

"He'll be in soon, Allie," Sandy said. "You know he has trouble with these things."

"What, you mean emotions?" Alison asked as she sat down on the worn couch in the living room.

Sandy didn't respond, simply gave Alison a look that told her to mind her words.

"How's Brian doing?" Alison asked, trying to conceal her interest. "I mean, does he still come by to see Eva?"

"He's doing well," Sandy said. "He picks Eva up every few months. He's due for another visit next month. Do you think you'll be here for that?"

The question was a loaded one, and Alison understood that the real question was if she would be staying indefinitely or not.

"No mom, I can only stay a few weeks." Alison said, looking over at Eva, who was coloring with the remnants of a box of crayons. Some were little more than colored pebbles. "I'll have to be out for my next assignment. And you know he and I can't be together, not as long as we're both fighting this fight."

"Why don't you stay, honey? Eva misses you," Sandy looked down at the stained apron she was wearing and brushed it self-consciously. "We all miss you."

"I can't. You know I can't." Alison felt her pulse quicken as she fought back against a confusing slurry of emotion. To calm herself, she continued to watch as Eva colored a rainbow. It arced high above a stick family of five like a protective dome. "Not while those in power still exert the kind of control..."

Sandy held up a hand to stop her. She knew the rhetoric, that hand said. Alison had given her mother the explanation time and time again, and Sandy didn't need to hear it all again. Fine, let this visit be as complete as it could be, Alison thought.

Jack walked into the room during this pause and looked down at Alison. She took her gaze off Eva and looked up at her father. He was an imposing figure; a broad man, who looked like he'd been destined to lift heavy things and turn heavy bolts. How much of that was genetics and how much could be attributed to his work assignments, she couldn't tell.

“Hi Daddy,” she said. The tone she took wasn’t completely under her control as she felt herself slipping backward in time.

His expression softened. Jack leaned down and kissed Alison on the forehead. “Welcome home, Allie.”

CHAPTER 4

John did take over the Urban Tactics lectures from Vesnina a week later. The extra work of preparing an additional lesson plan was a welcome distraction from the constant ideological struggle that continued inside him. Being faced with Lockwood during each of his Live Piloting classes, however, hadn't helped him. For these reasons, John only remembered his upcoming meeting with Jim the night before it was scheduled to happen. And so, he found himself spending a sleepless night pulling and compiling data so he would have something to give Jim out on the ridge. As stolen data siphoned onto a new small red chip at the spliced access port near his boots, he looked out over the darkened base below.

Lockwood would be asleep, that is, if he hadn't been pulled off on another ill-advised excursion by his fellow cadets. John smiled for a moment, lost in the thought of Zak having friends close enough to get in trouble with. He pushed the feeling away and refocused on his task. The usual assortment of fresh training materials and machinery specs were already loaded onto the chip. What he was pulling now were personnel records pertaining to who had been transferred out of the school recently. An uptick in deployments was interesting to John, and the

Harbingers might see some use in knowing exactly who they were dealing with out in the field.

As he loaded these files, he remembered his conversation with Alison and worked his way back through it. He tried to pin down exactly why he'd suddenly decided to request that Jim meet him in person out on the ridge. This trip into his memory turned out to be a mistake, as he found himself running back into what had caused his distress in the first place.

He'd been able to mostly ignore Lockwood during his Live Piloting classes, only interacting with him briefly when necessary. It had become obvious to him, however, that these tactics could only work for so long.

John poured a fresh portion from the nearly empty whiskey bottle in front of him and stood up. His mind was racing and sitting down was only aiding his building anxiety. He took his glass and walked to his wall of awards and certificates in wooden frames. He sipped his drink slowly and placed his hand on the glass in front of a framed news article. It was from the dedication ceremony at the newly created United Entities Mechanized Warfare Academy. In the photograph, John was shaking the hand of some politician or other who had been available for the event. It was possible it could have even been the person the base was named for.

John looked at the version of himself in the photograph. Even then, his eyes had looked tired and lost. He could have retired then and declined the appointment to the position at the school, but something had kept him working, something he couldn't quite pull from the air.

He shook his head, realizing that was a lie. He knew why he had stayed active. To stop would have been to surrender and relegate himself into obscurity. Even when the photo had been taken, John had been on the road to defecting. He'd known that leaving his post with the United Entities would have made him worthless to the Harbingers. Deeper than that, though, he simply hadn't been ready to become obsolete. The man in the photo was undoubtedly him, but something had changed in the intervening frames.

Not a week after the photo was taken, John had made his first contact with the Harbingers of the Fall. He'd made a connection at a small, dirty bar in Tonopah and began making scheduled information drops. In his first drop, he included a text file with some personal writings alongside the requested information. No one had said anything to him about the text file then, but he continued to send short essays on various topics along with the requested information at his scheduled drops.

The first indication that anyone had even been reading them came while he was watching news coverage on a demonstration being put down by force near the nation's capital. A sign that one of the protesters had been waving through clouds of chemical smoke made it uncensored through the broadcast and into his room. "Stability Serves The Masters," it said. At first he'd chalked it up to commonplace confluence of ideas. He and the fervent crowds of protesters were of the same mind, and it only made sense that they would be thinking similar thoughts. But it had continued to happen. During security briefings where he was only included as a matter of precedent, he heard his own words read aloud. They talked about his words as dangerous new rhetoric that must be stopped.

That had been years ago now. He'd had correspondence with leaders in the Harbingers since then that confirmed how important they deemed his words. Some of them had even been codified into a loose framework they'd begun calling the Doctrine. He'd become the Voice of the Fall.

John wasn't sure how he felt about being a voice for a movement. It was easy for him to sit in front of a screen and pound out angry words. It was easy for him to throw ideas into empty space. In many ways, the practice was therapeutic for him. The fact that the ideas were routinely quoted by bright-eyed revolutionary youth when they believed no one else was listening was strange.

Alison had echoed his own words the last time he'd seen her. John wondered how out of touch he had become, isolated in the Academy tower. He was far away from the front lines, safely tucked behind thick concrete walls while continuing to educate the next generation of oppressors. The hypocrisy of his actions every day wormed its way into his heart.

John brought his glass to his lips and drained it as he turned away from the frames on his wall. He sat back down at his terminal and continued working to assemble his respectable cache of information for the drop tomorrow. He wasn't sure yet if this drop would include a new essay. He wasn't sure he had another grand revolutionary edict in him. Being rendered obsolete could be nice, he thought to himself.

What place even was there in this world for someone like him? He was wavering back and forth on issues of morality so often that he couldn't count on himself to teach a course correctly, or to even remember when his next intelligence drop would be. His position was a tragic misplacement of trust. The school had a traitor, and the rebels had a pampered drunk. Lockwood had a careless protector. And his own family, they'd merely had the outline of a father and a husband. One that they'd tried desperately to color in themselves, only to find it vacant when they needed him most. He didn't want to touch that stovetop today, but he had no control over the thoughts as they returned to him.

He felt powerless against the torrent of memory that awaited him. John cast an unwilling glance over at a photograph on the wall that had become a blind spot over the years. His eyes could usually slip past it, out of fear that it would catch him by surprise. A smiling family beamed out at him from a photograph faded by years of sunrises and sunsets in this room.

Suddenly, and against his will, he was back in another time. When it happened, they'd been trying to reach him for some reason or other. Was it a birthday, he wondered? Was it his? They'd arranged a transport visa through the proper channels and had set out to reach him while he was back in the country on leave for a week. If he'd gone home to meet them there, or even met them halfway somewhere, they wouldn't have been driving through the night to reach him.

When they didn't arrive, he'd known something was wrong. The report came to him in the form of a physical letter, typed on paper and sealed in an envelope. It slid underneath his door late in the evening, and John had stared at it for an hour, terrified to reach down. The anonymity of a letter absolved anyone of the responsibility of being there when he found out.

Eventually, he picked it up off the worn stain-resistant carpet and held it in his hands. He ran his fingers along the crisp edges for a long time, feeling the lightness of the thing. His heart raced the same way it had on countless occasions just before he kicked the door in on an enemy terror cell. Then, suddenly, he torn the letter open and read the crisp, direct words inside in a frenzy. He crumpled the paper in his hands, feeling his fingernails bite into his palms.

The car carrying his family had run off the road on their way to him. No foul play was suspected, and a technical glitch in the car software had been blamed for the crash. Whoever had signed the note had offered their sincere condolences and offered to extend his leave by a number of weeks.

If it had been an act of terrorism, or even another vehicle, he would have had somewhere to direct his anger. But since it had no place to land, it curled in around him like a thick cloud of smoke.

Eventually, he made the drive back to his home after all. Once there, he sat in his car for hours, staring out through the window at their bright red front door. It was duplicated thousands of times inside the tiny droplets of water that clung to the glass. Helen had wanted to paint their door red for years. John couldn't remember when they'd actually done it, but he did remember the smile on her face as they stood together looking at it.

"What do you think?" he'd asked.

"I love it, John," she'd said. "Thank you."

"You're welcome," he'd said and leaned down to kiss her.

"It looks awful." She had laughed and looked up at him with caring brown eyes. "But I've always wanted a red door."

By the time he finally decided to get out of the car, he had been staring at the door for so long that his eyes were raw and dry. He opened the door of his car and walked through the soft rain. It had been almost a mist, like walking through a falling cloud. He stopped in front of the red door, picked up a stone frog near a pot of wilting lilies, and removed the spare key from the hidden compartment there. The key, sharp and unused, slid into the lock neatly. He opened the door and continued to stand in the rain, looking into the shadows within.

The idea of going into the house felt wrong somehow. He felt like burning the entire place to the ground rather than face what was inside. Instead, he stepped across the threshold, the hushed sound of the rain disappearing behind him as he closed the door. He walked through the house, slowly. His tears passed effortlessly down his face, through his untamed beard and onto the floor, leaving a dotted trail on the tile behind him. He made no attempt to wipe them away. The effort would have proven fruitless.

His fingers passed over surfaces as he walked through room after room. Walls, picture frames, bookshelves, countertops, and knick-knacks with meanings faded by time. His path ultimately led him to the bedrooms. Feeling unable to face the horror of entering Mary's room, he'd leaned in and quietly closed her door, as if she were sleeping inside and he didn't want to wake her.

He turned to his own bedroom, the one he had shared with Helen. The door was open, as it always had been when he'd been able to spend more of his time there. He reached inside and turned on the lights, letting the scene wash over him as if it were a photograph. His tears became unrelenting sobs as he stood in the doorway. It would have been better if the room were perfectly clean. On the bed he saw a pile of clothes that needed folding. A pair of slippers, never to be used again, were tossed into one corner. The bed wasn't made, as if Helen just left and would soon be coming out of the bathroom, wiping away the remnants of toothpaste from her mouth.

John sank to his knees then and gripped the worn carpet with both hands. His screams had alerted the neighbors, and police eventually found him motionless in the bathroom with a bathrobe clutched to his chest.

Now, back in his room in the desert, high above the Academy, his tears were flowing freely once again. They danced along rough stubble and down onto his desk. With this pain unleashed inside him once again, he found himself opening a blank document on his terminal. He began typing a resignation letter from the Academy, citing his emotional inability to continue on.

The act, and his conviction connected with it, cleared his head somewhat. Tomorrow, he decided, he would say many of the same things to Jim and also vacate his position with the Harbingers of the Fall. Let everyone solve their own problems. He'd decided that his place as a cog spinning between them would be over soon.

When he finished his resignation from his post at the Academy, he opened another blank document and began a final essay for the Harbingers of the Fall. John doubted if this one would ever receive the same veneration as his others, but he wrote it anyway.

~

John woke earlier than he could normally manage, feeling well rested and confident. He planned to turn in his resignation with Katherine and have that checked off his list before he headed to the Urban Tactics course. The decision to retire had helped him with the immense weight his shoulders had borne for years. Every movement as he got ready, and every floor the elevator climbed toward the Vice Admiral's office seemed to lighten the load. On the top floor, the elevator doors opened, and he was presented with a clean white hallway leading to Katherine's front door. He marveled at the fact that the entire floor was dedicated to her quarters. Sure, most of it was meeting rooms and suites for foreign dignitaries. But a significant amount of room was still dedicated to her working and living spaces. She even had an office in the administration building on the other side of the base.

When he reached Katherine's door at the end of the hall, he raised one hand to knock but hesitated. He thought back on what had led him there. Images of things he'd done under orders, and the things he'd done for the Harbingers passed through his mind.

John tried to make a mental calculation. Had he done enough to quit now? Were his scales even? Would this surrender leave him free, or burdened in the end? Before he could decide, the door opened. Katherine stood in the doorway, dressed and ready to start her day. She looked surprised.

"John, good morning." She took a step back into her quarters. "I was just headed out. Is there something I can help you with?"

"Yes," John said. Then, realizing his hand was still raised to knock on the door, he let it fall. "I can come back if this isn't a good time, sir. Or I could schedule something with your aide."

"How many times..." She began to chastise for not using her first name, but evidently read the seriousness in his expression. "No, now is fine. Please, come in and take a seat."

John followed her into an office just inside the door and sat in the offered seat. The view from Katherine's quarters was very similar to his own, with one major difference. From the top of the tower here, the base wasn't visible below when simply looking out the window. In order to see the walls, he would have to walk close to the glass and look down. He preferred the view from his own quarters. Being able to see the base below kept him grounded. If he had the view from here, he might have been able to forget how enclosed he really was.

"You said you had something to tell me?" Katherine had already taken her seat behind an acre of polished glass that served as her desk. She looked across it at John with her eyebrows raised.

He broke his gaze from the window behind her and refocused on Katherine herself. He cleared his throat and lifted the two flimsy sheets of paper in his hand into view above the desk. After placing them on the desk with a deliberate motion, he turned them around so that the words were facing her.

Quietly, she reached out over the glass and pulled the offered papers into her own hands. She leaned back in her chair and read what he had written. In the silence, John could actually hear the wind rushing by the windows outside. Being this high off the ground was unsettling. It's probably why he had chosen urban tactics instead of the Air Force all those years ago.

"We can't keep your courses staffed without you, John." Katherine put the resignation letter on her desk. "This says you want to be relieved of duty at the end of the week. I'm sorry, but I'm not going to be able to allow that. I know you're long past the customary retirement age, but you can't leave now."

"I'm tired," John said. "I've given everything I have."

Even as he said it, he knew it wasn't completely true. He had more to give, he just wasn't sure which side, if any, deserved what was left in the tank. Which engine would he pour his last measure of energy into? He wanted to hold onto it, use it to power his own engine until he ran out and drifted on into the void. He was tired of shifting gears constantly. He was tired, yes, but he hadn't given everything, not yet.

"Can you stay on until the end of this cycle?" Katherine asked, almost pleading. Her tone caught John by surprise. Normally cool and short, sometimes bordering on clinical, she sounded concerned. "I can authorize your resignation at the end of the semester if that's still what you want. I suppose if you decided to press the issue, you could probably push this resignation through over my head. I wonder if you wouldn't mind just thinking about it for a few days?"

The weight John had felt falling away as he rode up in the elevator began to pile on again. Maybe he could stay. He could finish his courses and leave without the burden of his students also on his shoulders. He could still back out of his duties with the Harbingers tonight on the ridge.

"John," Katherine said, pulling him out of his daze again. "Will you at least think about it?"

"I'll stay as long as I can." He stood and walked back to the door. "But no longer than that." He'd meant that last part as a joke, but it had come out stiff and cold.

Katherine said something else before he left her office, some words aimed to thank him, but he wasn't listening. Once he was on the other side of the door he sighed deeply and headed for his classes. Perhaps tonight he would be able to offload a different burden.

~

"Watch this, Allie!" Eva yelled as she leapt from the branches of the tree next to the house. She landed on the ground and collapsed into a roll, and sprank back up with her arms out wide.

"Be careful!" Alison snapped at her automatically. "I mean, please be careful. You could break your neck."

"I was being careful. I was jumping carefully." Eva stuck out her tongue. "You sound like mom."

"Yeah, well you sound like me." Alison shook her head and sat up, brushing the dry grass from her hair. "Want to go for a walk?"

"Sure!" Eva said, finally letting her arms drop to her side. "An exploration, you mean?"

"You could call it that." Eva had a wandering spirit that Alison liked to think came from her.

They started walking down the main drive that led to the house. The branches of the aspen grove were knit together in a canopy of rustling leaves. As they walked, Alison occasionally kicked a rock off the drive and into the trees. She liked to think that if she walked this path enough times, she'd eventually clear them all and the path would be completely smooth. Of course, she knew that weather and erosion would always bring more rocks to the surface, but the task was pleasant and nearly automatic by now. She looked down at Eva beside her, and noticed that she too was occasionally kicking an errant rock into the trees.

"Hey, why are you doing that?" Alison asked.

"Doing what?" Eva sounded defensive, as if she thought she was in trouble. "I'm not doing anything."

"It's nothing bad," Alison laughed and kicked another rock. "You're kicking rocks off the road."

"Oh. I don't know," Eva kept her eyes down, looking even more intently for errant stones now. "You and Daddy do it. I just want to do it too."

Eva stopped suddenly and kicked at a larger stone, this one half buried in the hard-packed dirt. When it didn't come loose, she immediately set to work trying to extract it with her hands. As Alison watched Eva work, she wondered idly what other habits and quirks the family had given her. Eva finally got her fingers beneath the rock and pried it out of the ground. Alison was impressed by how large it was and bent down to help Eva move it off the road. In the place where it had been, there was now a large depression in the road. When Eva stood up, she clapped her hands together sending a cloud of dust drifting down the lane.

"You gonna fix that?" Alison asked, pointing at the hole in the road. "Always be sure that what you're doing to fix something doesn't actually make it worse."

"Now you sound like Daddy." Eva stuck her tongue out like before, but she quickly set to work scooping some dirt into the hole.

When they continued down the road, Alison was lost in thought. Was her commitment to the Harbingers akin to removing a rock and leaving the hole unfilled? Returning to a place of uncertainty that had been coming more frequently than she'd like, she wondered if there was some truth to what Phillips had been saying on the ridge. She shook her head and pushed back on the idea with effort. No, she thought, her work with the Harbingers was more like destroying an established interstate. What they were doing was clearing the ground for fresh roads to be built. Just when she'd decided she was done with this bout of mental gymnastics, she stared to wonder what the rocks represented in her analogy. Were the countless rocks that would be upturned akin to human lives? In the end, was it worth the effort and the loss to clear the landscape?

"Allie what's that?" Eva pointed off the road to a dense area of brush where a wheel could be seen sticking out.

"Good catch!" Alison left the path and walked to it. She pulled away some of the branches and uncovered her ATV. "I thought you might want to take a ride."

As an answer, Eva began to help with the branches and other forest detritus. When they had it cleared, they mounted the machine and set off back for the house. Her father would be happy to see that she'd kept it in such good shape, but it could use a bit of work before she headed out to get her next assignment.

CHAPTER 5

During his evening rounds through the grounds of the base, John stuck to his typical routine. He let his eyes fall into a natural rhythm, searching the deepest shadows of the Academy. His ears keyed in on rogue sounds and assigned each one a meaning. Some sounds were easily explained. Wind bumped a sheet of metal against one of the maintenance sheds. A long, drawn-out cry came from one of the dozen or so feral cats that had somehow made the base their home. Another class of sounds was only slightly harder to recognize: an unintelligible whisper, the sudden zip of a uniform, or the soft promises of young love. As he passed a dark corner near one of the cadet barracks, one of the second class of sounds stopped suddenly, then resumed once they thought he was out of earshot.

He made his way to the garage, found his usual truck, and got inside. After working through the social conventions with Adams through the radio, he was out past the wall quickly. The rolling door shut behind him, and he was alone once again.

John took his time getting to the drop point on the ridge. As he meandered among the dunes and sagebrush, he went over his arguments in his head as best he could. John had only spoken with Jim directly on a few occasions, having mostly interacted with Alison when an in-person meeting was required. Each time he had met Jim, he'd come away with the feeling that Jim was getting more out of the encounter than John fully understood.

When John had first started his life as a rebel informant, that feeling made him feel useful. More recently it had begun to make him suspicious. If he was being used, he wanted to know how. Tonight would be different though, tonight would bring those feelings to an end. He was going to amicably withdraw from the Harbingers, and let them drift away by themselves. The Harbingers were strong enough now, he was sure, that the structure would hold without his contributions. It might even flourish when someone inevitably filled his position as the resident rhetoric craftsman.

How ironic was it that he should be worried about the structure of a movement whose deepest stated goals were to destroy the very societal structure it resided in? Perhaps that little hypocrisy was necessary in order to achieve this goal. It would have made a good topic for him to explore in an essay, but he allowed the thoughts drift away as he neared the ridge. Instead, he began going over his speech. The words were neatly arranged in his mind, and all he needed to do was get them out in the right order.

John parked at the edge of the ridge and flashed his lights twice, then once more after a brief pause. He turned off the engine and stepped out into the cool desert air. The wind was at a low for the area, but still occasionally gusted up the ridge and tugged at his clothes. He pulled out a cigarette and lit it by flicking the end. As he drew the smoke in, the tip glowed fiercely in the night. He exhaled and looked down at the cigarette, watching as the glowing edge of the paper and tobacco crept slowly down the length of it. The burning edge.

"Are you going to smoke that or just watch it burn?" Jim's voice came from the darkness.

"I don't want it." John laughed, thinking about the question metaphorically. He shook off the accumulated ash and offered the rest of the cigarette to Jim as he joined him at the truck.

"Thanks," Jim said, taking the offered cigarette. "So, why am I here? What's so important you had to talk to me directly?"

"I want out," John said simply, his prepared speech evaporating from his mind.

"I thought you might say that. I'm sure you understand that I wouldn't be here just to relieve you of duty. I've got more important things to do, we all do. The next time you want out, just don't show up for your next drop."

"Sure," John said, a little crestfallen. "That makes sense."

Jim was right, though. If the Harbingers were going to accept a resignation, John would have never heard from anyone in the Harbingers again. No, Jim being here could only mean that he intended to persuade John to stay.

"We only need a few more weeks," Jim said, smoking the cigarette slowly. "Then you can leave knowing you did all you could to help the cause."

"What I've done isn't enough?" John asked.

"No, it isn't," Jim said. "Not yet. We have one more task you can help with. It's big, John. We've got our own mech pilots in training. Our technicians are working with the information you've supplied over these years so that we can create our own units. We will soon have actual mechs waiting to be piloted. But, what we need is one of the training pods to bridge the gap, and we need it soon. Getting the amount of information stored on one of those pods out of the Academy would take too long."

John looked out over the landscape as he waited for Jim to deliver the specific ask. Would this really be the last time, or would the Harbingers try to string him from one seemingly important task to the next?

"We need you to leave the garage you use to come out here unlocked on a specific night coming up. Just leave a point of access for our team to enter." Jim took a long drag from his cigarette and then looked at John. "We also need you to deactivate the automated security on the base so we can move a small team in and retrieve a simulation pod."

"Are you serious?" John asked, shaking his head. "That kind of breach could expose me, you have to know that."

"We've thought about that," Jim said. "Command wants to send a second team to extract you while the other one deals with the pod. They think we could use your skillset directly within our ranks, especially now that we've got our own pilots. And having the Voice of The Fall closer to home wouldn't hurt either. You're being wasted holed up in that school."

John took a long, deep breath and exhaled. He wished he hadn't given Jim his cigarette. "I don't know what anyone is fighting for anymore Jim. I'm not sure if what I have to say is worth the risk."

"I'm sure that's how you feel now," Jim said. He must have sensed John's thoughts and offered him the cigarette back. John hesitated at first but took it.

"I think your doubt has more to do with your isolation than anything else," Jim said waving back toward the Academy in the distance. "You're locked up in there and you've lost sight of what's actually going on out here. Did you know the glorified health lottery isn't accepting anyone over the age of forty now? Or that families are being expected to live on rations only half as nutrient as they were two years ago? Will you just consider joining us? Come take a look at what's going on out here and if, after seeing what's at stake, you still want to leave, we won't stop you."

John looked back at the Academy. It was a hulking complex of structures surrounded by massive walls. The central tower, black as the night that surrounded it, reached high into the sky like a broken lighthouse. He put the cigarette to his lips and inhaled.

"I asked to resign from the Academy today as well. I think I'll still be there until the end of this cycle. Two months. I can give you until then to get this plan worked out. Let me know when to let the teams in. Just promise me you'll do your best to keep it quiet."

"Of course, John," Jim said. "The Harbingers owe you a lot for the words and information you've contributed over the years. We wouldn't be the same without you, and we can't do what we're planning without you either."

"I'm not sure if that's a comfort for me right now," John said. "But I think you're right that I've lost touch with things outside. If I had someone else inside, someone I could talk to, maybe I could have sustained my resolve."

"You know how it works," Jim said. "Even if we do have other operatives inside with you, we couldn't tell you. Operatives are stronger in isolation. You're more attentive to your task and less likely to make mistakes."

"I know all that," John said, taking one last drag off his cigarette and handing it back to Jim. "I think I may have written that part. Send your teams to get the training pod. I'll do what I can to help. I'll think about going with your second team, but I already feel like I'm running on empty."

John sat back at the desk in his room. He turned the red chip he'd loaded with data over in his fingers. He'd intended to give it to Jim out on the ridge two nights before. Instead, he'd somehow found himself committed to the cause more deeply than he had ever been. Sometime before the end of this cycle, he would leave a door open, disable the automated security on base, and be whisked away into the actual ranks of the Harbingers. The cause he'd watched falter and flail in its infancy was now strong enough to orchestrate a raid and bring him in. Maybe what he'd been doing would count for something after all.

John looked at the chip held between his thumb and index finger and thought about wiping it clean. One of the documents on it, his last personal message to the Harbingers, had been meant as a cry to reappraise the scope of the conflict. It was a short piece that likely wouldn't have seen more than a handful of readers before being discarded. Some of the words inside it, words like 'lost' and 'depleted,' still rang true to him. Others like 'faithless' and 'disillusioned' somehow didn't, not quite. He hadn't been able to end the piece with a concrete suggestion for what the Harbingers of the Fall should do next. John hadn't been able to bring himself to condemn either side, at least not completely, and he'd ended it cryptically.

John spoke his words from the piece aloud, recalling them clearly. "I fear now that the actions of the Harbingers and the crimes of the United Entities have begun to burn in such a way that it will never end, merely smolder on. I urge any reader to consider their place in this conflict. Consider the fact that it will take more than the sacrifices of a single generation to heal the damage done by our disease. The cause of the Harbingers of the Fall may ultimately demand the sacrifices of your children as a price for the future you seek."

John ran over these words again in his mind, remembering how they'd flowed from him like water. He thought again of wiping the chip clean, but instead stood and walked to the framed photos and certificates on the wall. He stood in front of the picture of his family, then lifted it from its place and held it.

There was no glass in the frame. He hadn't replaced it since the night he'd broken it while halfway through a bottle of whiskey. By opening the back of the frame he was able to slip the red chip behind the photograph. As he hung the photograph back in its place on the wall, he let his fingers rest there for a moment. Someday he would revisit the words and find out which ones still felt true.

~

"Not that one," Jack said from beside her. He reached out and pointed at the lug nut down and away from the one she'd been about to tighten. "Just remember to move in a star pattern. I don't want your wheels coming off halfway down the drive."

"I know, Dad." Alison rolled her eyes but moved to tighten the one he'd indicated. She knew the process and would have done it properly if he hadn't been hovering behind her making her nervous. "This isn't the first wheel I've put back on this thing."

"You sure? Because it looked like you were about to just go around the lugs in a circle."

Alison looked over her shoulder at him and smiled. Just a few years ago they'd have fought about this furiously. She wasn't sure when, but more recently these kinds of interactions just ended with them lightly jabbing at one another verbally. The argument they would have had sort of drifted in space between them as some sort of vague possibility both real and imaginary. Given the scope of the real-world conflicts going on around them, and their acute awareness of them, the smaller disagreements and differences seemed much less pressing. Also, perhaps she was just older, and this was how relationships progressed.

She finished tightening the last lug nut, following the star pattern he'd taught her when she was Eva's age. As she stood up, she accepted help from one of her father's strong arms.

"Just make sure you watch that belt," Jack pointed to the spot on the ATV where a worn drive belt had caused him to make all sorts of concerned noises. "If it goes out on you, you know how to replace it right?"

"It wouldn't be the first time I changed a belt in the field," Alison took her tool back to the back of the ATV and put into the trail box. "But yeah, I'll keep an eye on it."

He eyed her a bit warily but then shrugged and jerked his head slightly. The movement was so slight that anyone else might not have even noticed it, but what it said was, "Good job, now do you want a beer?"

"Sure," Alison said. She closed and latched the trail box and then walked with Jack to the back of the house where there was some shade.

Alison sat down in an ornate old wooden chair that looked like it had once been part of a set. Jack went inside, and Alison could hear Eva asking him for something. Whatever she'd asked for, he would probably do. Unlike when she'd been young, her father had a hard time saying no to Eva. So, Alison had a few minutes to herself in the backyard. She was only able to close her eyes for a moment when she heard the back door open again.

"What'd Eva want?" Alison asked.

"I'm not sure," Alison's mother said. "Something about a rocket ship or something. He's probably stuck for a minute."

"Sorry, I thought you were Dad."

"I just wanted to talk to you," Sandy sat down on a plastic chair beside her. "You're leaving in a week and I just wanted to talk to you before you left."

"What about, Mom?" Alison closed her eyes and continued to lean back. She wasn't in the mood for another round of guilt to stay.

"I don't know," Sandy's voice betrayed a sense of sorrow. "Just anything."

Her mother had never tried this particular tactic in conversation, so she opened her eyes and looked over. "What do you want to know?"

"Really. Just anything you want. What were you and your father doing?" Sandy didn't know the first thing about machines of any kind, so her asking about what they'd been doing with the ATV was a desperate grab.

"Just taking a look at some of the parts that wear down a bit quicker than the others." Alison pointed at the vehicle. "I've put a lot of miles on that thing."

"Really?" She let the question hang in the air, vague and directionless.

"I went all the way to the ocean this last time. It was beautiful. I mean to be clear, things are as bad out on the coast as they are here, maybe worse. But the change in the scenery was nice."

"Did you get in? The water I mean. Was it cold?"

"Yeah," Alison looked up at the sky, remembering. "Yeah, it was really cold. You don't expect that, with everyone saying how much warmer it is or whatever. But I went in all the way up to my chest. You get used to it pretty fast though."

"I've never seen the ocean," Sandy said. Her tone wasn't exactly morose, but it seemed to be mourning something. "I hope Eva can see it someday. She should be able to see whatever she wants."

Alison looked at her mother with a new sense of wonder. It had never occurred to her how trapped Sandy might feel, here at the house. Even before she'd expressed the urge to join the

Harbingers, Alison had wanted to travel. Her mother had always tried to gently guide her back to reality whenever she got too far along in her hopes. Now, here she was saying she wanted Eva to see the ocean.

"I went really far north too. That's what took the longest." Alison felt like her mother wanted more, and so she decided to provide it. "There are still forests up there. The trees are huge and old. After I dropped off my intel in some mountain town, I spent a day in the woods just wandering around. I know it's really not that big, but I felt like I could have walked forever and never come back. I was scared I'd get lost, so I came back before it got dark."

"Good." Sandy pointed at the trees that surrounded their home. "Bigger than these?"

"Oh god, yeah." Alison mimed a broad tree with her arms. "They were huge. Like buildings but made of tree parts. I really didn't know they got that big. It was a lot like being in the woods around here, just so much bigger. There's so much out there. I wish you could have seen it too."

Alison surprised herself with her last words. She wasn't sure why she'd said them, but it was true. For every conversation argument they'd had over her leaving, Sandy had dug her heels into the ground here even harder. Alison understood now that she'd just wanted to keep her safe. Sandy was so planted here now that she may as well be one of the trees around the house.

"If Eva wants to see them, she will." Alison reached out and touched her mother's hands, where she'd begun to clutch at her apron again. "Things will get better."

"I know, honey." Sandy reached up with one hand and wiped away tears before they could fall. "I just want to make sure you stay safe."

"I'll be okay," Alison said quietly. "I can take care of myself. You and Dad made sure I know what I'm doing."

She squeezed Sandy's hand and then let go as her father pushed open the back door. He was holding two brown glass bottles with stoppers in them.

"Guess I should have brought three," he said.

"I don't need any of your backwater hooch," Sandy stood up to give her seat to Jack. "You two enjoy. I'll go make us some dinner."

Before Alison could say anything, Sandy was back inside, and Jack was handing over one of the brown bottles.

"They're good I swear." He popped the lid from his bottle and took a long draught. "I mean they're good enough. Not like my last batch."

"Whatever you say, Dad." She took a drink of her own and looked at it. "Tastes like a wheat field. I can even taste a bit of the dirt."

"You make your own hooch then." He laughed and took another drink.

~

When John arrived at the training fields, his class of pilot cadets had finally managed to get the left arm of their mech working. They'd been working on it for days, and he had been starting to worry. But now they were running it through stabilization protocols and had it moving with some amount of accuracy.

The mech had been cleaned of most of the grime, but a white ring around the hull still showed where it had been submerged for quite some time. Along one side of the mech, a spray-painted name had taken residence: Cronus. John would almost have preferred they call it the Phoenix. Terrible name or not, the mech itself was working quite well. With a couple more weeks of work, it would be ready to join the ranks of the training fleet they used for unit drills.

A loud bang rolled across the training fields then, and John felt himself flinch. The Cronus had belched a prolific cloud of black smoke. For a moment it encompassed the entire mech, as well as the surrounding class of cadets. His first instinct was to run toward them in case anyone had been injured. But as the smoke cleared, he could hear the class as they coughed and scattered. No one looked injured.

John started walking toward them to ask what had happened when another bang, and a smaller plume of smoke, came out of the mech. This time John saw where it was coming from and stopped walking, any fears for their safety mostly abated. They were attempting to use the jump jets and had forgotten to prime the ignition lines before they fired them. Another bang reached him, but this time the smoke was followed by a number of white-hot jets of fire from a number of nozzles along the body of the mech. It lifted a few feet straight up, and then settled back down to the ground shakily.

The cadets around it began cheering, some still coughing. John allowed himself to smile briefly before setting his face into a stern look of disappointment. They hadn't technically been cleared to use the jets yet, and he would have to reprimand them for it. He walked toward them, relishing the looks of concern and dread that flashed on their faces. These were replaced by the neutral expressions expected when in front of a superior officer by the time he reached them.

"That was a lot of smoke for the amount of cheering I just heard, cadets," John said. "You haven't been cleared to leave the ground yet, and I distinctly believe I saw this mech come off the ground. Would someone mind telling me I'm wrong about that?"

"My apologies, sir." It was Lockwood talking from the back of the group. "I finally worked out the electrical issue we've been fighting, and I got excited. I asked Samson to fire the jets to see if I was right."

"I said," John began sternly, "Someone please tell me that I didn't see that."

"Oh. Well," Mark Alder spoke up quickly. "What you saw was a mirage. It's very hot out here and that made it look like the Cronus was floating. Uh, sir."

"Thank you, Alder," John said. "I'm pleased we've cleared up that issue. I just came out here to let you know I'm going to give you full clearance to use any ambulatory feature on the mech you haven't used. And before you get any ideas, this does not include the weapons systems."

John turned to leave and allowed his smile to return. It was promising that they'd begun to move on to the final aspects of the mech. It meant they were ahead of his projections. He watched from a distance as they continued to test the thrusters.

CHAPTER 6

Alison ate dinner with her family on her final night at the house. They managed to get through the entire meal without any talk of her departure the next morning. It was amazing how fluid relationships could be when united by a common goal. They'd all wanted the same thing for the past few weeks: to be a cohesive unit for however long it could last. At times she'd even been able to fool herself into feeling stable. The restless feelings inside her had quieted, and she'd settled into the routines of the house. Alison adopted the chores she'd had when she was younger. One of those was making sure to dump whatever scraps they'd accumulated throughout the day into the compost bin outside.

After dinner Sandy and Eva began their nightly ritual of cleaning the dishes together, and Jack stepped outside to enjoy the night air. Alison followed him out with the compost and headed to where they had their bin. It was near a toolshed and would look to anyone wandering by just like an old oil drum. On previous nights, Alison had retired to her room after this chore. She would read one of the few books in the house or update her maps until it was time to put Eva to bed. Tonight however, after dumping the day's scraps, she headed for the wooden bench hanging from the old tree in the yard. Jack sat there, with one of his homemade beers in hand, looking out at the twilight woods. She sat with him as the light faded from the sky in the west and then felt a chill on her skin as the night crept in from the surrounding tree line.

When all but the final wisps of color had receded into the distance, Jack finally spoke. "You should stay," he said. He didn't look at Alison, simply continued to watch the darkness. "Let them go fight their wars and just come home. Eva is young enough still that we can explain this to her. Even if you left us, your mother and I would miss her terribly, but you know Eva's place is with you."

"I can't leave the Harbingers," Alison said. "I'm doing this for her. You have to understand that. Everything I'm doing, I'm doing so that she has the freedom to be whoever she wants to be. I can't, I won't, let her be oppressed the way we are."

"You talk about this oppression as if it's the only thing there is to a life," Jack said. "Sure, your mother and I have nothing in the way of wealth. And, sure, everything we do serves whoever the great masters of our civilization are." He waved one large absently out toward the trees. "But we have enough to live, and we've been allowed to stay together."

"Not everyone is this lucky," Alison said shortly. "Things are getting worse every single day, Dad. And what if Mom gets sick? Or Eva? The Wellness Exchange, that damn health lottery, is cutting down submission quotas every day. And rations are being squeezed so tight that other families are having to make some very hard decisions. If they were going to be able to stabilize this bullshit for everyone, they'd have done it by now. But they haven't stabilized it for everyone, they've done it for whoever they deem worthy."

She looked over at Jack, trying to read his face. She found him hard to read, as she always did, and so she continued. "They're using us, Dad. We can't keep letting them skim our smartest children from the top and then leave the rest of us rotting out here. There are people dying by the thousands of things they could cure with a single goddamn pill. We're starving to death in remote labor camps to supply their Enclaves with everything they want. All so they can protect their own way of life."

"Are those the reasons you tell yourself?" Jack asked.

Alison didn't like what his tone implied and shifted uncomfortably in her seat.

"I know you were young when you had Eva." He turned away from the trees and looked at her. "I understand the fear you have of being a mother, but I see in you everything that I see in your mom. I see the way you look at Eva when you think no one is watching. She needs someone who will love her that completely."

"I can't." Alison choked on her words, then continued with effort. "I can't let them keep her, keep us, controlled like this. Letting them do that, when I have the ability to do something, it's impossible."

"I suppose you make a bit of sense," Jack said. "You always have. Without the illegal crops I'm able to bring in, I'm not sure how I could keep all of us healthy. Does Brian feel the same way? Because I see the same look in his eyes when he comes to take Eva with him."

Bringing up Brian stirred another level of the settled dust within Alison. She closed her eyes to block out an urge to cry.

"You've seen him more often than I have, Dad," Alison managed. "His position at the Core Utility is really important. They need him there when the Fall finally begins."

"Is that what you're doing?" Jack asked, his words cutting deep once again. "Waiting for the grand moment? Can't you do your waiting here, with us? I promise you time moves just the same here as it does out there, doing whatever it is you do."

"I'm a courier of information. If I don't do my job, information in this part of the country is crippled." She looked out at the mountains, distant shadows on the horizon. "It might not be glamorous, but it's not enough to just wait for the call, Dad. I have to do this."

"Can't they find someone else?" His tone softened. "Someone else could surely do what you do."

"Just stop it." Alison stood up and walked out a few steps. She turned around to face him, tears brimming in her eyes. "If I stayed here, I'd never be able to leave. If I could trust myself to leave when I finally got the call, I'd stay. I'd stay and…"

She stopped and thought about all the things that could be if she stayed; of all the things she'd been able to do here for the last few weeks. She could watch Eva draw the pictures that got hung up on the wall. If she stayed, Alison could read Eva every word of the few books they had, over and over, until they both fell asleep each night. She could teach Eva about the desert plants: which ones were edible, which were poisonous, and which were the best to smell just after rain. They could wander the desert together.

Alison was lost in these images and began to trace a path through time with her daughter. Eva would grow older and begin school. At the age of twelve, she'd take the Comprehensive Assessment, and if she was smart, the government would whisk her away into one of the Enclaves. She'd probably never come back home again. Even if she did, Eva wouldn't be the same girl. And, if she wasn't deemed worthy, she'd be assigned a work path, and she would live out her life according to that path with any deviation severely punished. And all of this was assuming that the world wouldn't get worse.

Alison felt her resolve tighten within her. She turned away from her father and finally let the tears fall. She listened as Eva and Sandy cleaned dishes inside. The sound spilled out into the yard along with the warm light.

"No," Alison said. "I can't stay here. Eva deserves the freedom to choose what she wants to do with her life. She deserves to stay with her family, no matter what scores she gets on some damn test. She shouldn't have to work in whatever oppressive factory or farm they've got pumping out resources for the Enclaves. And if she gets sick, she shouldn't have to listen to a fucking radio broadcast to find out if she'll be treated for it or not. Anything I can do to free her from the…the goddamn monsters in their castles, anything at all, I have to do it. I can't stay, Dad."

From behind her, Alison heard the ropes of the bench swing as her father stood up. His soft footsteps as he approached were reassuring. They were the same footsteps she'd heard her entire life, the same boots even. He placed a hand on her shoulder and turned her back toward the house, and him. It was only now that she realized he'd been crying too. When her tears threatened to erupt into audible sobs, she buried her face into her father's shoulder. He didn't have to tell her he understood. She knew.

Just as she was about to head back inside, Jack stepped back and reached into one of the oversized pockets of his coat. He pulled out an object wrapped in clean white cloth.

"Your mother would never let me hear the end of it if she knew I was giving this to you," he said, holding out the object. "She's convinced you shouldn't have one."

Alison recognized the shape of it immediately; it was his old-style revolver. The fact that he had a firearm wasn't news to her. He'd always had a shotgun for safety in the house, and a couple of small-caliber handguns he'd used to teach her how to shoot. All of them had been illegal of course, but no one in the area cared because he supplied them with illegally grown food to supplement their rations.

"This was your grandfather's." He unwrapped the weapon, revealing a polished dark metal barrel and cylinder. The grips were wood, almost as dark as the metal frame. "It's old, but I've taken good care of it. Do you remember how to use one of these?"

"Sure I do, but I've never fired this one," Alison said as she took the gun from him. "All I remember are the .22 rifles and revolvers we used for target practice."

"That's fine Allie." He drew out a small cloth bag filled with loaded cartridges and handed those to her as well. They jangled lightly, a sound that belied the deadly power within. "Take these too. I loaded them all myself, and they'll fire. This is almost the same thing as what we used when you were little, just bigger and more powerful. Be careful with it, Allie."

“Dad, I don’t think I’ll need this,” Alison said. “I’m a courier. I take information from place to place. If they discover who I am, this isn’t going to stop anyone.”

“Every time you leave this house, I’m afraid you won’t come back.” He looked at her sternly. “Every single time you leave, I have to come to terms with the fact that I can’t protect you out there. At least now I’ll know you have some defense.”

“Thank you, Dad,” Alison said. She shook her head and put her arms around him.

“Give ’em hell, kid,” Jack whispered.

John sat at the end of the short bar in Recreation Level 5. His presence in the bar had clearly been noted by the other patrons. Wherever he walked, a circle of vacant seats and space developed. The cadets seemed afraid to talk openly about their lives within earshot, and the staff were probably keeping their distance for similar reasons. It didn’t matter to John. He wasn’t there to socialize, and the bartender occasionally broke through the invisible barrier to resupply his glass. His glass was nearly full, and so his bubble would stay sealed for a while.

Across the room, near a table against the window, was the reason he was here. Lockwood was there with Mark Alder, one of the other cadets in his Live Piloting course. Lockwood seemed normal enough, if a bit timid. He was at least a bit drunk, because he’d shed a significant amount of the timidity John typically saw from him in class. The other cadet with him was egging him on. It was good that Zak had someone to encourage him, but hopefully the two of them didn't rustle up too much trouble tonight. Another stunt like the one they'd pulled, and John might not be able to help.

After a few minutes, another cadet joined them at the table. A woman a year ahead of the other two put three drinks down on the table, and then leaned into Mark. She only stayed there a moment, enough time to establish contact with him and then stepped back. John found that interesting. It would have been easy for her and Mark to peel away from Zak, to leave him alone at the table, but she seemed to be actively working against that outcome.

From his vantage point across the room, John had expected to watch as Zak was eventually worked out of the group like a splinter. Instead, the three of them remained an animated group of friends, with only a passing gesture or look to indicate that the woman and Mark were even a couple. Zak, he realized, had friends that cared about him.

John wasn't sure why he hadn't expected it. For some reason, he had expected Zak to be living a life of sadness, devoid of companionship. A subtle trick of the mind, he supposed. John had allowed the tragedy of Zak's family to color his entire perception of the boy. Seeing him at the Academy, mostly happy, jostled the picture he'd built around the boy over the years.

He'd built his image of Zak almost completely from paper records. After the initial incident, he had stayed updated on everything that happened to Zak for years. He'd watched as Zak had moved through the state system for orphans, those that had been deemed promising enough for development. Every foster home, every standardized test, every medical checkup had been funneled his way. But John had eventually checked in less frequently, and then eventually he'd stopped altogether.

When Zak had shown up in his class roster, it had been years since John had last seen the boy's name. And now here he was, just another student at the Academy. He drank with friends at the bar, piloted and fitted the mech in his class, and seemed to be thriving. The real version of Zak was smiling. In all of John's imagined futures, he'd never envisioned Zak smiling. The mood of the whole bar was heightened tonight.

Classes were winding down and preparations had begun for the graduation ceremony for the higher-level cadets. In just a few days, relationships of all sorts would be pulled apart by duty and distance. Lockwood and the other cadets in his Live Piloting course still had another year before they would have to leave the Academy behind. John could tell, though, that the friendship between Lockwood and Alder would survive. They seemed like a symbiotic pair, each one filling the shortcomings of the other. Alder, with his gregarious nature, drew Lockwood out of the shadows and into social light. Lockwood, by contrast, had made Alder a more focused and altogether more effective cadet. There was even a reasonable chance they could be grouped together into the same mechanized armor unit at the end of their training. Bringing in soldiers who already shared a bond was often useful on a battlefield.

John smiled. Seeing Zak like this had made him more secure in his conviction to leave both the Academy and the Harbingers behind. A somewhat fantastical plan to retire and make a home somewhere remote had even begun growing as well. He had never even bothered to think about things like that before, but he found himself imagining a cabin near a lake somewhere where the water was still potable, and the fish were still edible. He visualized being able to disconnect from society whenever he wanted and live off the land. These were obviously not the most realistic goals. Any large body of clean water would be completely off limits to habitation, or so crowded with people making homes there that it wouldn't stay that way for long. But perhaps his status would at least afford him a place inside one of the Enclaves when he retired. It wasn't completely out of the question, maybe even likely, that they would want to post him somewhere safe when he left. He allowed himself to dream, an alien feeling, and sipped his whiskey.

John might be able to let go of all of this after all. He could fade away and let the world continue to spin off its own accord. It was a foreign thought in his mind, and John felt it race around, scrambling for purchase. The thought didn't have a place to live. He looked down at his drink, breaking his gaze away from Lockwood's group as two more cadets joined them at their table. The ice in his whiskey had begun to melt. It wouldn't taste quite the same now.

John watched through the side of the glass as the water from the ice drifted downward to join the amber drink. Before more damage could be done to his drink, he drained the glass. He caught the eye of the bartender, who immediately moved to grab another glass. Wordlessly, John slid his empty one forward on the bar to signal that he was finished for the night.

As he passed by Zak's table, he did his best not to look to closely, but did manage to catch a real flash of joy in the boy's eyes as someone told a joke. Once he was inside the elevator, he felt the familiar lurch as it propelled him upward.

In his clouded mind, the thought came back to him almost as an accusation. Zak might be okay. John had joined the Harbingers, at least in part, because of what had happened in that apartment so many years ago. He had been trying to make the world into a place where things like that weren't possible anymore. With every information drop and within every attached essay he'd included with them, he had been working to create a world where Zak could smile. He hadn't considered that it was already possible.

~

The house was quiet as Alison woke early in her childhood bedroom. A breeze pushed in through her partially open window, bringing with it the soft sounds of morning. This far out of the city, there was only an occasional rumble from vehicles passing on the low-traffic roads near the home. She had to leave today, and she knew it. If she didn't, her next courier assignment would have to be scrapped, and the Harbingers would assume she'd been compromised.

Brian would also be there in a few days, and it wouldn't do for her to be here when he arrived. He would take Eva back to the city with the complicated-but-plausible cover story they'd all agreed on years ago. It had always seemed unfair that Brian got to take her all to himself when he came, but it would be impossible for him to stay outside the Enclave in Tonopah for long. They had worked out this plan themselves after Eva was born.

Every detail had been debated and agreed upon by both of them, but that didn't mean the arrangement didn't sting.

Alison sat up and placed her feet onto the cold wooden floor of her room. All her things were still here, just where she'd left them. Her room always felt as if it was waiting for her to sink back into it and continue along the course that had once been set before her. A desk in the corner was a mess of paper and art supplies. She'd had aspirations of being an artist back before her scores on the Comprehensive Assessment had come back years ago. A small slip of paper, handed to her by a distant and distracted administrator, had told her she'd been assigned to work in a faraway manufacturing plant, no doubt creating some instrument of oppression or other.

While she had never admitted it directly to anyone but Brian, she'd been crushed when the assessment hadn't selected her for placement inside the Enclaves. Something about being told so directly that she wasn't worth protecting had been devastating.

Alison walked over to the desk, her weight causing the boards to creak beneath her feet in familiar places. She found the slip of paper right where she'd left it, inside the worn cover of a book on the art of cartography. She held the paper in her hand and read the words:

Subject: Alison Harrow

Control Number: 0013529

Determination: Unsuitable

Recommendation: Labor Unit 2602, Light Duty Ordnance Assembly

It was strange to think about how much a small scrap of paper had changed her life. She'd read the words on the paper at the testing center and come straight home. Her parents had seen the look on her face, they must have, because they hadn't attempted to talk to her. Alison, the crushed and confused girl she'd been in the past, had refused to come out of her room for two days. After that, she refused to go to her assigned trainings. For her parents, this hadn't come as a surprise. Many people who weren't selected to live in one of the Enclaved zones in a major metropolitan center went through a period of noncompliance. Most people eventually fell into step with society.

Alison hadn't. Instead, she'd found a thread of the Harbingers of The Fall sticking out somewhere and pulled until she somehow scored a meeting. Late one night, she slipped out of her bedroom window and made her way to an abandoned grocery store a few miles down the road. It could have easily been a trap baited by government intelligence operatives, but it wasn't. It had been Brian. He'd offered her the first glimpse of what a true purpose could feel like.

After learning that Alison had been assigned duty in an ammunition factory, Brian had tried to get her to accept it and work as an agent inside the system. That was where most of the Harbingers of the Fall existed, hidden in plain sight, working their assignments and waiting for orders. Many of their members even existed inside the Enclaves, like Brian. Alison had refused to pretend, refused to become a cog in that machine, and Brian had worked out another role for her as a courier. She'd flit from town to town with information, always on the move to the next clandestine exchange. She had eagerly accepted the opportunity, and then Eva had come along.

Alison placed the scrap of paper that detailed the life she'd rejected back into the book. All of this was for Eva now. If it had just been for spite, she might have caved and taken her spot in the factory. She and Brian had kept up their meetings, long after they were strictly necessary. And so, between one trek across the desert and another, Eva had come to be.

Neither of them had known what to do. Alison was barely twenty and legally a fugitive from duty, though a low priority one. Brian had already been entrenched inside the machinations of the GovNET Core Utility in Tonopah, so they'd made the arrangement. Alison's parents had taken Eva in when she was born. Alison took on the role of a sister who returned to visit her family whenever she could manage the trip. Brian would take her into the Enclave occasionally when he could, existing for Eva as an uncle. Eva had never bothered to ask who Brian belonged to, and simply accepted him and moved on.

Brian and Eva still had a relationship that bordered on parent and child when he was around. Alison knew this, not because she'd seen it, but because of how Eva talked about him. Even as she resented him for his place in Eva's life, she wondered about the life the three of them could have built in another time. Would they have become like Alison's own parents, living illegally on the fringes of society, paying off the government patrols whenever they came through? It was possible they'd have managed to shield themselves from the worst things. But there had always been reality, pressing in on all sides, to make her decision easier.

Her decision to leave Eva with her parents had been the hardest thing she'd ever done. Alison thought back to the days and weeks after she left on her first assignment and began to feel a great weight settle in on her. Guilt from multiple directions threatened to pull her back down into bed, to lull her into inaction. She closed her eyes and pictured her idealized version of Eva. The image of a woman with a fiercely unrestrained thirst for knowledge and adventure flashed before her. This version, should Eva choose to inhabit it, would only be possible if Alison continued her sacrifice. The only way the next generation of children would see a future with any opportunity for freedom would be if she, and countless others, pulled as hard as they could on the ropes they'd fastened to the rotten tower of Stability. Bring it all down and let the world be made anew.

A sound startled Alison from her memories, and she looked around her room to find the source. It came again, a soft knock at her bedroom door. She started to get up to open it when a piece of paper slid underneath. On it, in the careful letters of a child just beginning to put sentences together, was a note and a drawing.

"I will miss you," it read. A stick-figure family was drawn underneath, with hearts and stars surrounding them. Each person was labeled.

"Mommy," "Daddy," "Eva," and another figure with a backpack labelled "You."

The dining room was quiet as Alison took her seat in the chair that had been hers for as long as she could remember. Her mother set plates of eggs and potatoes in front of each of them and then sat down herself. A silence followed, filled with all the things they wished they could say. Then, in the way that only a child could, Eva broke the tension.

"Why do we have to eat so many potatoes?" she asked as she poked at them with a fork.

"We've been over this," Sandy flashed a look of exasperation at Jack. In that look was a measure of relief. "They're easy to grow and easy to keep hidden, since they grow underground."

"Why don't you just grow other stuff underground then?" Eva speared one of the potatoes and Alison could tell that the gears in her head were turning. "Why just potatoes?"

"We grow other things too," Jack said calmly. "And, in a way, we do grow them underground. We dig trenches and grow things at the bottom. That way, if anyone comes by, we can cover them."

"Still too many potatoes," Eva said. "I want to see where you grow the food."

"I'll take you with me the next time I harvest," Jack looked at Eva approvingly. "Put you to work."

"I didn't know it was going to be work." Eva put the piece of potato in her mouth and made a face. "These are fine."

"I used to get tired of them too." Alison leaned over to whisper to Eva. She knew her father would hear, but that was okay. "If you go with him to the trenches, you can sneak some extra fruit if you're careful."

Alison's father made a show of admiring a forkful of his own sliced potatoes and stuffed them in his mouth. While he did this, Eva shared a conspiratorial smile with Alison.

After they finished, Alison headed back to her room to gather her things. She didn't have much. A large backpack held most of her larger supplies. A satchel she wore slung on her side she reserved for the things she might need access to more frequently: a compass, map, and other survival aids. She retrieved the gun, wrapped in its clean cloth, from the top drawer in her dresser. Feeling its weight in her hands, she considered where to pack it. After a few moments, she decided to put it in the satchel. If she was going to carry a weapon, she may as well have access to it quickly.

The drawing Eva had slid under her door that morning was laid on her bed in a shaft of light spilling in from the window. The smiling figures stared up at her, holding hands. This too she folded and put into the satchel.

When she left her room, the house was quiet. Everyone was already outside in front of the house, waiting for her to come out. Every time she left like this, it felt like the last time she would ever see the house, their faces. As she moved through the house, she let her fingers run over familiar surfaces: the corner of the wall in the hallway that turned toward the living room, the familiar grain on the back of her father's wooden chair, and then the cool metal of the doorknob as she pushed out into the morning light.

She descended the steps of the porch and moved to hug them each in turn. Sandy, her arms stronger than they looked, squeezed her for so long that Alison wondered if she'd need to say something. When she finally let go, Jack's embrace gave her warm and even pressure that eased immediately once she started to pull away. Finally, there was Eva, staring up at her with a smile that mirrored the ones on the picture she'd drawn. Alison picked her up and held her tightly in her arms. This embrace, she realized, was a mirror of the one she'd just shared with Sandy.

After a long time, Alison leaned down and placed Eva lightly back onto the ground. With enormous mental effort she walked to her ATV, loaded with supplies and cleaner than it had been in years. As she put on her helmet, she took a final look at her family. She tried to take a mental snapshot of them standing in front of the house. Her father wore a grim but admiring smile. Sandy crossed her arms tightly across her chest, and in her eyes, Alison could see one last plea for her to stay. And then there was Eva, jumping and waving both arms wildly as if she wouldn't be seen otherwise. Alison turned on her ATV and headed down the overgrown dirt driveway, headed for the main road. As they began to get smaller in her side view mirror, Alison turned her head toward the road ahead.

~

The air was already hot on his face, and the sun had just risen above the mountains. John took off his cap and wiped sweat from his forehead. The action would be starting soon, and he wanted to watch all of it. While the cadets could technically still fail his Live Piloting course, the final assessment was more of a formality than an actual test.

Instead of a practical scenario based on real-world battles, he'd drawn up something he thought would be interesting to watch. He'd taken up a position on top of the wall that went around the base. A few other people had managed to find a reason to be there as well. Vice Admiral Katherine Scholl was there, looking out into the desert with a pair of binoculars resting on the concrete ledge in front of her. Against his instinct, he walked up beside her and peered through his own pair of binoculars toward the large open expanse of land to the west of the base.

There, he saw a lone mech standing in the open. It was the large Neith class mech the students had named the Maratus long ago. Lockwood, Alder and a few other cadets were inside that unit. It was essentially a massive command center suspended in the air by eight powerful legs that spread out radially. On top was one massive gun, and a number of other armaments and senor arrays. This type of mech would, on operations that required it, serve as the center for a unit's command and control. It was a daunting presence, just sitting out in the desert near the base. Underneath the mech was a single armored truck.

The scenario John had devised was simple. Half the class would be stationed aboard the Maratus, with two cadets in the truck below. The other half of the class would be piloting any of the other mechs they wanted. The goal of the command mech was to protect the truck, and the goal of the other lighter mechs was to take it out. To make things more interesting, however, John had allowed the cadets in the lighter mechs a three-day head start to prep the battlefield any way they saw fit. Based on the amount of time they'd spent out there, he expected quite a show.

The main gun on the command mech swiveled toward a rocky outcrop to the north, and two of the legs shifted so that they would protect the truck beneath from anything in that direction. John couldn't see any of the smaller mechs on the battlefield and enjoyed the mystery.

"I thought there were supposed to be two teams out there, John," Katherine said. "I count one solitary mech and a truck."

"Just wait." John pulled his binoculars down to get a better view of the entire field. "They're out there."

Almost as if in response to his words, there was movement to the east. Two mechs rose from the sand like sleeping giants waking from a century of rest. Sand cascaded from the sides of their sleek metal frames and they began to advance on the central mech.

"Oh, I do love a good trick play." Katherine picked up her binoculars but didn't use them. Instead, she smiled broadly as two more mechs rose from the sand to the west.

The command mech executed a smooth series of movements in response. First, the main gun fired on the rocky outcrop to the north. A massive colorful explosion of green paint indicated a direct hit on anything that might have been hiding behind the rocks. At the same time, the mech's main body pivoted to the east and began firing its smaller weapons systems at the mechs coming from that direction. The main gun pivoted then and moved to attack to the west.

Rounds impacted one of the smaller units to the west, and the unit capitulated into the sand, disabled. A sudden cloud of red near the command mech showed where two of its legs had been disabled by incoming rounds. The large unit corrected quickly for the two, now useless, limbs. As it stabilized itself, the main gun got off a clean shot on the two units to the east and dropped both of them.

Mere seconds had elapsed, and all but one of the smaller mechs had been neutralized. As the main gun swung around to this final unit to the west, something new happened. A wall of smoke engulfed the smaller unit, and it was impossible to know where it was.

"You can never go wrong with a good smokescreen." Katherine shook her head.

"It's a classic for a reason," John said.

For a few long moments, the only movement below was the thick black smoke that rolled slowly into the sky. Then, out of the cloud, an agile Lupine class mech on all fours came sprinting out into the open at full speed. It darted suddenly to the side and narrowly avoided a volley of green paint rounds. It made it to within a few hundred yards and then released a barrage of its own. Simultaneously, every one of the command mech's weapons systems hit the Lupine class at what was essentially point-blank range. Even using these dummy rounds, it physically blasted the mech backward in a bloom of color.

It kicked up a cloud of dust as it fell, temporarily obscuring their view of the battle. John scrambled to get his binoculars up, and aimed them at the truck beneath the command mech.

"Well, I'll be damned," he said. "Crafty bastards did it."

The truck below was coated entirely in red paint. While none of the smaller units had survived the encounter, they had technically won. John dropped his binoculars down.

"Quite a show, John," Katherine said. "It's a shame we won't get any more of these out of you." She was, of course, talking about his resignation.

"Someone else can direct for a while." He tapped his optics to switch on his direct communications with the cadets below. He started to hear them talking to each other but was distracted by Katherine.

"It won't be the same and you know it, John." She patted him on the shoulder and then turned to leave.

As he watched her head for the door, he heard the cadets cheering on the open channel.

"Thank you, cadets." John said over the radio. "I'll have your final evaluations available by the end of the day today. Please put out that fire before it becomes a problem Zimmer. All of you return your units to the training hangar and make sure get them cleaned off."

"Losers clean," Zimmer said to the cadets on the command mech. "I'll see you guys tonight in Rec. Five. And, before you get all bent out of shape, we set off some flares behind the rocks out there and dug some trenches last week. Just because tactics are old doesn't mean they're not still useful."

John smiled and switched off the channel. Though one side had technically won out, the skill demonstrated by both sides had been near perfect on both sides. He felt comfortable leaving these cadets, leaving Lockwood. They were as ready for the battlefield as he could make them. He had one more final exam to administer for the Urban Tactics course, and then he'd be done with all of his official duties with the United Entities Mechanized Armor Corps. By the end of the day, he would be cleared of everything. After that, he'd go on one last stroll to the ridge and then return to the base and leave a door open. That was it. He was almost through.

The Urban Tactics final that John had devised was altogether different than the one he'd drawn up for his Live Piloting cadets. Most weeks, he'd just copied the mech exercises over and adapted them as best as he could to the urban tactics setting. He felt he owed it to the class, especially Vesnina, to give them something new and challenging at least once.

So, in one of the practice fields to the south of the base, he'd had some first-year cadets clear out part of a medium sized hangar. It held an assortment of construction equipment and was one of the larger structures outside the walls of the base. After enough space had been cleared, John had personally set something special up inside the hangar for the class.

All he told the cadets was that they needed to breach and secure the hangar. John hadn't given them any more instruction than that. In fact, he hadn't even bothered to meet them beforehand to send them on their way. While this probably seemed like indifference to the cadets, the real reason was that he was waiting for them inside the hangar.

Ten minutes into the cadets' prescribed assessment time, he heard the quiet crunch of tires as an armored transport vehicle arrived outside. Shortly after, he heard the first sounds of activity from two places. The first was the large main rolling door at the front of the hangar. The second was a small back door. He had to give them credit for attempting a simultaneous breach, but they were in for a surprise no matter what their tactics were. He wanted to show them the value of being overmatched.

He turned in the dark hangar and walked over to the surprise he'd prepared for them. Under cover of darkness one night, he'd moved an Ursidae class mech from the training mech hangar and into this one. It was so large that it took up nearly half the space. He mounted the entry ladder and made his way into the mech. Its systems were already powered on and ready to go, so all he had to do was close the rear hatch and take his seat. As he pulled it closed, he heard the telltale sounds of flashbangs and smoke grenades going off in the hangar.

John could only see the main rolling door from his position in the cockpit. When it went up suddenly, he assumed the smaller door behind him had also opened. At first the cadets would have seen only the confused tangle of construction vehicles. John lifted the frame of the mech from its quadrupedal position and onto its rear legs. He now towered above the small team of cadets before him. They'd been taking cover behind a forklift and were unprepared for an attack from above.

John fired his forward mounted guns at the two unfortunate cadets who had first entered, and they fell back with blue paint covering their uniforms.

The rest of the cadets retreated and took up positions outside the large entryway. John moved his mech forward and, as he neared the opening, the door began to come back down. Smart, John thought, a mech in closed space would be much more vulnerable. They were trying to trap him inside the hangar. He longed forward and caught the door with one large extremity before it could close and then rammed it back up. As he stepped out into the midday light, none of the cadets were in sight.

By turning the unit around, he managed to locate about half of the rest of the cadets. They had taken up positions along the roof of the hangar and opened fire all at once. Small arms fire wasn't particularly effective against mechanized armor, but with enough concentrated firepower it could do some damage.

They were more prepared than he thought they would be. He calmly acquired a target lock on three of the cadets and prepared to volley more paint-laden rounds toward their position on the roof when his proximity alarm went off.

A jolt in the frame of his mech indicated that he'd somehow struck something. His target locks vanished as his mech stumbled backward, trying to compensate for whatever had just happened. Real structural damage had been done to one of the legs of his mech and he was going down fast. His mech hit the ground hard and alarms of all kinds began to scream for his attention. The tactical simulation program running inside the mech was also telling him that the simulated damage from the dummy rounds the cadets fired had already reached a critical level. He twisted the body of his mech to attempt a recovery from the fall, and finally saw what had caused it.

Vesnina stepped out of a badly damaged armored personnel carrier with her rifle shouldered. She'd rammed him at full speed with the APC. As she approached his mech, the rest of the class encircled his mech behind her. John laughed aloud and shook his head. In a way, he was disappointed he wouldn't be able to give them a long speech about the value of understanding limits. He'd been planning to close it out with the message that despite any odds, a soldier must press on. It seemed that they already knew this, however.

Vesnina was mouthing something John couldn't hear, but her intentions were clear. She was telling him to come out with his hands visible. He saw in her eyes a fierceness he recognized. He'd seen it countless times while on the battlefield, from some of the most ruthlessly effective commanders he'd ever served with.

He felt his smile fade then, as the pride he had felt went cold in an instant. These cadets were well trained and would go on to become exemplary mech pilots. During the careers ahead of each student, there would be dozens, if not hundreds, of operations where their deadly precision would be put to use.

How many lethal blades had he unleashed on the world during his tenure at the Academy? John thought back to this morning where Lockwood and his fellow cadets had also exhibited their skills. Then, as sure of himself as he'd felt earlier that day, he suddenly felt lost in the dark again.

After the Urban Tactics final, John had gone up to his room. He had a decision to make; would he let the Harbingers of the Fall into the base to extract a training pod? Whenever he felt himself about to land on a concrete answer, some new or returning thought would swoop in and push the pendulum back in the other direction. John checked the time on a small clock near his bed and sighed. It was almost time for him to go. Slowly, as if he was moving through dense mud, he put on his coat and left his room.

The elevator lurched, sending him down to the ground floor for one final nighttime stroll through the Academy grounds. Normally he would have stayed in this evening. It was the night before the graduation ceremony and, for this special occasion, he usually let the cadets roam as far as they felt brave enough to go. Tomorrow the ceremony would separate relationships of all kinds, and John had always thought that goodbyes were important.

Whether or not he completed his task for the Harbingers, after tomorrow's ceremony he would be officially retiring from his service at the Academy. They'd even asked him to make a speech.

He wouldn't be able to see Zak through the end of his training. But despite his thoughts on the matter, things looked positive for the boy.

Out in the cool night air, he noticed a few cadets wandering the grounds at once. Some were too drunk to even care about his presence. John was actually surprised to see just how many of them were out. He made a mental note to put in a word with Katherine to implement security patrols at night after he left. Without him on base to perform his unofficial role of night watchman, the cadets would no doubt be venturing out like this every night.

As he made his way toward the garage, he began to worry that some of the cadets might take notice of him. If anyone discovered the missing training pod before he departed, they might also remember seeing him leave through the garage. Putting those facts together would change the nature of his retirement.

As he approached the garage, though, his fears subsided. Word must have spread quickly that he wasn't taking the night off of his patrol, because by the time he reached the garage, the number of roaming cadets had dropped to near zero. Inside, the truck he'd come to think of as his was right where it always was. He got in and turned the ignition while keying his authorization codes on the display panel.

"Didn't expect to see you tonight." Adams' voice came through the communications panel. "I thought you might let the kids have a little fun."

"They can have all the fun they want when I'm gone," John said.

"Yeah, man. I heard," Adams said. "I sure will miss our little talks when you're gone."

"Shut up and open the garage."

"Well excuse me, sir." Adams feigned injury, but John could hear the smile in his voice.

"Open the door and go back to bed," John tried his best to sound as natural as possible. "I'll make sure I lock everything up when I get back this time. You can stay up there." John shifted into drive and waited for the door to open.

It was a variation on the same conversation they'd had many times before, but the garage door didn't open this time. John's heart began to pound in his chest as he ran through a scenario in his mind where he was dragged from the truck and put in handcuffs.

"It's been a pleasure, sir," Adams said finally, and the garage door opened.

John didn't say anything back, in part because he didn't trust his voice not to reveal the fear that had welled up inside him in an instant. He also held back because these goodbyes had begun to wear him down over the past few days. He didn't trust himself not to reveal the malaise that had sprouted as the prospect of actually leaving had become reality.

John drove out into the desert, beginning his final winding drive to his usual spot. Once there, he got out of the truck and stood as close as he could to the edge of the ridge. This time, he wouldn't be dropping a red chip filled with intelligence and fuming screeds. Tonight, his sole purpose was to leave the rolling garage door unlocked when he returned to the base. The Harbingers' team would slip in and out through there. Jim had assured him they would secure the door when they left.

There would be no second team coming to extract him, as Jim had suggested at first. John had made the decision to withdraw from both the Harbingers of the Fall, and the Academy. He consoled himself with the thought that if he ever wanted to rejoin the Harbingers, all he would have to do was reach out to someone in the network with his intent.

On some level he knew that wasn't entirely true. Most people who left the Harbingers were considered expended ammunition at best. At worst, the people that left were seen as dangerous liabilities that required mending. He hoped, however, that his words and actions had secured him some special consideration.

He withdrew and lit a cigarette by flicking the end sharply. It popped alight, and he drew in deeply. John closed his eyes and exhaled, envisioning the smoke as his anxiety leaving his body. The practice was nearly automatic at this point. Soon he was daydreaming about his fantasy retirement cabin near a lake somewhere. By now, the government would have informed him if he were going to receive a post like that, but he hadn't. His assigned housing was just a small two-bedroom home in one of the lower-level Enclaves in the southwest. The picture of himself by a lake had become a visual mantra of sorts though, and so he embraced the image.

When he opened his eyes, he examined the desert mountains in the distance, illuminated by a full moon. Above him, long wispy clouds hung motionless in the sky. The night felt completely still, daring him to be the first to move. For a long while, he waited to see if he could outlast the landscape but eventually dropped his cigarette onto the sand. He left it there to burn, its orange embers slowly crawling along the paper, as he got into the truck and returned to the base.

As John pulled into the garage, he waited to hear if Adams would contact him. Nothing came through, which meant he was probably asleep, as he had been on almost every night like this before. The plan was working so far.

John got out of the truck and walked over to the garage door. By pulling on a chain there, he was able to manually close it. When it was a foot off the ground, he stopped and contemplated that last measure of space. It was such a little thing, a foot of darkness.

If he closed the door, the retrieval team wouldn't be able to get into the base to escape with a training pod. The pod wouldn't be missed for several days at the earliest since the cadets had all completed their training for this cycle. The first person to notice it missing might not even report it, because the pods were routinely removed for maintenance. Even so, there was always the chance that this act would be traced back to him.

John dug inside himself, looking for a motivation strong enough to guide him in this decision. He remembered Lockwood's face, the one he'd worn as a child when careless bullets had torn his life apart. John was faced with the problem that had been swinging back and forth inside him ever since Lockwood had shown up in his classroom. Now that Lockwood was a part of the very military force John was trying to subvert, he wondered if he could support the cause that was trying to bring it all down. He allowed the jousting match to run its course in his mind.

As he hesitated, his fear of being discovered grew in intensity. Suddenly he let go of the chain. As he did, pain radiated in his palms. He'd been grasping the chain so tightly that red marks were visible. The door would stay open, he decided. Though Lockwood had somehow found peace inside this monster, it didn't change the fact that it was a monster.

John walked out of the garage, leaving the space for the Harbingers to enter the base. His final act in this conflict would be this largely forgettable shot at the looming beast. Inside the thick concrete walls of the base, the air was still. As he walked across the impeccably manicured grass of the parade field, he looked toward the main assembly hall. He changed course and entered the cavernous space through one of the side doors. The normal long tables used for meals had been pushed against one wall to make room for hundreds of white chairs. They all pointed toward a temporary stage that had been set up against one wall.

On the stage was a podium with the seal of the United Entities on the front.

John walked onto the stage and took his position behind the podium. Before him were hundreds of vacant chairs. Tomorrow they would be filled with the professional expectant faces of hundreds of cadets. They would want him to say something about his decades of service for the United Entities. Vice Admiral Katherine Scholl would expect him to say something about the manifest duty to protect Stability.

John looked up into the rafters where a large flag hung there in the stillness. There he saw the dual figures of a phoenix and a bald eagle, their wings bent protectively around a single five-point star. A banner below these figures bore the words: "Stability before self." All this was set in the center of a field of deep crimson red, a symbol of the blood that had been spent to secure their precious Stability. He felt ill and wasn't sure if it was the flag, or the thought of speaking in front of hundreds of future cogs in this oppressive machine, that caused it.

CHAPTER 7

Alison approached an abandoned gas station near midnight on foot. She'd abandoned her ATV three miles back. The noise it made, even running quietly, attracted far too much attention to bring it this close to the safe house. As she got closer to the station, she passed a wooden post marked eight times with chalk. She checked again, surprised. Why would there be so many here tonight? She pulled out her own piece of chalk, left another mark beneath the others, then crouched down below the level of the surrounding brush and opened her satchel. She removed the old revolver. She also took six cartridges from the drawstring bag her father gave her and loaded them into the cylinder slowly in the moonlight. Her fingers were cold and clumsy from inexperience, so the process took longer than it should have.

She was still hidden in the high sagebrush behind the building when man walked out of the rear door of the station. He unzipped his pants and began urinating out into the night. Behind him, all seemed to be well inside the station. Two figures lifted glasses into the air and then tilted them back.

Alison tucked the revolver into the back of her jeans, making sure to avoid snagging the hammer. The last thing she needed was to embarrass herself in front of a group of her peers. She stood and walked toward the man, who had by then zipped his pants back up and begun to walk back to the gas station.

"Are you a traveling man?" Alison asked. The man flinched and turned around quickly. The phrase she'd used was one the Harbingers of the Fall had stolen from the Freemasons. They used it, and other phrases like it, as a sort of middle finger to the power structure the coded phrases represented.

The man relaxed as he recognized the phrase. "Fuck you, who is that?" he asked.

"No one you would know," Alison said. "Just a fellow traveler here to get my orders."

"You came on one hell of a night, uh…" The man paused.

"Alison. My name is Alison."

"Well, Alison." The man spread his arms and took a step back toward the station. "Welcome to the end."

"What?" she asked, confused. "What do you mean?"

"What do you mean, what do I mean? Are you sure you're at the right party?" the man asked, his voice gaining an edge. Then he called back toward the door. "Hey, you better come out here. I think I may have said too much."

Another form stepped out into the night, and Alison recognized him immediately. It was Jim. He was holding a gun in one hand and a drink in the other.

"Jim, it's me," Alison called out as he pointed the gun into the night.

"Alison!" Jim said in a carelessly loud tone, clearly drunk. "About time you showed up. It's time!"

"Time for what, goddamnit?" she asked.

"Command has tipped the domino." Jim's face tightened in the moonlight, attempting to convey sincerity and seriousness. "It's the beginning of the Fall. We're lighting the fuse, knocking the chair out from under them!" By the end, he was almost yelling.

So that's why there were so many members at the safe house tonight. Whatever plan they had been working toward all these years was finally being put into motion. As a courier, she knew only a little of the grand blueprint of the Fall, so she wasn't too surprised to find that it had begun without her even knowing.

"What's happening? I mean, specifically, what's going to happen?" A buzz of excitement and fear rippled through her.

"I'm not really sure," Jim said. "I just got word that if everything goes according to plan, there will be a massive friendly force headed our way by this time tomorrow. We're supposed to assist them with fuel and then continue on with them. I think they're mounting an attack out at Taycher Base. I'll know more when that happens. But tonight, tonight! Tonight, we drink to the end. We're going to burn this motherfucker to the ground."

Alison had never seen Jim this drunk before. Usually he was calm, mildly buzzed but clearheaded. This side of him was new and manic. She wasn't entirely comfortable with the way he was casually waving the hand holding his pistol around.

"Fuck those privvies, man," the formerly urinating man said.

"Fucking right!" Jim said. "Fucking right," he repeated, a bit less enthusiastically.

Alison could see, even in the moonlight, that Jim was having trouble with some rogue thought. The man's remark had also struck her as overly flippant. She had met Jim a number of times at bonfire parties out in the desert. The organic nature of an event like that had made for an effective meeting point. Cadets from the base had often frequented those parties, and Jim had interacted with them at length on occasion. Alison had made it a point to never get to know any of the cadets that had come crashing into the firelight, but she'd also never truly imagined them as a mortal enemy. But now that the switch had been pulled, they very clearly stood on the opposite side of the line. Jim had known many of them through the years and, like her, had probably never really expected to see the line drawn up.

"Get me a drink," Alison said, and headed for the door of the convenience store.

~

The deep rumble of an explosion woke John from a light sleep. His nerves had kept him awake for most of the night, and so he was even mor disoriented than usual. His eyes struggled to adjust in the low light as his room, high above the base below, seemed to sway. He threw his covers to the side in an attempt to get out of bed. His bad leg tangled in the sheet, and he fell to the ground. Another explosion rocked the base as he scrambled on hands and knees to the window at the end of his room.

Below, bright flames had already enveloped one building. A massive hole torn in the base wall to the east also shone with flame, billowing thick black smoke into the early morning sky. It was barely bright enough outside to see the mountains on the horizon. He could see people streaming in through the new access point. It wasn't supposed to happen like this. He'd left the door open for a just small team to enter the base. This wasn't supposed to be happening. They'd used him.

The small, distant, sounds of gunfire reached him from below. He used the desk next to him to pull himself to his feet. As he watched the scene unfold below, his breath fogged the glass, and he impatiently wiped it away.

"Oh, no," he whispered, then shouted. "Shit!" His voice echoed in the room.

A cadet barracks below exploded, scattering burning debris. He turned and shoved at his desk, sending his computer terminal and an unfinished glass of whiskey crashing to the floor. His chair fell behind him and he reached back for it, intending to push it away too. Instead, as rage built within him, he lifted it and pivoted, flinging it against the window. The wooden frame of the chair buckled against the glass. Crisp cracks radiated outward from the point of impact, but it did nothing to halt the scene below.

"No," John whispered, placing both of his hands against the cool glass. "What the hell are they doing? They can't do this. They can't do this, they can't."

He could see where the rebel forces were going. They were using information he'd given them, and they were headed for the central mech hangar. The fires were spreading from building to building, too fast to be purely organic. They were burning buildings on purpose. The cadets, incapable or unprepared to put up a fight, were being mown down by the invading forces. Cold whiskey, spreading along the tile floor, reached his foot and pooled there, sending a chill through him.

John backed slowly toward his bed and sat down, trying to figure out what he should do. Smoke, caught by wind, blew toward the tower and enveloped him in temporary darkness. Alarms were just now beginning to sound, but it was already too late. A fluctuating orange light from the fires below passed through the smoke at his window. Then, as his door behind him crashed open, John became alert. Before he could reach the gun on his nightstand, he was forced backwards onto the bed by a pair of strong hands. Bright flashlights made it hard for him to make out details, but he managed to see a number of figures clad in dark grey tactical uniforms with no insignia fanned out around him.

"This must be him," the man holding him down shouted to the rest of his team. "Verify."

It took John a moment to understand that the last part was intended for him. "Sergeant Major John Phillips, United Entities Mechanized Armor Corps."

"Not anymore," said another voice somewhere near the door. "Gather your things. You're leaving. Command wants you with us when we leave."

"Departure in two minutes," another voice said. He was having trouble keeping track of the people moving around in the fluctuating darkness. The pressure on his shoulders shifted, and he was lifted from the bed. John stumbled, half blind, as sounds of gunfire, some from below and some in the hallway outside, echoed through his room. He was able to get dressed and put on his coat before a figure at the door called in. "We have to go," said the voice in the dark.

The smoke at his window cleared for a moment, and he managed to get a look outside. The damage that had already been done was almost inconceivable. Just minutes before, the school had been in a collective deep sleep, preparing for the graduation ceremony in the morning. As the group in the room began moving toward the door, John went back toward his window. He looked down and counted the rows of cadet barracks. There it was. Lockwood's barracks was still intact. Swarms of rebel forces were continuing to make their way toward the mech hangar at the center of the base. Another explosion rocked the tower from below as another hole was blasted in the outer wall of the base, this one to the west.

The walls of the room trembled, and some of his wooden frames clattered to the floor behind him. Mechs began pouring out of the main garage below, tearing and blasting the new hole in the western wall open further as they made their way through. The impacts of high energy rounds seared points of light onto his retinas and he blinked away hot tears.

John was pulled away from the window sharply and pushed toward his door. He stepped on one of the frames on the floor and lost his balance. He fell to his knees, where he was faced with the photo of his family. Resting inches from his face, his wife and daughter stared back at him through time. Would they understand the man he had become?

As he was yanked up from the floor, he was just able to reach out and pull the photo from its glassless frame. As they moved out into the hall, he pulled the crumpled photo to his chest. All along the hallway, doors were open. A frightening dark silence came from each one as they made their way toward the elevator at the end of the hall. A familiar urge to vomit filled him as he and the team were sent toward the ground. The back of the elevator afforded him a view of the base. The scene that rapidly approached as they descended was of a dark campus punctuated by areas of flickering light. What he was able to see inside those patches of clarity provided enough detail to understand what the whole picture must have looked like.

A group of cadets lined against a wall suddenly dropped to the ground. John couldn't be sure if they did so because they'd heard something, or if someone had heard them and took them down. In another patch of light, he could see a large contingent of rebel soldiers carrying a large object, straining with the effort. It could have been the training pod, but the size didn't look quite right. It was too small.

Then, in another patch of firelight, John could see a girl, Cadet Vesnina. She was terrified, and then she was on the ground. Smoke blocked his view, and he wasn't able to get another look.

John raised his eyes, instead focusing on the eastern sky where a brightening pale blue gradient signaled the beginning of a new day. The attack would be over before the sun could even break over the horizon.

CHAPTER 8

Smoke rose from a point on the horizon to the south, a dark column that rose high into the sky and then bent with the prevailing winds to the east. The distant sound of something exploding reached them like thunder. Alison and Jim were standing in front of an extinguished campfire, the detritus of a night of revelry strewn around their feet.

"That's got to be Taycher base." Alison pointed out toward the smoke. "They really did it."

"We should get inside and get some sleep." Jim shook his head in a solemn gesture of disbelief and drained the last of the beer in his hand. He pointed toward the abandoned gas station. "Everyone else is already passed out. Today is going to be a long day, and whoever is coming from Taycher won't be here for a little while still."

"I couldn't sleep if I tried," she said. "Plus, someone should keep watch."

"Suit yourself," Jim tossed his empty bottle into the embers of their extinguished campfire. "I'm going to at least make an attempt."

He walked to the station and Alison was alone. She watched as the smoke reached high into the atmosphere and then fanned out quickly, like blood spreading from a wound. She watched it for a long time, wondering what the next stage of her life would look like. During each of her courier assignments over the years, she'd told herself she was pushing the clock closer to the beginning of the Fall. Now that it was here, she felt unsteady. She'd always wanted the world to change. Now that it had, she wasn't sure it was ready. She wasn't sure if she was either.

~

When the elevator reached the ground floor, John was pushed out gently. The unit fanned out around him, and they walked forward toward the large smoking central mech garage.

"I want to see Jim," John said to the group. When he didn't get a response, he cleared his throat loudly. "I'm not going any further unless you take me to him. This is all wrong. He told me this would be clean."

"Shut the hell up," one of the people behind him said. "This place is crawling with armed privvies and I need to concentrate."

"We're going there now," another of the soldiers said more evenly. "Command asked us to retrieve you personally. Just follow orders while we make sure you get there alive."

John wasn't used to being talked to this way, but he knew when he was outranked. In this case, he'd been relegated to a position without rank altogether. He continued with the team, almost as if in a trance, trying his best not to notice when they weaved around the bodies. Scrawled along one of the walls they passed by was a message: "The Fall Begins." The paint was still wet, glinting like blood or oil in the firelight.

The team pushed forward, pulling John along with them like a lost child. When they reached the central mech garage the sound there was almost deafening. Automatic rifle fire was a constant jittering hiss as the rebels fended off forces trying to make their way into the cavernous space. The mechs themselves, somehow powered up without credentials, were roaring to life two and sometimes three at a time. When they did, the ground trembled as they immediately dashed for the ever-widening hole in the side of the building. A confusing cacophony of human voices added a third layer of sound. Orders were being called out all around him. Orders to barricade doors, place blast charges, abandon a position, retreat to the exits, or to hold the line. All this at once, yet everyone seemed to know which order was for them, and which they needed to ignore.

John breathed in the thick smell of exhaust from so many mechs powering up. A number of the units used a form of cold fusion that vented steam, which had produced a murky fog in the predawn light. Shafts of light sliced through the space, making the garage look like a cathedral under siege.

"Keep moving," one of his team said. "We're headed for the command mech, over there. Just keep moving."

John could see it towering high above the other remaining mechs in the garage, its eight legs sticking out radially. This was one of three battle-ready command mechs they had in the hangar. The other two were already gone, it seemed, which would account for the size of the hole in the wall.

John stumbled as he was ushered forward at an accelerated rate. The chaos stirred something inside him he couldn't understand. He found himself clenching and unclenching his fists as he made his way around a mech just as it came to life. The lights on the front pierced through the haze, and it immediately began to move, pounding the ground and jarring his bones.

When they reached the command mech, he was pulled up a loading ramp and inside the cargo bay. One of the doors on the catwalk up near the training pods was blown open. A firefight began with the government forces. Bullets rained down onto the mech garage floor. They ricocheted off the cement and remaining mechs, sending sparks flying.

"Get this fucking door closed," someone yelled from deeper inside the cargo bay of the command mech. "We've got our targets aboard!"

The mech was powering up, a low droning sound that quickly became more akin to a jet engine. As the eight legs hoisted the central module into the air, the cargo ramp began to rise, slowly obscuring his view of the ongoing battle below. John walked toward the ramp, taking in as much detail as he could. Nearly half of the mechs in the garage were already gone. Just before it closed fully, at least three of the smaller mechs simply exploded as if they'd been hit with rockets. The rebel forces were sabotaging the mechs they couldn't take with them. It was a solid strategy. They would have control of the only contingent of mechs in this part of the country, at least until an airstrike took them out.

That possibility should have terrified him, but his mind didn't have room for fear as he struggled to keep pace with his own thoughts. While the air defense capabilities of the command mech he'd been loaded into were extremely advanced, it would be only a matter of hours before something made it through and then it would all be over.

Suddenly, John recognized the feeling he couldn't identify earlier. He was thrilled by this chaos. It had been a long time since he'd been in the middle of something this complex, this high stakes. He'd missed this, he thought, then he shook his head, disgusted. These were children, or very nearly so. He turned around to confront the team that had taken him in but was surprised when all he saw was woman standing there, waiting for him.

"Hello John," said Vice Admiral Katherine Scholl. "Pleased you could join us."

John stood in silence, trying to piece together why she was there. His first instinct was to salute. Then, suddenly, it all fell into place. She'd been with the Harbingers of the Fall the whole time, just as he had.

"When I tried to resign, you asked me to stay," John said quietly. "The same night, Jim asked me to stay on too. I thought it worked out well, the best of both worlds."

"We thought you might put it together yourself, but I wasn't sure I could convince you to stay unless the Harbingers also needed you here," Katherine said.

"Needed me for what?" John asked, his rage returning. "It wasn't supposed to be like this. You… We were only supposed to be taking one of the damn training pods. Jim said it was going to be a small force. No one was supposed to die, Katherine."

"People are dying every day, John," Katherine said, her voice retaining the same cool, even tone that revealed nothing of her emotions. "Whether you still see it or not, things outside the

Enclaves are worse than they've ever been. We didn't need a training pod. We've had the information necessary to train pilots for some time now, as you can see. Even I didn't know the scope of this attack until it happened. But believe me, if we are making a move like this, it must be time."

"What do you mean?" John asked.

"I think we're ready to bring it down John. Everything," Katherine said. "We're on our way to a secure location where you and I will be read in on the whole plan. That's what I've been told."

"What else have you been told?" John asked, doing little to conceal his anger now. Exactly where his anger was coming from, he wasn't completely sure. He himself had written time and time again about the need for swift and calculated strikes just like this one. In the essays he'd passed along with his gathered intelligence, he had also written about the compartmentalized information structure that was clearly at the center of the Harbingers' power structure.

"Listen, John." She held her hands out in front of her like a person calming a scared animal. Her voice also betrayed an unfamiliar tenderness. "You provided some of the formative strategies for all of this. You know what you're supposed to know. I'll tell you everything I know, because I think the need to keep it from you has passed. But before I do, you have to understand that you probably know more than I do about the overall strategies at play here."

"I didn't even know this was happening!" he yelled. But she was right. If they were using his ideas on how to execute an attack like this, then they could also be using other strategies he'd formulated during those late nights at his terminal.

As if reading his thoughts, Katherine spoke again. "Your writings are widely distributed among the Harbingers, even some of your more esoteric essays. Parts of it are quoted like gospel for god's sake. You're the Voice of the Fall."

"So, the attack was successful," John said, changing the subject. He didn't want to think about his direct role in what was happening. "They...We, I guess, stole a fleet of mechs and now we're headed for some kind of haven. I don't believe for a minute we'll get there. The defensive capabilities this unit are advanced, but eventually something is going to punch through. And, if they drop something big enough on us, it won't even matter if the guns take it out early."

Katherine looked around suddenly, apparently making sure that no one was too close to their conversation. "Come on, let's get upstairs. I'll feel more comfortable having this conversation on the command deck."

They took the main stairway up two floors and entered onto the command deck. It was a large room compared to the small cockpits of the smaller mech styles. A pilot console and chair was positioned in the middle of a broad windshield that dominated the forward bulkhead. Along the walls were various stations for communications, sensors, weapons and other essential systems. Each one was staffed by a person wearing the same muted grey uniform as the team that had abducted him. While the mech was operating more or less as it should have, the staff seemed to be struggling to keep up with the task of keeping it that way. John was actually vaguely impressed they were doing as well as they were. He and Katherine were likely the only people on board who had ever stepped foot inside an actual command mech before. He turned to her to comment on this, but she spoke before he could.

"The priority extraction target of the attack wasn't these mechs," she said. "Although without them, we probably wouldn't have gotten out of there with it."

"With what?" John asked. "What the hell did we take?"

"I'm not sure it has an official name. The people working on it on the other side of the base only ever referred to it as 'Ston'". I'm not clear on the specifics, but from what I gathered, it renders air power virtually obsolete. Anything coming in from above can be neutralized instantly at a variable distance. If it works like we want it to, it will be like our entire core of mechs is traveling under a protective dome."

"Does it work?" John asked, momentarily forgetting his anger. Technology like that could change everything about how battles were fought.

"Well I hope so, or we're all going to burn to death in this metal box. Now it's your turn."

"My turn for what?" John felt his curiosity break as a wave of fury built back up.

"Tell me what else you know. This plan is following a strategy of yours I read from years ago." She looked at him expectantly.

She had called this 'his' strategy, and the worst part was that she was right. He paused and took in the scene around him again. The radio chatter coming through the communications panel was a constant overlapping clamor of activity. The woman working on parsing it seemed to be at a loss as to how to operate the station effectively. John pushed past Katherine toward the console. Katherine followed behind him, adopting a look of stern confusion as he remained silent. He listened to the radio traffic, trying to pick out anything that would confirm a suspicion that had been growing since they boarded. Every voice that came through the console sounded confused, even scared. No clear voice of authority cut through the noise.

"It's nationwide," he said, finally. He knew it was true, because it was following one of his strategies very closely. "Nationwide or perhaps even global. That's why we haven't come across anyone trying to stop us yet. No one knows what's going on because it's happening everywhere. Right now, as a dozen or more of these high-profile attacks are going on. Hundreds or even thousands of smaller actions are also underway. Trashcan fires, riots, roadside bombs, anything to create chaos and distraction. If even a handful of the larger actions are successful, the ramifications could be catastrophic for the United Entities."

The woman at the communications panel had stopped working and was listening to John speak with a rapt expression. Katherine motioned for him to elaborate.

"Slowly all radio traffic is going to go dark," he continued. "The people behind those transmissions will be found if they don't stop broadcasting on such high frequencies. Others are probably already staying dark as they try not to call attention to themselves. And there are certainly some who have switched off these frequencies, knowing that we're able to listen. It would be good for us to get onto our own coded frequency as soon as possible. We'll need to make it local to our core, too. We can't broadcast too widely, no matter how many layers of encryption we use. If we're using the wider frequencies, tracking us is as easy as looking for a lighthouse."

He reached past the woman at the comms panel and began priming it for new settings. When it was ready for the new inputs, he turned away and waved his hand at the panel, turning it back over to her. The woman looked down at a sheet of paper in her hands and began to work at inputting the new frequency codes. As soon as she finished, more controlled radio traffic came through. This would be only communications from the other stolen mechs traveling with them.

A voice came through clearly. "Command unit three, are you with us yet?"

"Command unit three reporting in," the woman at the panel said. "We had some technical trouble here, but we're on track now. What is our heading?"

John returned to the back of the room. He leaned against the cool metal bulkhead and closed his eyes, trying to form a picture in his mind of what the country must look like. Military installations everywhere would be under siege or have been gutted like Taycher Base. Many would simply be sabotaged, like the few mechs this force hadn't been able to take. He shook his head as he encountered a new hiccup in his mental picture.

He opened his eyes, hoping to find someone there for him to bounce his thoughts or his anger off of. No one had followed him. Katherine had taken the pilot seat and was working on directing the surrounding forces into a close formation as they moved across the desert. He wondered where they could possibly be going that would be safe. If his writings were really at the center of the strategies at play here, then they must know it was basically pointless to engage in a large-scale operation like this. All this would serve to do was change the hands that wielded power. None of this made sense to him.

Attacks just to commandeer technology and weaponry weren't in line with the professed goals of the Harbingers of the Fall. Acts like this were far more likely to create smaller factions and a struggle for power that would just result in more of the same for the people. That had been the final conclusion of the paper he'd written on this strategy. His entire thesis had been that the most effective way to bring down an institution as large as the United Entities would be a slow and steady crawl.

There was only one exception he'd written about that would make large-scale attacks viable, but it had been nothing more than a footnote. He'd said that if the ruling class, in a spastic fit of irony, created a technology that could cripple its own power, all measures should be taken to obtain it. The experimental Ston device that Katherine had described didn't quite fit that description, but she'd had incomplete information about it. Perhaps it was some sort of game-changing technology. Or, more likely, whoever held the reins for the Harbingers of the Fall had gotten tired of waiting.

He rubbed his eyes, trying to keep his thoughts together. With his eyes closed, searing flashes of what had just happened at the base came forward again. He saw the indiscriminate destruction, and the unwarranted loss of life. His anger returned, as if it had been pressurized within him, and it threatened to explode. He had nowhere to direct his fury, and so it turned inward. Had he wrought this entire nightmare? What he'd seen surely was just a small part of an expansive campaign of violence. He felt lightheaded, partially from the light swaying movements of the mech, but also from the steady course of adrenaline in his system finally starting to subside.

He braced himself on the bulkhead and took another look at the command deck. Katherine was moving around to each of the stations, correcting people where necessary, but everything seemed to be working well. His impulse to join her and guide these people as they put what was likely years of training into practice for the first time was nearly overwhelming. He'd spent so many years at the Academy training and preparing pilots that he had learned how to teach without considering the consequences. He could stride into the room in front of him and begin teaching again, this time for the opposing force. And why shouldn't he? Katherine was right, when she'd said people were dying every day. Alison had said the same thing to him when he'd been on the ridge with her.

He shook his head. No. He couldn't involve himself that directly. Not yet. Instead, he turned and headed down the stairs. The narrow hallway on the deck below led to various amenities that were only available on a mechanized armor unit this big. Ahead, he could see a room with some tables and chairs bolted to the floor. A number of excited looking people were gathered there talking in whispers about their conquest at Taycher. Some, he saw, were more solitary, perhaps experiencing the first of what would become a lifetime of moments spent contemplating the morality of killing.

Instead of going into that central room, he ducked through a doorway into a dark bunk room. Inside, there were three beds, one on top of another, set into the wall. There was scarcely room in each of them to lie down. His knee protested the awkward way he needed to tilt his body, but John managed to climb into the middle bunk. Once there, he felt his body relax. He closed his eyes and felt tears streaming from his eyes, running back along his temples.

When he opened them, the subdued light from the hall illuminated something on the bottom of the bunk above him. Dozens of names, complete with ranks and titles, had been scratched carefully in different handwriting all above him. Anyone who'd been assigned to the bunk he was lying in must have contributed their name. Among the names were also an assortment of phrases, symbols, and crude drawings. John read through the inscriptions, running his fingers along the intermittently smooth and coarse metal. A history, recorded sporadically, that was now obsolete.

The mech's new crew would be sleeping in these bunks soon, with the names of their enemies staring down at them. No, that wouldn't do. He made a decision then. He'd worked for years to bring down the systems of oppression he saw controlling the world, and now that things were finally underway, he couldn't abandon it. If he truly meant any of the words he'd written and sent to the Harbingers, he needed to stand behind them now. That would start with erasing the names of the enemy above him.

He climbed out of the bunk and made his way down another flight of stairs to the cargo deck. This space, after the confined corridors and rooms of the crew deck, felt cavernous. In reality, it was just a series of four bays with doors that opened outward to receive cargo or personnel. With the central module of the mech lowered to the ground, the rooms could be loaded simultaneously from all sides of the mech. Or, on a battlefield, they could offload ground troops and assault vehicles quickly.

Now, each of the four bays were loaded with a seemingly random assortment of equipment and vehicles. There were a number of people working to organize things as best they could. But without stopping to unload some of the larger vehicles, the process was largely one of inventory and less of organization. As he meandered through one of the bays, he came upon what he was looking for, a box of electric metal grinder tools and abrasive discs. As he was counting them, someone finally took notice of him.

"Can I help you?" a woman in muted grey coveralls with a clipboard asked.

"You can," John stepped away from the tools and looked her over. Her stern gaze told him that she wielded at least some authority down here. "I need you to get some people upstairs to clean the bottoms of the bunks. It shouldn't take long."

The woman looked at him as if he'd asked her to go get him a coffee.

"My name is John Phillips." He tried to stand taller, to assert a leadership role he wasn't sure he could command here.

The woman looked at him, her expression softening a bit. "I thought you'd be younger," she said. "Sure, I can spare a couple of guys for an order from the Voice of the Fall."

CHAPTER 9

The sun had turned the inside of the gas station into what felt like a sauna, making her head pound. She walked up and down the mostly bare shelves of the convenience store in search of the medicine section. Three grossly overpriced packets of aspirin still remained along with some allergy medication and bandages. She tore open two of the aspirin packets, popped the pills into her mouth, and dry swallowed them.

The front of the station once had a series of floor-to-ceiling glass panels. Only two dirty panels remained now. The others must have been broken and replaced with plywood long ago.

As she walked up to the glass and looked out at the horizon, smoke still rose into the sky. It had begun to turn white and thin out, and gradually thinned as it drifted into the east. Whatever was on fire out at Taycher must have already been burning for hours.

Alison heard a sound behind her and turned to see Jim walking up the medicine aisle toward her. He looked disappointed to see the empty shelf. Alison reached into her bag as he approached and offered him the last packet of aspirin. As Jim took the pills, Alison gestured toward the smoke.

"Must have done a lot of damage out there." Alison gestured through the murky glass.

"People have been quietly coming into the area for weeks," Jim said. "I'd be surprised if there was anything left out there."

"Weeks?" Alison looked at him angrily. "Why the hell didn't you tell me?"

"I had no idea what was going on." He rubbed his forehead. "They'll be here to pick us up soon. We should get everyone up. Can't let them miss the first day of the Fall because of a hangover."

Alison meditated on the change her life had just undergone. The Harbingers of Fall had managed to transmute itself from a mere organization into an event in history in a single night. She'd somehow found herself caught up inside what had once been a mere fantasy. The firm and tactile nature of reality around her struggled against the nagging feeling that it was a dream.

She nodded at Jim and stepped away from the glass. They headed to where the others were still curled up on the blankets and bedrolls they'd laid out on the checkered linoleum floor. Many of them were already awake, fending off a throbbing communal headache. The celebrations had depleted most of the alcohol they'd brought into the empty convenience store. Containers were strewn on the floor between the sleeping forms of her fellow... what? Alison wondered who these people were to her now that they were at war. She mentally shuffled through the countless documents she'd read while out in the desert ferrying words and intelligence from one place to another. Brothers and sisters; that's what the literature had used most commonly.

She adopted the term now in an attempt to embrace the grandeur and ambition of the moment.

"Good morning, brothers and sisters," she said. "Today, we are free entities of no country, united in the task of bringing down the flawed tower of society."

It sounded good to her. She'd stolen it from something John had written in one of his various essays. He really was good at what he did, she had to give him that. The group was silent for a moment.

"Five more minutes," a woman said rom inside her sleeping bag.

"Yeah, five more minutes and a gallon of water would be great," said another.

Another beat of silence, and then they were all laughing—from fear or excitement, Alison couldn't tell. She laughed with them, but for her, the laughter was unsettling. Now that things were actually happening, people would be fighting and dying in struggles all around the country, maybe even the world. Laughter at this moment felt wrong.

Once they were all up and as refreshed as possible, they headed to the roof of the building to watch for whatever was coming their way. It wasn't long before Jim pointed out a number of figures on the horizon in the direction of the smoke. Merely black specks at first, they were revealed to be a mass of mechs. When looked at through two pairs of binoculars, supplied by Alison and Jim, they could see that there were at least three massive command mechs and an assortment of smaller units moving toward the station. In addition to these machines were a number of armored supply vehicles pulling up dust trails below them.

"Should we be hiding?" someone asked as they took another look through Alison's binoculars. "What if those aren't friendlies?"

"There'd be no reason to head this way if they weren't," Jim said. "They're moving pretty slowly, probably keeping pace with the larger units. Looks like they'll be here in an hour, maybe two. We'll need to be ready to fuel up any of the trucks they have with them. Go down to the store and grab anything that looks like it would be useful. Alison and I will keep watch up here."

Everyone eventually cleared from the roof of the gas station, some immediately, and others only after taking another turn with the binoculars. Once they were alone, Jim and Alison sat with their legs dangling over the edge of the building. They were silent for a few minutes, looking out toward the approaching mechs. The way the mechs moved, slow but with such visible force, it felt like waiting for an oncoming tsunami.

Jim put his pair of binoculars down and opened his backpack. After rummaging around inside, he pulled out a matte black pistol in a holster attached to a belt. Alison watched him as he took the gun out and laid the holster and belt out flat beside him. The belt held a number of replacement clips, presumably loaded. Jim checked the gun to make sure all the moving parts still worked. Alison remarked on how much more careful and precise his movements were this morning. Then, holding it as if to fire, he rested his thumb on a small panel and aimed it into the trees below. After a brief moment, a red light at the back of the gun turned green, and a small screen there showed the number twenty, indicating the number of rounds in the inserted clip. Evidently satisfied, he put the gun back into the holster and stood up. He wrapped the belt around himself and practiced drawing the weapon a couple of times before he sat back down with Alison on the edge of the roof.

"Have you never seen a gun before or something?" he asked, smiling at her.

Alison flushed a little. She hadn't realized she had been watching him the whole time. "No, it's not that," she said. "I've just never seen one so new up close. My dad, he has a few of the old-style guns. He's always kept them around the house. Gave me one before I left, thought I might need it. I guess he was right."

"Where you got it?" Jim asked.

Alison drew out the cloth-wrapped revolver from her backpack beside her. Jim held out his hand to take it, and she placed it there almost reverently. He unwrapped it and checked to see if it was loaded. It still was, from when she'd loaded it the night before.

"Shit, this thing is old," he said. "Feels good though. But I wouldn't leave this thing loaded if you're just going to carry it around in your bag. You never know what'll set one of these old things off."

"Yeah, sorry. I should have done that already." She reached out to take it back from him. He gave it up, somewhat reluctantly. He watched her, with what she assumed was the same interest she'd had, as she unloaded the cylinder and placed the cartridges into the drawstring bag with the others.

"That thing is an antique," Jim said. "It's beautiful, but are you sure it still even works?"

"The other ones I used as a kid always did," Alison said. "They were smaller, though."

"Well, like I said, be careful with that." He gestured at her gun. "The rounds you're using aren't the standard inert rounds modern weapons take. Yours have actual gunpowder and a bullet in one metal jacket. God, those rounds have to be ancient."

"He loaded them himself before I left," Alison said. "He knows what he's doing."

"I'm sure, but the way they make them now, a bullet only fires with an electromagnetic charge." He smiled. "More efficient, and a hell of a lot quieter."

Talking about the antiquated mechanisms of the revolver immediately made her miss her father. Jack had always been one to stick to what worked, and it had come in handy throughout her childhood. They'd had a deep well with a hand crank they'd used to supply the neighbors with water when the shortages got bad. A wood burning box in their living room had provided heat during similar energy blackouts.

"I guess I'm just old school," Alison said as she put the gun back into her bag.

"Well, you're one better than most people," he said. "I'd bet the guys downstairs don't have much more than a knife on them."

Alison brought her binoculars up to her face and noticed something new in the distance. "Hey, there are a bunch of trucks about a mile out. They must have pushed ahead of the mechs. We'd better get down. They'll be here any minute."

By the time they climbed back down into the station, the others had noticed the approaching trucks. They waved down the first one, and it pulled into the station. A heavily armed man in dull grey uniform climbed out of the passenger side and aimed his rifle at the group. Jim pushed by Alison and went out through the glass doors of the convenience store.

"Stop where you are and identify yourself," the man at the truck shouted. His bearded face was angular and serious. "Keep your hands up and away from your weapon."

"Fuck, guys, we're friendlies," Jim said, but his hands went up. "The crops look great." He pointed with his hands still up back toward the truck. "Just radio that phrase exactly to Katherine or whoever's in charge back there."

The bearded man turned his head briefly to relay the information to someone still in the truck. The phrase must have gotten to the right person, because the man lowered his rifle, and his expression became less intense.

"Well, it's a pleasure to meet you all. Help us get these trucks fueled up, and we'll get you back to the main formation," he said.

They filled each truck with gasoline that had been brought in the week before as it pulled in—twelve in total—then packed themselves into them. Alison and Jim got into the last one and it pulled away from the station, headed for the approaching mass of metal machines still in the distance.

"Welcome to the rebellion, guys." The driver said. Her backward baseball cap and cheerful tone seemed incongruous to their situation, but a pistol on the dashboard managed to correct the image a bit. "We've got a route planned ahead for the other trucks that'll pick up some smaller groups like yours along the way. We're headed back toward the main force now. Once we arrive, you'll have to move quickly into wherever they station you. We can't afford to have any of the units stopped for any extended length of time."

"Is there anyone following you—following us—from Taycher?" Jim asked.

"I don't have that information for you. All I know is we're moving as fast as we can while keeping a pretty tight formation. The only forces we have moving outside the formation are these trucks doing pickups along the route. But I'd be surprised if we didn't see some action by the end of the day."

This seemed to satisfy Jim. Alison thought about asking where the main convoy was headed but supposed the driver wouldn't have that information either. Instead, she tried to peek through the front windshield. Occasionally, when their path bent just right, she caught a glimpse of the mechs as they loomed ever closer.

Around the hulking machines ahead of them, the air was thick with dust picked up by their massive footfalls. For a few minutes they were out of sight behind a rise in the terrain. Alison began to wonder how long it would be until they arrived when the road turned to reveal them, like a field of giants, crossing a low valley. She let out a gasp. Three eight-legged metal beasts, stories tall, strode toward them at a speed that was hard to calculate because of their size. All around them were smaller mechs of a wide variety of shapes and sizes. Some moved swiftly like large predatory dinosaurs, while others seemed to be pounding the earth into submission as they lurched forward.

A voice through the radio said, "Pickup vehicle, identify yourself."

"We reap as we sow," their driver said into the receiver. Then to the passengers, "Each pickup has its own bullshit code. It's crude, but it works. I'm the only truck that left with this particular code phrase so, theoretically, I'm the only one that can come back with it. They've got this pretty well orchestrated, honestly."

The voice came through the radio again. "You guys are headed for Command Three and Recon Seven. You must have someone special on board, Liz."

"How the hell am I supposed to pick the right mechs out of the lineup?" the driver asked.

"I'll bet they're the only two not moving," Alison said before she could stop herself. She pointed at one of the giant metal spiders and a smaller two-legged mech slowing down at the back of the main force. The voice on the other end of the radio must have assumed they'd figure it out, because no response came through.

As they covered the final stretch, the two command mechs that were still moving loomed high above them. Now that they were closer, she could see how fast the mechs were actually moving. The groans and impacts of the footfalls as they washed over the truck came like a hybrid thunderstorm and earthquake. All around them, a cloud of kicked-up dust limited their visibility to not more than a few dozen yards in any direction. The driver swerved occasionally as she gave each mech a wide berth. Then, as suddenly as the cacophony had begun, it was fading behind them. They were traveling over a broad, flat stretch of land, plowing over sagebrush that must be at least waist high.

When they reached the two stationary mechs, the bulk of the group continued to fade behind them. They exited the truck to see that the command mech had lowered its central module so it could take on passengers. Jim climbed out of the truck and called for Alison and a couple of the others to join him and he jogged toward the command mech. The rest of the group went toward a large bipedal machine that looked like an armored cargo container with legs and clambered up a ladder into it. She caught a glimpse of the interior of the unit and saw rows of seats set along the bulkheads like a military cargo plane.

As she approached the central module of the command mech, one of its cargo ramps opened, revealing a space similar to the personnel carrier. It was filled with an assortment of vehicles and haphazardly stacked crates. Jim waited for her at the top of the ramp and Alison walked by him just as it began to close. The personnel mech's engines roared to life outside and then whisked it away back toward the main group. Once their cargo ramp was closed, Jim motioned for her and the others to follow him up a staircase. They went up two decks and entered a command-and-control room. A sudden shift as the command module began to rise off the desert floor caused her to reach out and grab a handhold set into the wall.

She surveyed the deck before her. This was her first time anywhere near a machine like this, much less one this big. Being pulled into it, with so little time to process everything, was surreal. From what she'd seen in propaganda and entertainment, she had expected to hear orders being shouted from station to station and for there to be someone clearly in charge standing at the center, conducting it like an orchestra. But it was quieter than she'd expected.

While there were stations around the edges of the room and a small table with a holographic map displayed above it in the middle of the space, most of the operations seemed to be carried out without verbal commands. The only two people who weren't actively working with one of the terminals stood at the front of the mech near a broad reinforced glass panel that looked out over the desert landscape. The two people were looking out toward the main group as it continued to move ahead. Alison noted with unease that they were both dressed in what looked like the uniforms of United Entities military leadership. One, a woman with dark skin and sharp features she didn't recognize was conversing with a broad man in a uniform that looked older.

The woman turned to the room and said, "Get us moving, would you? We can't stay out here in the open. Push the structural tolerances to catch up if you need to, we should be fine." Then, seeing Jim and Alison, she strode over to greet them at the back of the room. "It's good to have you aboard, Jim."

"Happy to be here," he said. Alison braced herself against the wall again as the mech lurched forward. The sudden acceleration set off loud alarms at some of the stations making it hard to communicate, and Jim had to yell to be heard. "So, are you going to tell us what the plan is?"

The woman in the military uniform held up a finger and then turned her attention to one of the stations with a particularly high-pitched wail coming from it. As she worked, the man at the window also turned to help. As he did, Alison recognized him.

"Phillips?" she said almost involuntarily.

~

John looked around for the source of the voice, annoyed by the interruption. When he saw Alison though, his irritation dissipated. He held up a hand, telling her to wait a moment, then finished silencing the alarms at one of the stations. When the sound in the room finally evened out, he walked over to Alison, Jim, and the other new additions to the crew.

"I suppose we should have greeted you a bit more formally when you arrived downstairs," John said. After he decided to embrace his role for now, he was finding it easier to slip back into a leadership position, though he still wasn't certain he even had one here. "Right now, we're sort of preoccupied with getting this mech back up with the main group. There's not much you can do right now to help, so I'd recommend heading below deck and finding a place to store your bags. She might look big, but there isn't a lot of space on a rig like this, so fit yourselves in wherever you can. When we're closer to the main core, we can talk about assigning duties." Then, turning his attention to Jim, he said, "Jim, I'm sure Katherine will want you to stay up here."

He looked over the group for a moment, taking in their faces. Jim's and Alison's were familiar to him; he'd made contact with both of them for his intelligence drops on occasion. The other people were strangers, and their faces showed a mix of confusion and fear. John didn't understand, and he looked to Jim for some kind of explanation.

Jim pointed at his arm and raised an eyebrow. It took John a moment, but when he looked at his own arm, he understood immediately. John felt on his jacket for the United Entities patch sewn there and gripped the edge of it with his fingers. He pulled at it sharply and was relieved to find that the seam tore easily, and the patch came off.

He looked down at the patch, studying the mix of symbols there. The phoenix and eagle stared up at him accusingly. He dropped the patch on the ground unceremoniously and looked back up.

"I've been working for the Harbingers from inside the government for years," he said. "I haven't had time to find something else to wear yet. Welcome to the first day of the Fall, soldiers. Head downstairs and take a breath. Get something to eat from the supplies in the mess hall."

This display of allegiance seemed to soothe their concerns a bit, and the group started heading below. Jim stayed behind and John guided him over to the central map table. Katherine was already there, examining a projection of the terrain ahead of them.

"So, you're in charge here?" Jim asked when they stopped at the table.

"I'm just following orders like everyone else." She didn't look away from the map as she zoomed in on a city, Tonopah, that was ahead of them. "My orders are to get this force to Tonopah and take out some high value targets in the enclaved zone. After that, the plan gets less specific. I assume that means someone else will step in with whatever the next step of the plan is." She looked up from the map and raised an eyebrow.

"Hey, don't look at me." He held his hands up defensively. "All my orders ended once I boarded this mech. I'm just along for the ride now I guess."

"We all are," John said, mostly to himself. "Each of us only knows as much as we need to know to keep us moving. Some of us seem to know more than others, however."

He looked at Katherine and Jim, and a flash of anger surfaced in him again. No matter how many times he'd convinced himself over the past few hours that the measures being taken were necessary, the image of the base burning in the predawn light was something he couldn't seem to shake.

"You're right John," Katherine said. If she saw John's anger, she made no indication. "I probably know more than either of you about this. But even what I've got is pretty limited. I told John most of this already, but the primary reason for our attack on the base was to lift a piece of technology called the Ston. It's supposed to provide air cover, which is why they want us traveling in such a close formation. My orders are to get us through Tonopah and on a straight heading, just a few degrees off due north. I've got a kill phrase that someone will use at some point to let me know my authority is to be handed over. Before you ask, I can't tell you the phrase. That would defeat the purpose."

John saw Jim relax at the mention of a kill phrase. "Did you have one too?" John asked.

"As a matter of fact, I did," he said. "It was the same phrase the driver of my truck used to verify his identity. When I heard it, I knew that my part in this was complete. What I do from now on is just support the next person in the chain. I know this is a sore subject for you John, but do you have any orders, anything at all?"

"I didn't even know this was happening," his voice betrayed his anger more than he would have liked. "I have no idea what my role in this is supposed to be. I didn't even want to be here until..." He stopped talking, and took a deep breath.

"You were one of the primary extraction targets at Taycher," Katherine said. "You've got some role in this thing. You came up with a lot of the procedures and thinking behind all of this, so I'm sure they've got some plan for you ahead."

John felt like she was being polite, trying to make him feel useful. He didn't need or want that, and so he changed the subject. "The targets in Tonopah, what are they? Or can you even tell us?"

"I don't see why not," Katherine said as she zoomed in on a large building in her map of the city. "The west coast of the United Entities is much more spread out than everything further east. So, our target is the major GovNET utility there. There are some lower-level targets too, but this one is the main concern. We take it out, and we cut off information moving through the region. Then like I said, we're headed north."

"What's north?" Jim asked.

"Not a lot as far as I can tell." Katherine pulled back on the map and showed them the heading she was supposed to lay in after Tonopah. "Just mountain ranges and open land."

"There has to be something," Jim said. "We have to stop sometime."

As her group started heading below, Alison made a point to be last in line at the stairs. When it came to her turn, she didn't descend. Instead, she turned and watched John as he worked with Jim and the woman at the map in the middle of the room. Eventually, John looked up and noticed her. He excused himself and made his way over to her.

"You seem to be fitting in nicely," Alison said. "Finally decided to commit to the cause?"

"Sure, I suppose," he said. "They...we took out Taycher and the Academy. I was brought here, and I just found myself filling a power vacuum. Most of these people have never seen as much as a light-duty mech up close. If this is going to work, they'll have to learn fast, and I've been teaching this stuff for over a decade. Listen, let's take this conversation up top. I could use some fresh air."

Alison hadn't realized it, but she also wanted to be out of the mech too, so she agreed. John took her to a metal ladder set into a bulkhead. It led up to a small hatch in the ceiling that opened out onto a broad viewing platform on the top of the mech. Alison was blasted with a stinging desert wind as she climbed out onto the metal hull. It ripped around the mech as it continued working its way back toward the main group. They were noticeably closer now, but it would still be some time before they caught up and could settle the mech back into a more manageable pace.

"It's good to see you with a purpose," Alison had to speak up to be heard over the wind and the deep percussive gait of their mech. "Last time I saw you, it looked like you were giving up. I guess I kind of needed to make sure you were still with us."

"To be honest, it just feels good to be relevant," John said. He looked out ahead of them, and Alison still wasn't quite sure she believed him. "They're actually using a lot of the intel and theory I passed through you for this operation. So, in a way, we've got you to thank for anything we accomplish."

"I'm flattered, but you don't give credit to the messenger any more than you blame them. If they're using your work, this is your victory."

John looked at her for a long time, as if deciding whether or not to trust her. "That's kind of what I'm afraid of." He clenched his jaw for a moment. "What if all of this doesn't help?"

"The true criminal act here would be to do nothing." She raised an eyebrow. "That's another one of yours, isn't it?"

"Sort of. It's something a lot of people have said in different ways through history. I think that's my biggest fear. When I was alone, this was all just academic speculation. How could I have written things like 'dismantle at any cost' without understanding how high that cost would ultimately be?"

"It was a school that trained people to become cogs in a machine designed to crush and subjugate an entire population," Alison said, allowing her voice to rise. "You should be happy to see a place like that burn."

"Happy? How can I be happy to see any of this? I've lived through enough tragedy. I feel like an old man meddling in the affairs of the young, just hoping to feel useful again. When I said that inaction is immoral, I never thought about the morality of the action itself. It wasn't just the Academy, you know, not if they're actually following my strategy."

"That makes sense," Alison said calmly, but the thought was new and exciting. She watched as John felt the spot on his jacket where he'd torn off the United Entities patch. "If I remember right, this kind of activity would only work if it was coordinated across the map. The broader the simultaneous action, the more likely some will succeed."

John looked at her again for a long moment, his eyes searching hers. "None of that was in any of the documents disseminated widely," John said. Alison felt a cool rush of fear. "You weren't just passing my information along, were you? You read everything that I passed through you, didn't you?"

She shrugged, hoping that the gesture looked relaxed. "It's not like there's much else to do, alone in the middle of the desert."

"I can't really blame you for curiosity," John's face softened a bit, and Alison thought she saw a faint smirk. "You're right though. This only makes sense if we're working in cooperation with a broad series of attacks. Otherwise, our little force would've been stopped by now."

"Why are we grouping up like this anyway?" Alison asked, pointing at the mass of machines they were slowly gaining on. She was pleased to note that John had used the term 'we' without hesitation. "If we're such a target, there's no reason to group us all up like that. We should be scattering to the wind in hopes that some of us survive."

"That would be true, and it probably is for most of the other attacks going on right now," John said. Alison got the distinct feeling she was being lectured to. John had assumed a solid stance and looked at her only intermittently. It was probably a habit borne from his years at the Academy.

"It would be true," John paused, as if for dramatic effect. "If we didn't have something that makes a tight formation completely logical."

"Okay, sure," she said. "You've got my curiosity. What do we have?"

"You're to tell no one any of this, of course, but above that group is an invisible barrier," he said, pointing ahead. "Anything that comes within a predetermined distance at any angle higher than the surrounding trees and hills will be stopped instantly. I'm not sure about the mechanics of the thing, but I've been assured it will work."

"I hope so," she said, squinting out at the forces ahead of them. Nothing in the air above them seemed to indicate anything unnatural was occurring. "Otherwise, we're standing in a barrel just waiting to be shot."

"Something else doesn't make sense to me though," John said. He walked away from the hatch to the railing at the front edge of the platform. She followed, content to soak in as much free information as John was willing to divulge. "You see, we've had people like me in places everywhere for quite some time. Corporations, schools, government agencies."

Alison thought of Brian, working in the luxury of the enclaved GovNET Utility in Tonopah. "Sure, I've met a few embedded operatives, you included."

"They wouldn't risk exposing assets like this unless they have an endgame," John said. "And with the Harbingers, there is only one endgame. At least as far as I know. So, either they've found a way to leverage these attacks in such a way that everything comes down, or they're not telling us the whole plan."

"What could they not be telling us?" Alison asked. She didn't like this line of thought, and the implications ran wild in her mind.

"It could be a number of things, really," John said. "They could be like every other group in history and simply plan to leverage themselves into a position of power. Or they could have something that truly makes this all worth the risk. There could be some angle I'm not seeing yet because I'm too close to one facet of the problem. Or—and this one is the one I'm most afraid of—whoever is making decisions could just be stupid. Maybe they decided it was time to strike because they feel like they've got the numbers or just because they got tired of waiting."

Alison leaned against the railing with John, feeling the wind as it rushed over the hot metal of the mech, then over her. It pulled at her clothes and played with her short hair in sporadic gusts. During the break in conversation, she let the information rest in her mind, trying to make sure she remembered everything. Alison noted the more relaxed set of John's shoulders. He seemed deep in thought, so she left him alone. She closed her eyes and listened as the wind rushed by her ears. The smooth movement of the mech high over the desert almost felt like flying. Then a distinct rise in sound came from behind them, causing her to open her eyes and turn around. A formation of small black dots resolved in the sky, headed toward them.

“Phillips.” She pulled on his arm, to break his trance, her eyes still trained on the dots in the sky. “We’re not going to make it. Oh, shit, John, we have to get back inside.”

“What are you talking about?” He turned and his eyes followed her gaze. “Go, now. I hope whoever is at the sensor array knows what they’re looking at.”

~

They both made a dash for the roof hatch. As John opened it, the air around them suddenly heated up, and a deafening roar pummeled his ears. At first, John thought the mech had already been hit. After the initial shock, however, he realized it was the main gun on their mech firing. It loomed above the observation deck and had sent a volley arcing into the sky. That was good. Someone downstairs must have already noticed the approaching fighters.

Alison darted into the opened hatch and slid down the metal ladder nimbly. Inside, John could hear a new mix of alarms going off. He managed to get onto the ladder and began to descend when the mech lurched to the right, throwing him off balance. His leg, as uncooperative as ever, slipped from the rung. He was just able to catch the ladder before he hit the floor of the command deck.

“Forward!” he yelled to the whole command deck. “Do not take evasive action. Our only chance is to maintain this line and hope the main group slows down for us. Keep those guns firing and alert the others. Our sensors probably picked these guys up first.”

He skipped the last few rungs of the ladder in a sprawling leap. When he landed, he lost his balance and was steadied by Alison. He pushed off her in an effort to get to the sensor array console as quickly as possible.

"Multiple targets inbound," Katherine called through the radio at the front of the mech. "We're sending coordinates now." She pointed at the woman working the communication controls, who nodded and turned back to her console to execute the order. "Please respond. We also request you slow the main force; we're not going to make it into the formation in time."

"We have the coordinates," a voice came through the radio. There was a pause that stretched on, and John wondered if they would ever return to the communication. "Maintain speed, Command Three. I'm not sure we can coordinate a defensive barrage and a slowdown simultaneously. These pilots aren't ready for that."

"Well, we're not ready to die!" Katherine yelled through the radio, losing the calm demeanor she had exhibited before. "Don't bother returning fire. If the device doesn't work, we're fucked anyway."

"We'll do what we can, Command Three," the voice said. "Someday, we will all fall. Fall with grace."

The phrase was a familiar one, a mantra often quoted as a toast among fellow members of the Harbingers when they were securely among comrades. John noticed a distinct wave of calm wash over the people on the command deck, as if the words had somehow smoothed the raw edges of their fear.

The first round from the approaching jets finally hit their mech and everyone was jolted to the side. It must have been a fairly large ordnance. Smaller rounds wouldn't have even been noticeable through the thick armor of their unit. Through the front glass of the command deck, he watched as another strafe of explosions bloomed from the ground all around them. The smoke broke around the glass as they pressed onward, the frame of their mech straining for every inch.

"How far out are they?" John asked Jim, who had taken over at the sensor array. "How long do we have?"

"Shit. Not long," Jim said, flipping through the controls as fast as he could. "Maybe a minute, two at most. Fuck, they're fast."

Suddenly, a bright light filled the room through the front glass of the command deck. The other mech that had stopped with them earlier was hit. It twisted, mid-stride, and tried to correct with a newly damaged leg. The limb failed, and the mech plummeted to the ground. Its impact sent up a cloud of dirt and smoke as the mech ground to a halt. John's command mech passed over it deftly in a mad scramble across the desert.

"Stop!" John yelled toward the front of the command deck. "We have to stay over them. They'll die out here if we leave them."

Katherine hesitated. Then, making a decision, she worked the pilot controls and the mech came to a sudden halt. The sound was like a steel mill at quitting time. They stood over their fallen comrades, and a ringing silence filled the command deck.

John strained his eyes as smoke washed over the front glass once again. When it cleared, their main force was closer. An intense surge of relief surged through him. The others had managed to come back for them. Overhead, the jets passed by in a tight formation, their shadows racing along ahead of them, on the desert sand.

With a screaming roar, they came into view in the sky ahead of them. They'd skipped John's mech in favor of an attack run on the main core of mechs. John watched with everyone else on the command deck as the fighters fanned out to begin firing. Then, against all logic, the jets at the front of the formation seemed to impact an invisible wall. Three white-hot explosions bloomed in the sky. They were quickly followed by two more impacts before the rest of the fighters became aware of the danger ahead. Those that weren't immediately disabled or shattered attempted sudden maneuvers to avoid whatever had stopped their progress. It was too late. Two or three managed to avoid direct impacts, glancing off the edge of the invisible wall, but they still lost control. Each one arced through the air almost gracefully, spewing trails of bright smoke as they fell from the sky.

"They're gone," Jim said quietly, looking down at his sensor panel. "They're just gone."

CHAPTER 10

Alison stood at the back of the command deck, feeling equally stunned and useless. She still gripped a handhold tightly, expecting to be viciously tossed to one side or another by the next direct hit. Ahead, their main force loomed closer than ever. She still wasn't sure exactly what had happened, but she allowed herself to relax a bit. They must have managed to turn the whole formation around like Katherine had said. The mechs at the edge of the core parted in front of the windshield and circled around them.

"Recon Three, do you copy?" Katherine said into the radio. She was talking to the downed mech that was still below them.

"We're here," a voice came in. "All present and accounted for, but we've got significant damage to one support piston. I can get us moving, but nowhere near fast enough to keep up with you."

"Do what you can," she said. "We have a scheduled rest up ahead just after we get through our tasks in Tonopah. We need to cover the ground by nightfall. Meet us there. We'll leave a truck with you for support."

At the mention of Tonopah, Alison thought suddenly of her family. They lived only a few miles outside of town. She hadn't even thought to track the direction they were headed in until now. It had only been a couple of days since she'd left her home. Where could this convoy be going at such speed that took them through Tonopah?

She began to wonder if her family even knew what was happening. It was still early in the day. Right now, Eva might even still be in bed. Sandy would be inside prepping whatever breakfast she had planned. Alison's father would be out on the back porch, watching as the sun rose from behind the mountains of her childhood home. She'd told him once while looking at those rocky points that she would be a mountain climber when she grew up. In a way, that had become true enough. She'd summited a few peaks during her courier routes, but more often had found herself picking her way through low canyon passes to save time.

Alternatively, she thought, they could be huddled together in front of their broadcast wall, desperately hoping for information. Surely, they would have already seen the smoke from Taycher in the distance. And they'd be able to see the smoke from the decimated fighter squadron soon enough as well.

"Alison." A voice startled her. It was Jim, turned momentarily away from his seat at the sensor array. "You need to head down below deck and find a place for your things." He gave her a look that she assumed was supposed to be reassuring, but she felt like a child being told to go to her room. He turned back to talk with John, and Alison stood there for a few moments in defiance, listening.

"Tonopah, eh?" Jim asked him. His tone was casual, but Alison could hear the concern hanging at the edges. Any family or friends Jim had would be from Tonopah as well, or at least the surrounding areas. "Any idea what's next after we take out the targets there?"

"Listen." Alison heard irritation rise in John's voice. "I know just about as much as you do. Stop assuming I know what's next. I was the pawn in this, remember?"

"Hey, I just did what I was told." Jim held his hands up in front of him. "We all only know what we need to know. I'm sure we'll all learn more when we get wherever we're going."

"This is bullshit," Alison said. The two men turned, surprised. They obviously hadn't expected someone else in their conversation. "You both know more than you're saying. John, why are we going to Tonopah? You wrote this fucking plan. You need to start owning it."

"I already said this. I only wrote it as a broad possibility," John said, his frustration seeming to sublimate into despair. "I never expected it to be used. It wasn't meant to be a viable strategy. The only thing we can do now is use our tactical advantages and keep the enemy at bay for as long as possible."

"What then?" Alison asked, pointing out the window to the north. "What's the tactical advantage of going to Tonopah? Let's work this out now."

"The GovNET utility makes sense as a target of course. But it's also just the closest civilian population," John said. "Maybe that's it. The taller structures there could provide enough cover for a brief rest period. I honestly don't know. I'm sure a number of people traveling with us have snippets of information and specific instructions on when and where to divulge it. My bet would be that the scheduled rest period after Tonopah is meant to provide time for new orders to find the right people."

"Well, when you know what the hell is going on, see to it I'm one of the right people," Alison said. Having the conflict drawn toward her home so suddenly had turned her excitement into a confusing mix of anger and anxiety. She turned away from them and headed for the staircase to the lower decks.

In the first bunk room she found, there were two people working with metal grinders. Sparks rained out as they sanded the underside of the bunks. She moved to the next one, but found the lighting felt too intense for the confined area. The thought of sleeping on one of the bunks, with the next one mere inches from her face, sent a shock of adrenaline through her. No, she would have to find somewhere else to rest. She went in search of a more open space.

A number of other rooms with bunk beds, these ones dark but equally claustrophobic, weren't good. After exploring the passages for a while, she heard the sounds of a small group and followed them, hoping a space large enough to hold a conversation would also be a space large enough to sit and think. As the voices grew louder, she noted the familiar sounds of cutlery on plates. John had said something about food earlier, hadn't he? A dining room would do.

After some confusing twists and turns that may have taken her down hallways she'd already seen, she came out into a refreshingly large space occupied by a number of people. The light inside the room was just as harsh as the hallways, but at least there was space. She didn't have to listen for long to know what they were talking about. They had all been down here when the fighters were on approach and were just now getting word about what had happened.

"Hey, you!" one of them yelled. The voice was too large for the space, as was the man it came from. "Were you upstairs when it happened?"

"Yeah, sure," she said, taking a seat at one of the long metal tables.

"Oh, hell, yes," the man said. "I want to hear everything. It's just my fucking luck something happens when I'm down here."

He made his way over to Alison, pulling the others along with him as he crossed the room. Once they were around her, her sense of claustrophobia returned in force.

"Well?" one of the others said. "What happened up there?"

"We were attacked by some fighters," Alison said. "I'm not sure what you want from me. We took them out, or they got taken out by whatever we've got."

"Details, honey," the large man said. "We're currently inside history as it's being made."

"We're always inside history as it's being made," she said, letting her distaste for the man seep out. "That's how the process works."

"Well, fuck me," he said, his slick grin momentarily washed away. "Sure, but some shit is more important than other shit."

"Listen, you're going to have to get the story from someone else," she said.

"Fine, whatever," the large man said. He pushed off from the table. Had he really been leaning over her? "We'll go ask someone else, doll."

As they left, she lowered her forehead to the cool metal table and wrapped her arms around her head to create a dark space. Her breath filled the small area she'd created, fogging the table. As the voice of the large man faded down one of the tributary hallways, she lifted her head. She hadn't fought off a bout of claustrophobia this intense in years. There was a reason she'd taken her assignment as a courier and not inside an underground camp.

Fortunately, she'd become very good at the job, and it was one that would continue to be valuable now that the Harbingers were acting out in the open. Her knowledge of the terrain would make her useful when it came to getting information from one group to another. She allowed herself to dream that she might even become an asset in a strategic capacity. Her knowledge of this region could be applied to troop movements, or even battle strategy if she got the opportunity. Her next assignment would probably come during their next stop. She'd be given some packet of information and be sent off to one of the other cells on the western coast. Good, she thought to herself. She couldn't imagine being holed up inside the belly of this metal beast for any longer than she had to be.

A deep vibration passed through the mech and Alison rose from her seat. Something must be happening outside again. She headed for one of the small doorways and this time she made a better effort to learn the route. After a few turns, she was pleasantly surprised to discover color-coded lines on the floor. They were faded by years of shuffling combat boots, but she was able to find a green one labeled "command deck" and followed it. In places that must have had higher traffic, she lost it, but with some guesswork, she was able to find her way back to the central stairway. The entire time, the metal deck beneath her feet continued to vibrate strangely occasionally. When she climbed the main stairs to the command deck, she found that a number of people had done the same.

Beyond the crowd of people, she could see the skyline of Tonopah before them. They were moving through it at an alarming pace. The line of mechs in front of them were keeping the pace as well.

"Command Two, get back in line with the main column," Alison heard John say. "If we're going to cut through this place like a goddamned jungle, we may as well make sure we're limiting the collateral damage."

Someone must have relayed the command because the rogue mech drifted back into line with the rest of the main group. Even in this tight formation, traveling along the main thoroughfares, the damage they were doing was extensive. As they followed along a highway, they were bringing down overpasses, crushing vehicles and an occasional building. Alison's anger flared, seeing the damage to this familiar place firsthand. She calmed herself by reminding herself what they were actually doing: they were advancing a military force as fast as they could through a city. It was amazing they'd been able to limit the damage as much as they had.

"Why couldn't we have gone around the city, for fuck's sake?" a voice from the crowd asked.

"Not that it's any of your goddamn business, soldier," Katherine said, turning away from her station at the front of the room. "But we have high priority targets in the area. Now, I want all nonessential personnel off this deck."

Katherine turned away from the group. They grumbled a bit but dispersed quickly. Again, Alison managed to hang back, postponing her return to the cramped rooms below. John, out of breath from his constant movements from one station to another, looked up from one of the panels and spotted her lingering. He nodded at her, then up toward the ceiling, indicating he wanted to talk on the observation deck again. Then he tapped his wrist and used hand signs to relay "2300." She nodded and turned back to the main stairway. Just having a limit to how long she would have to stay below helped to calm the nagging dread the bulkheads induced.

~

John looked back down at the panel he was working on. The woman he was training had only cursory training on the mech's systems, so he'd spent a lot of time correcting her mistakes. A well-trained pilot from the Academy could have, theoretically, done all the required tasks to operate the mech from the main pilot seat. The additional stations, and a competent team, certainly aided in making the task easier, but they weren't technically necessary.

And so, John was coaching the relatively inexperienced rebels through their first real interaction with a live mech. After some thought he realized that, taking into account their inexperience, they were all doing quite well. The quiet concentration with which they operated the controls struck him as the most surprising. The cadets he'd taught at the Academy had typically joked around and bantered with one another at the slightest provocation. With these rebel forces, though, they went about their tasks, vocalizing only when necessary. Perhaps it was the immediacy of the situation, or the concentration required, but John suspected it was a sense of purpose that had somewhat lacked in the cadets. Sure, his cadets had held their duty in high esteem, but none of them had seen combat yet, and only a handful had really understood the seriousness of what they were being trained to do. These rebels, pulled from the wastes and the outskirts of the Enclaves, had already fought just to be alive. With that simple distinction, John saw that the Harbingers of the Fall might actually succeed in whatever plan they were acting out.

He continued moving from one station to another and soon found he had to check in with them less frequently. The main task of moving the mech and keeping all its systems nominal became easier as his new students acclimated to where switches and buttons were positioned. They had all trained, John learned, on improvised simulators with incomplete information pulled together from disparate sources across the nation. After a while, he eventually found himself with nothing to do for long stretches of time. During these, he wound up looking out the broad front windshield.

"Our target is approaching, John," Katherine said from beside him. "It's the tall one with the curved top over there. Once we bring it down, it will disrupt official communications for most of the western region."

"Sure, that makes sense," John said, trying to see if he could spot the building she was talking about. He found it standing a bit higher than the surrounding structures. "Any more targets out here I should know about?"

"I'm sure there are a few," Katherine said. "But the other targets have been communicated to different people on the other mechs in our core. No one has a full target list."

As she spoke, one of the mechs ahead of them fired at a building to the east. John had only moments to size up the target before the round exploded, taking out the lower floors in mere seconds. It looked like an ordinary administrative building but must have had some specific tactical use he wasn't aware of. The destabilized structure fell as if in slow motion as it collapsed, sending up a huge plume of dust and smoke.

John shook his head with admiration. The round had been laid in with expert precision. The rebel forces were filling their roles smoothly, and John was beginning to integrate himself into their operations. He felt more purpose on the deck of this mech than he'd ever felt while in his room at the Academy. Still, there was a distinct lack of specific direction that held him back from feeling at ease.

"Still no word on what our next orders are going to be?" John asked. "Are you still in charge?"

"I am." Katherine said. "But when we get to the next phase of whatever operation we're working on, I could be taken out of command entirely. To be honest, it might be a relief if I was." She stared out the window for a moment in silence, and then looked down at her console. "Go work with the main weapons bank and get them ready to fire once we're close."

"Yes, sir," John said.

"How many times, John? Unless we're court marshaling you, call me Katherine." She smiled, but John could sense a layer of weariness behind it. "And I really doubt we'll be court marshaling you at this point."

CHAPTER 11

Alison made her way back to the dining area after she went below. Others found their way into the room around her as anticipation and boredom spread through the lower decks. Since the dining room was one of the largest on the crew deck, it quickly became thick with conversation and speculation. Alison sat at a table near one of the walls in the room, her head cradled in her arms again. As the seats around her filled up, most people apparently assumed she was asleep.

The theories being passed around varied from outright ridiculous on one end to dangerously plausible on the other. None rang completely true to Alison. The more fantastical theories posited an uprising of the entire civilian population of the United Entities. Some even went so far as to suggest the war was already over. The more realistic suspicions included aspects of what Alison already knew to be true; that the Harbingers had compartmentalized nearly every aspect of the plan to make sure as much of it was carried out as possible with as little information distributed as possible.

Another theory, one that was both plausible and fantastical, suggested that their coordinated attacks might be spreading beyond the region and covering the globe. If the goal of the

Harbingers was to truly be effective, it stood to reason that all power structures and systems of governance needed to be eradicated. Destroying one would simply leave a power vacuum, and there would be an invasion from some other power in weeks, if not days.

A theory Alison found deeply disturbing was merely whispered. Two people had taken a seat at her table, again mistakenly assuming she was asleep, to share this particular conversation. What had unnerved her the most about the conversation was how irreverent it felt. During her infrequent but geographically widely spread conversations with other members of the Harbingers, she'd become accustomed to a structured mentality of deep respect for the cause. These two people, however, spoke with dark notes of doubt in their voices.

The theory the two had whispered was that the Harbingers of the Fall, the entire operation, was organized and cultivated by the government itself. Thinking about this had caused her stomach to drop. It was possible, even dangerously likely, that the government would want such an organization to exist. It would gather all their enemies under a single umbrella. Even the use of double agents would make sure the organization never strayed too far from the herd.

But, Alison reasoned, they'd just taken down, at the very least, Taycher Mechanized Armor Base. Real people had died. They were literally stomping through the enclaved heart of Tonopah right now, taking down high value targets. Those in power in the United Entities wouldn't have allowed that kind of destruction, would they?

A sudden vibration passed through the hull of the mech. This one she recognized; the massive gun on top of the mech was being fired. The room grew quiet as the dull, rhythmic sound of the guns played like a drumbeat. Alison raised her head slowly, making a mild show of pretending to wake up.

"How long have I been out?" she asked the whispering people at her table. "What time is it?"

"Almost midnight," one of the men said. "I've got bunk time scheduled in an hour if you'd like to join me."

Alison didn't justify him with a response, but simply pushed away from the table and headed for the exit. She found the familiar faded green line on the floor and made her way back up to the command deck. She would be late, but hopefully she could still take John up on his offer to get some fresh air on the outdoor observation deck. Even the few minutes she'd be able to spend in proximity to the large viewing window would be enough to make the trip worth it.

When she reached the main stairway, she was surprised to find two guards blocking her path.

"Um, excuse me, guys," she said. "I've got an appointment, I guess."

"We have orders to keep nonessential personnel off the command deck," one of the guards said, clearly elated to exert some authority. It sounded like he'd practiced this.

"Sure, that's great," Alison said. "I need to see John. I mean Sergeant Phillips. Hell, whatever we're supposed to call him."

The same guard spoke again. "Mr. Phillips is busy. We were asked to make sure that—"

"Sure, I get it. Nonessential personnel. Whatever." Alison raised her voice a bit, hoping someone with more than three lines memorized might overhear and come help. "He asked me to be here, and I'm here. Just go check. I promise I won't do anything."

"Just go ask," the second guard said. "Why the hell would she lie?"

As an answer, the first guard marched up the stairs and Alison could hear him conversing in dismissive tones.

"I'm sorry about him," the second guard said. "He's just excited to be doing something. We were going a bit crazy downstairs."

Word quickly came down from inside the room to let her pass through, and she ascended the final flight of stairs onto the command deck. As she passed by the obstinate guard, she relished the pained look he wore as he made his way back to his post. John was already waiting by the ladder near the back of the room, apparently eager to get up and into the open air. If anyone noticed them, they were too busy to care for very long.

Together, they again climbed out onto the observation deck. Above them, a cool moon shone down, casting the long crisp shadow of the main gun onto the reinforced armor hull before her. Behind them, Alison could see a cluster of buildings in flames. That must be why she'd heard the guns go off before she headed upstairs.

"Those buildings look at you funny or something?" she said, raising her eyebrows.

"That was the GovNet Utility we talked about," John said. He waved his hand dismissively. "With any luck, it'll disrupt communications for a few days. And a few other targets in the area the other units worked through."

Suddenly, she remembered that Brian had worked near those buildings. Her first instinct was to panic, but it was late, near midnight now. There was no way he would be there still, especially now that things had begun with the Fall. She wondered if Brian would be joining their group at some point. He might even be inside one of the other units with the group now.

"Who even decides what's a target?" Alison asked, trying to keep John talking. "I mean, who's in charge?"

"I have no idea," John said. "Katherine has authority here right now, but I'm not sure exactly how they've structured it. She's gotten some of her orders through Jim, who got them from someone else, who probably got them from someone else. But for the moment, she's leading the pack."

"How do we even know where these orders are originating from?" Alison crossed her arms in front of her against the cool night air.

"We won't know until we settle down," John said. "And even then, we may be simply moving on to the next page of instructions."

For a moment, they stood together, swaying slightly from side to side as the mech worked its way across the desert toward their first rest point.

"What if no one is at the head of all of this?" Alison asked. She felt comfortable asking John this. He'd let her in on his own fears earlier, after all. "At least, what if it's not someone we'd like. What if when you follow all the lines of communication back to the source, we're just another tool in a game for power?"

John shrugged and patted his shirt pocket, looking for a cigarette like he had so many times before on the ridge near the Academy. He didn't find one, but instead withdrew a folded piece of paper. He stared at it for a moment with a look that was hard to read. Alison crouched down and took off her bag. She rummaged inside and pulled a crumpled cardboard pack of cigarettes out from underneath her travel rations, gun, and other assorted supplies.

"If we are just a pawn in yet another game for power..." John said as she shouldered her pack again. "If we're just one more tool in whatever game is being played, at least we tried."

Alison, surprised he responded to her question, handed him a cigarette and took one for herself. "But what if we just make things worse?" she asked.

"I'm not really sure what could be worse," John said. "You laid it out for me. So did Katherine downstairs. They own us. They own the land. They own the goddamn rain that falls from the sky, or at least they think they do. Realistically, I have never thought of the Harbingers of the Fall as a perfect solution. But maybe there isn't a perfect one. The United Entities do have their own logic in what they do, you know."

"Bullshit," Alison said. She lit her cigarette by striking the end with her finger. "Those assholes, locked away safe, have no idea what it's like outside the Enclaves."

"No," John said. "They don't. But that doesn't make all their actions inherently wrong. The medical lottery, cruel and barbaric as it seems, is in place to limit the spread of antibiotic resistant pathogens. The enclosed farms are there for similar reasons. The Comprehensive Assessment is there to make sure, as best as they know how, that the brightest of humanity aren't unutilized. There were some real problems brought on by the Decline, and they're dealing with them in the ways they've learned how."

Alison didn't know what to say to this, so she smoked her cigarette. It burned quickly in the wind. She'd heard these arguments before, of course. Some of it she'd gotten while in school. Other parts she'd heard from the family that lived closest to her childhood home. They had been staunch supporters of the government, though it hadn't stopped them from taking the contraband food her father offered them.

"They're wrong, of course," John said.

Alison let out a lungful of smoke she hadn't realized she was holding and coughed. Hearing him say that was a relief. She needed to know why she was there, on the back of a giant war machine, the city she'd once called home burning behind her.

"Humanity can't be saved like some species of endangered fish," John said. "You can't control enough of the variables to make it feasible. The Harbingers have at least that much going for it. They—we—understand that the whole thing is just too flawed to correct at this point. Humanity has drifted too far off course. The only way we'll survive is if we start again."

"And you think it'll work?" Alison asked.

"I'm not sure. Your guess is as good as mine at this point. Besides, that's not even the real reason I'm still here." He said it with an air of finality, as if he'd just come to the conclusion himself.

"Why are you here?"

"I killed a boy's family." He looked down at his unlit cigarette. "Early on in my career. I even received a medal for the operation. Nothing was the same after that one. I continued kicking down doors though, crushing rebel encampments. It was all I'd ever known how to do. I even led raids from a command mech just like this one once I joined the Mechanized Armor Corps. The whole time, the memory of that boy, sitting alone while his mother bled out in front of him…it burrowed deeper into me.

"I tried to push it away, to ignore it. I focused on my work harder and harder, until it was my family that paid the price. I focused on the wrong things, and then it was too late. That's when I made the turn that brought me here."

He unfolded the piece of paper he'd been holding to reveal a photograph. In it, the smiling faces of a woman and two children stood next to a much younger John. He was smiling in the image as well, an unguarded smile she'd never seen him wear. Alison looked down and saw that her cigarette had burned away completely. She let the filter go, and it was carried away on the wind. She wanted to ask him what happened, to understand how the man in front of her had ended up here, but she didn't. It was enough to know he was there because of his family. How they fit into the puzzle exactly wasn't all that important.

"I think we're here for the same reason," she said. "Maybe not exactly the same reason, but they're attached to the same thread. I have a daughter back there. My parents took her in just after she was born, and I came out here to do whatever I could to fix this world for her."

Alison was crying, the tears blowing back from her eyes. John was right. Even if this turned out to be the wrong move, if this just shifted power into someone else's hands, it was the only move she'd had. John put his photograph back into his coat pocket and reached over to Alison. He put a hand on her back, a gesture that reminded her of her father, and did nothing to stop the flow of tears.

"We'll be grounding the mech soon," John said, wiping at his own eyes. "We'd better get back downstairs. Wouldn't want to miss the next page of instructions."

~

Alison was still on the command deck as their convoy of mechs organized into a circle in a patch of desert crisscrossed with seldom-used paths. Once they'd descended the ladder, John had asked her to stay and no one had argued with him. The three command mechs gathered at the center, and the other mechs found room where they could settle down and offload their passengers. Each of the lighter mechs were left with at least one person to pilot it in case of an emergency. The three command mechs held on to three people to maintain the continuous scans that would warn of anything coming.

Alison managed to be one of the first to emerge from her mech. Everyone not tasked with watch duties walked toward the center of the formation where a truck was parked. The air felt fresher than she could have imagined, and she took her time covering the distance to join the crowd. Whatever was going to happen would happen whether she was there or not. She wanted to enjoy the open expanse of stars above her, and relish the feeling of unbound movement.

As she walked, she oriented herself on where they were. She'd exited the city a number of times on this side for various courier missions and recognized these crisscrossed paths and the surrounding hills. Her family home was on another side of the city, out toward the eastern edge. She hoped that it had been spared from any damage from their forces. The Enclaved center of the city hadn't fared very well. Entire buildings were missing from the skyline. How much of that had been intentional targeting, and how much had been collateral, she wasn't sure.

She covered the last few yards to the crowd and waited near the outside edge for something to happen. It didn't take long. Once the crowd had coalesced and quieted down, Jim and Katherine, the woman John had said was in charge, climbed on top of the truck to use it as an impromptu stage. Alison could see John standing near them, but he hadn't scaled the vehicle himself. Katherine had changed her outfit, and now wore a dull jacket the color of dust instead of the crisp blue one she had been picked up in. Alison looked at John again and noted that he, too, had changed out of his government uniform. Good, Alison thought, it wouldn't do to wear the oppressor's uniform now. Still, the crowd felt tense. It was as if they were waiting for someone to shout the first anxious question about what was happening.

"I've been in contact with Central Command," Jim said, and an audible sigh of relief washed through the crowd. His words promised many things in a single breath. The very fact that there was such a Central Command served to establish a framework for understanding their place in the world now. And the mention of direct contact seemed to mean that they would be given a concrete goal now. His words came as a surprise to Alison, but she supposed that maybe he'd communicated with them when she wasn't on the Command Deck. Even if he hadn't been in contact with them though, saying he had was a useful tool.

"I know many of you want to know what's happening," he continued. "And I'll tell you as much as I can. But, as you all know, our greatest ally is controlling the flow of information. What I can say for now is that we're headed north."

The crowd was silent, hanging on every word as he spoke. The wind washed his voice out, but Jim did his best to make sure everyone could hear.

"We'll be working our way to a base of operations where we will join with any of the other forces in our region that have survived. We've received codes to identify them, and codes to identify ourselves, should we intercept one another. Of twenty operations in this sector of the country, we've been able to positively verify that twelve have been successful enough to report back to Central Command."

The cheers that erupted from the crowd seemed to catch Jim off guard. He lost his footing and Katherine reached out one hand surreptitiously to steady him. Alison found herself swept up in the swell despite her doubts. Just as the cheering began to subside, Katherine stretched out her arms to quiet the crowd. The effect was impressive. By appearing to quiet them down, Katherine captured their attention and projected leadership.

"My information from Central Command is largely the same," Katherine said. Her voice was just as loud as Jim's, but she didn't seem to be struggling to project. This wasn't her first speech to a group of assembled soldiers. "We still have one mech behind us, damaged in the initial firefight as we were leaving Taycher. They won't be here soon enough for our liking, but we will not abandon them. A small team will head back to service their mech if that's possible or extract them if it's not. A mountain range close to our current location will provide better coverage as we wait for them. Once the repair team gets them up to speed again, they will meet us in the range. I have mechanics selected already but need volunteers to help with other tasks the team may have. Anyone willing to assist our stragglers is welcome to step forward."

Before Alison could think, she felt herself walking forward. She and a number of others emerged at the front of the group. Katherine, looking down from her perch on the truck, counted off some of them. When she got close to Alison, John nudged her leg with his elbow, and she stopped counting. Alison looked up at Katherine with an indignant scowl but if she noticed, she gave no indication.

"That should do it for now," Katherine said to the group. "We'll be heading to the range as soon as we can get mounted up. Those in the repair group get together and outfit two of the trucks for the mission."

As the group dispersed and headed back to their respective posts, Alison approached John. "What in the hell was that Phillips?" she asked a bit too loudly. "Who the hell are you to decide what I volunteer for?"

"Alison, calm down," John said. "It's not what you think."

"I'm not some child that needs protecting. I know this area better than anyone. I could actually do something instead of riding along in a goddamned sardine can."

"That's why I didn't let Katherine pick you," John said. "We're going to need a few good scouts to go ahead of the main party. We're traveling in such a tight formation and we've got no eyes ahead."

Alison's anger lifted a bit, but she still felt there was more to his explanation than he was saying. "You don't get to save me, John. I'm just like the rest of these people." She waved a hand back at the thinning crowd. "We all want to make a difference in this, and you're not going to stop me from doing that. I've given up too much to just be protected from it all now that I'm here."

"I'm not saving you," John said. "Jim is heading up the scout team and specifically requested you. Report back to Command Three and await your orders."

He said it with an air of authority he hadn't used with her previously. She gritted her teeth but saw it for what it was. He understood her point, and he was treating her like anyone else under his command. She thought back to their conversations on the observation deck, and immediately regretted her decision.

"Now, soldier," John said before he turned away.

CHAPTER 12

After they successfully relocated their mechs to the mountainous region Katherine had indicated to the northeast, they set about creating a camp while they waited for their stragglers. Alison, and two others waited for Jim inside a central tent that had been erected for those who were most closely involved in the planning and execution of their journey. In another part of the tent, Katherine and John leaned over a projected three-dimensional topographical map of their area. The map looked just like the one on the Command Deck inside the mech, but Alison suspected that everyone wanted to be out of there for a while.

Outside, there were three small single-seat ATVs with extra red jugs of gasoline strapped to the hoods. They were of a different manufacturer than the one she was used to, but the mechanics would be the same: four large wheels mounted to a frame with handlebars for steering. Additionally, she'd seen a larger truck loaded with fuel and water next to the ATVs.

Alison, fully equipped in the manner she would be for a courier assignment, waited for instructions with the two other scouts, Marcus and Rhone. She didn't know them very well but was familiar with them by reputation. They were known for taking and completing even the most rigorous assignments in the western region. Up close they were just two gritty-looking men who looked like they belonged in an old-style western. In a way, she was a lot like them. Her clothes were the same muted browns and tans, and her visible skin had the same dry, taut appearance. The packs they carried contained similar water containers, rope, and other supplies expertly packed within them. One difference between her and the others was in what they did as they waited for orders.

While the other two fretted with their bags, making sure they had everything they would need, Alison simply knew her pack was well stocked. She remembered where everything was and didn't feel the need to verify what she already knew. This allowed her to pay attention to what John and Katherine were doing at the map. They were talking in low tones, but Alison had spent years mastering the art of looking like she wasn't listening. So, after a while, they began to speak a little louder, seemingly confident no one was paying attention.

"We don't know the final rendezvous point yet?" John asked. "No one has come forward with a goddamn clue about that?"

"No one in our party seems to know anything," Katherine said. "Either they have orders not to give it to us until we get closer, or someone else will intercept us with the information."

"Are you serious?" John asked. "We're just blindly moving along the last known heading, hoping someone will give us a hint?"

"Not exactly," Katherine said. "But yeah, basically."

Alison had noted which direction they'd been traveling and knew of a few outposts out ahead of them. She didn't see a good way into the conversation but spoke up anyway. “I’ve taken a few courier assignments that led me this way.”

John and Katherine turned to her in surprise, as did Marcus and Rhone.

“Ember Springs is the last one I did,” she continued. “Took intel from Taycher up there. It’s a small town in a mountain range along our heading. I’d never been that far north before.”

“Either of you make drops along our route?” John asked the others.

“Now that you ask, yeah.” Rhone looked up from his pack. “I made a drop out at Ember Springs recently too.”

“Alright, I guess that’s our best guess right now,” Katherine said.

Jim strode into the tent then with a wide grin then, and Alison’s attention moved involuntarily to him. “Did you know the driver's seats in the trucks we stole are leather? A goddamn military resupply truck with leather seats. I wonder if they’re heated.”

“They’re not,” John said as he left the map and walked to the group. “Now that you’re all here, gather around. We’ve got a heading for you, and now a possible destination. Jim, you will take this route.”

John traced a path along the map, following dry riverbeds, trails, and an occasional main road. The path flowed a few degrees off true north to the west, deviating only to avoid larger geological features.

“The rest of you will spread out, still following the same bearing, but pick different routes to cover more ground. Keep an eye out for anything or anyone that might be important. You’ll check in with Jim to fuel up or report anything you see. However you want to work that out will be fine. You'll have short-range radios, and he will have an encrypted radio in the truck he can use to report back to us. Your mission is to make sure the path ahead of our force is clear of anything that would hinder our progress."

As John talked, Alison noticed one of the soldiers at a radio terminal in the tent begin talking and writing frantically on a notepad. She tuned out of the briefing and tried to determine what was happening. John was in mid-sentence when the radio operator finally called out.

"Sir," she said tentatively. Alison recognized her as the same woman who'd been operating the communications panel in the command mech. "We've got a problem."

"What is it?" Katherine asked, clearly annoyed at the interruption.

"It's our stragglers, sir. They're in trouble." The radio officer handed Katherine a piece of paper with hastily scribbled notes on it. "They just got into the city, and they're being followed by someone."

"Shit," Katherine said. "Are these coordinates right? Everybody out. We'll finish this briefing later."

Alison attempted to hang back as she'd been able to do before, but Jim pushed her along as ushered the team outside.

~

Inside the tent, John took the piece of paper from Katherine. Written on it were coordinates that indicated an area on the other side of the city in the same direction they had come from Taycher. The page said the forces following their straggler were mechs, but that should be impossible. He'd seen the remaining mechs go up in flames as they'd left. Anything left behind wouldn't be able to power on, let alone follow them.

"We can't have our damaged mech make its way to us now," Katherine said. "That would give away our position and theirs. What do you think?"

"Are you sure they said mechs?" John asked the radio operator, still looking at the paper.

"That's what they said, sir." She looked as if she was trying very hard to remember every detail correctly. "They reported seeing an unknown number of large heat signatures approaching from the southeast. Then they went silent. Something about wanting to stay dark."

"Good," John said. "Someone's got some brains out there. If there really are mechs on our tail, they'll be scanning the frequencies just to look for radio sources. There's no way they will hear anything distinct. It would just be noise to them, but it's not hard to determine the direction of a transmission. What about the repair team? Are they still reporting?"

"Last time they did was an hour ago," the woman at the radio said. "Everything was fine. I can check again." She reached for the controls.

"Get away from that!" John snapped. "Do you want to get everyone killed? I just told you anyone following us is listening for transmissions. Dial the intensity down and... you know what? Just get out of the way."

John moved over to the radio panel and helped the woman aside. He felt an instant of guilt, being so harsh with her, but a single errant radio burst could mean death for anyone out there. He worked the controls for a moment, bringing the range down on the transmitter, and said, "Maintenance One, bring down your transmission radius and respond. Repeat, bring down intensity and respond."

"Affirmative, base. You're coming in weak."

"Our stragglers have just reached the city, but they've got someone on their tail," John said. "Hold your position and await further commands. Maintain radio silence unless ordered to respond."

No response came through the radio. John nodded with approval. He walked back to the map being projected on the table and panned back to a view of their current dilemma. He keyed in the new coordinates listed on the sheet of paper, and a red marker appeared on the map a few miles outside the city. Already displayed on the screen were the locations of their main fleet, repair team, and straggler mech in the city. Together, the points made a straight line cutting almost perfectly diagonally across the map. The swath of damage cutting across the city would probably have been enough to give the followers a good shot at finding them, even if they didn't pick up on their transmissions. John's group was going to have to move quickly if they were going to get away without being discovered.

"We can't risk the safety of the main core for one crippled mech in the city." John hated how cold the words sounded. "We may have to leave them behind." He said the final words in a near whisper, almost to himself.

"I agree," Katherine said. "And we need the techs on that repair squad if we're going to be able to maintain our other mechs the rest of the way. But our people aren't going to respond well to that. We have to make at least some effort to retrieve the soldiers out there."

"The repair team is closest, but they're not equipped for a firefight. We'd be sending them in almost blind as well."

"Not if your scout team provided intelligence." Katherine pointed to a location on the map. "Look, they could travel quickly to a position high enough to watch for enemy movement. I know they're not equipped for a firefight, either, but if they're as good as Jim thinks they are, we could do this without the enemy even knowing."

"It puts even more assets at risk, Katherine. Are we really going to send a maintenance crew in to extract our people, and then also send our best reconnaissance out there?"

"If we don't do it, I'm telling you, we'll have a mutiny to deal with," Katherine said. "We've got a few former military types who would understand. But that won't be enough to stop anyone who decides they don't want to continue listening to people whose last job was training the enemy."

"Sure," John said. He knew she was right. After a moment of thought, he wondered how much of his resistance had to do with sending Alison into the field. "I'll get them back in here and bring them up to speed."

~

Two hours after midnight Alison left the encampment with Jim, Marcus, and Rhone. Despite John's misgivings about it, they were going with the plan Katherine had drawn up. The reconnaissance team made their way around the edge of the city, sticking to back roads whenever possible. Just before sunrise, they were in position, scattered a few miles apart along a span of low foothills with a clear view of the city. By using short-range radios, they were able to communicate with little fear of their transmissions being intercepted. The repair team should have made contact with the crippled mech just as the scouts took their positions above.

The city looked entirely abandoned even through Alison's binoculars. She was lying prone on the top of the hill to reduce her silhouette against the sky behind her. Alison kept a continuous watch in the direction the enemy mechs were supposed to be. Every so often, she flipped through the various filters on her binoculars. The infrared, motion enhancing, and a standard optical were the most useful. The rest of her team was scanning the area as well. If everything went well, the repair team would be able to get the mech up and running before any of the enemy forces knew what was happening. But if there was enemy movement, Alison's team would be able to send out a warning to abandon the repairs on the mech and retreat with their trucks to cover.

Watching where the enemy was supposedly camped made her uneasy. This stalemate had already gone on for too long, and someone should have made a move by now. She dropped her binoculars down for a moment and tightened the hood of her thick jacket. Then, watching the area for a bit without her binoculars, she noticed something. It was a flicker of movement two hills closer than she'd expected. She picked up her binoculars and saw an enemy mech take up a position on a faraway dune. It stood in the open for a few moments and seemed to be scanning the city. They were probably just looking to see if everything was in the same place, but this was the first visual confirmation that the forces following them were actually mechs. Without looking away, she used one hand to click the transmit button on her radio.

"We've got a peeping tom on the ridge," she said. "Looks like a small biped scouting the city. Our boys better get that mech moving soon or just pack up and leave it. They don't have a lot of time."

The sensors on the enemy mech probably wouldn't be sensitive enough to register the addition of the repair team visually. They might notice an increase in heat if their team attempted to fire it up, however.

"Bad news," Jim said over the radio. "I've got word we don't have the mech running yet. This is going to get dicey, guys. They're going to need our eyes."

Light from the rising sun glinted off another mech as it crested the hills just at the edge of the city. As she adjusted the focus on her binoculars, a number of enemy units came over the dunes, and she had to decrease her magnification to keep them all in view.

"We've got some fast-moving mechs headed right for our team," Alison said. "Can we please let someone know what's happening?"

"They know," Jim said over the radio. "They're getting everyone out of there in their trucks now. Repairs were abandoned on the mech."

Alison looked toward the city where the mech had been being worked on. She couldn't see the site directly from her angle, but her binoculars could still register a heat signature there. Between two buildings, she caught a glimpse of their trucks fleeing as quickly as they could. She let out a sigh of relief and panned back over to the advancing enemy mechs. They were working around the edges of the position of the crippled mech.

"They should be able to get out," Alison said. "The enemy mechs are spending a lot of time flanking our empty mech."

As she said this, though, the heat signature representing their mech began to move.

"What the hell?" Marcus or Rhone said over the radio. "Jim, our mech is moving down there. I thought we pulled everyone out."

"I did too," Jim said. "What the hell are they thinking? They don't stand a chance."

Almost as if to answer Jim's comment, their mech made a move. When it finally came into view between two of the larger structures, Alison was able to appreciate the damage to it for the first time. The mech was dragging one of its legs, almost completely useless. The rest of it looked to be slightly bent out of shape. Its angles were no longer square. But the guns were evidently still operational. Bright flashes began throwing uncanny shadows through the narrow streets and alleys below. The encroaching enemy mechs reacted quickly. None of the first shots connected, and the crippled mech managed to make its way slowly to the northeast.

"Jim, they're drawing the enemy mechs away from our trucks," Alison reported. "Whoever is piloting that mech isn't going to make it."

"Fall with grace," Jim said. Based on the volume and clarity of the message, she could tell it had been broadcast on an open channel at full power. Everyone would have heard it.

Alison's heart raced as she watched their crippled mech lurch wildly away, firing in any direction it could. What might look like the blind panic of a cornered animal was actually a calculated sacrifice in a greater game. When it was finally hit by a series of rounds from one of the enemy units, it stumbled forward and collided with a weakened building. Somehow the mech managed to push off the crumbling structure with one arm and continue on, putting more distance between it and the fleeing trucks.

Smoke and dust rose out of the city, obscuring Alison's view so she could only see the mechs' heat signatures in the haze. Soon, even those details faded as hot smoke and scattered fires made it impossible to distinguish one orange shape from another. It was over.

"We've done all we can from here," Jim said, his radio tuned back down to a tactical radius. "Gather back on my position. We'll move in behind our repair group and make sure no one follows us home."

CHAPTER 13

John and Katherine had received constant updates from Jim during the brief battle inside the city. The idea to have someone stay inside their damaged mech had been John's. The sacrifice had effectively served to draw the enemy off their fleeing trucks and steer them away from the trail of the main core, for a little while, at least.

Jim must have relayed the orders accurately, because the ploy had worked. No one else knew the pilot had been ordered to stay behind, and it might be better that way. Movements need martyrs. To whoever survived the building global firestorm, the fallen mech pilot might even become part of a grander legend. The story would be made stronger if people believed the act had been swiftly done without coldly calculated orders from a superior officer. It was a small detail, but one they might be able to use to their advantage when they informed the main group of the outcome.

Both teams were on their way back. Two small blue markers at the edge of the command mech's sensor range began closing in fast. John waited a few moments, watching the blurred edge of the screen, fearing that another marker would come into view indicating that someone was following.

If something larger had lumbered into range, they would have had a problem. He was still unsure of the scale of the enemy group that was tailing them now. Jim and his team had reported at least three or four well-armed mechs. That could be all there was, or just the tip of a much larger spear, but from where? John still couldn't imagine where any sizeable force of mechs would be coming from.

When nothing came into view after a few more moments of looking at the map, John left the canvas tent. Katherine was already waiting outside, looking uncomfortable in the dull wrinkled rebel outfit they'd been able to find. On John, the loose uniform hung naturally, but on her, it looked like a costume.

"Good showing, I hear," Katherine said when he reached her. "We've got a batch of returning heroes to welcome. Somebody will have to give a speech when they get here."

"Don't look at me," John said. "I'm about as inspirational as...well, I'm not sure."

"That's bullshit," Katherine said. "Do you really think no one knows you're a primary voice of the Doctrine? Enough people know, and word spreads fast in a community this small. They've been waiting for an excuse to hear the Voice of the Fall."

John had begun to hate that unofficial honorific. It was one thing to drink a bottle of whiskey and write abstractly about how he would change the world and another entirely to get up and speak to an assembled group of people hanging on his every word. Speaking in front of the gathering crowd of eager listeners without so much as a drink in him was daunting. Indeed, the general lack of alcohol in this damned caravan had begun to affect him. As the trucks in the distance got closer, he found himself fantasizing about the spilled whiskey in his quarters back at the Academy. There had even been a new bottle in the drawer. Why hadn't he thought to grab it when they were leaving? All he'd taken was a photograph.

He drew it out and unfolded it carefully, afraid of it being tugged away by the wind. He stared down into the faces of his family and asked himself the same question that always came to mind when faced with their images: would they understand the man he had become? He hoped they would understand his betrayals, his mistakes, and his choices.

He folded the image, taking care to follow the existing crease that ran over none of their faces. The fold itself separated them from him, on the paper as in life. He looked up toward the approaching trucks and stepped out in front of the gathered crowd. He could still feel the corners of the photograph in his hand and managed to suppress the desire for a flask instead.

When the trucks finally pulled up in front of the group, there was a roar of applause and cheering. Riding the wave of applause, he walked out to shake the hand of a man who approached him. The man, who had clearly emerged as a leader of some kind out there, saluted John after they shook hands.

"It's good to have you back, soldier," John said. "We're all happy to have you back."

"It's good to be back, sir," the man said. "But we wouldn't be here if it weren't for what Samson did."

Samson it was, then. It was good to know the name of the star of his speech before he began. The rest of the returning force disembarked from the two dusty trucks. John could see the ATVs and Jim's truck also approaching in the distance, but it wouldn't do to wait for them. Already, the applause and shouting had begun to quiet in anticipation. John spread his arms as Katherine had done recently, hoping the effect was as natural as she had made it look. The crowd responded and looked at him. He stood with the returned heroes at his back and addressed the crowd.

"Behind me," John began, pacing in the dirt slowly. "Behind me are men and women of extraordinary valor. In the grand tales they will tell of the Harbingers of the Fall, this moment may be a small thing, but we will know the truth. I don't need to explain the courage it took to stay behind and struggle valiantly to get our valuable mech back to us. I also don't need to tell you about the bravery it took to get these comrades back to us, once it became impossible to repair our mech in time.

"What I do need you to hear is of the extreme sacrifice made by one who is no longer with us. Pilot Samson has fallen."

He waited for a moment as a collective gasp rippled through the crowd. One person near the front even began to weep and was comforted by someone nearby.

"Because he stayed behind and drew the enemy away, we were able to bring our people back to us. The gift Samson has given our cause is beautiful, but not unique. There may come a time that each and every one of you may be asked to make a similar decision. Samson chose to protect the Harbingers. I believe you have within your hearts the courage to do exactly that, for the fate of humanity."

The crowd did not applaud, seeming to want more from him. He hadn't expected them to need anything more than a simple speech honoring a fallen comrade. What did they need? His pause had registered among the crowd, and he tried to read their faces. Without direction, he allowed his inner voice to spill out, if only to fill the growing silence.

"On your faces, I see ripples of fear, of anger, and of sadness. You're afraid, and rightly so, of being asked to make a sacrifice like this. I want you to know that if you are afraid, it will not be an order. One cannot order a soldier to their death without the soldier themselves already having accepted the order. Samson did not hesitate, did not need an order. He simply did as he knew he should.

"Of the anger I see, I welcome you to bathe in it. Anger, at the root, is recognition of wrongdoing. I need you, however, to direct your anger at the source of the misdeed. Marry it with the anger that brought you here in the first place. Build onto the anger inside you and give it context.

"And of the sadness, I have no advice. I have shared in my own losses. I have no grand words to help you through this one. I myself still wrestle with the aftershocks of my own grief. The only thing I'll say to you is, allow yourself to eventually transmute the grief into its more potent cousin: purpose."

John felt his words come from him with a life of their own. They might not be perfect, but in the absence of better words, these would do.

"All of these things I see in you should flow toward purpose. The forces that hold up the failing tower of society will not be swayed by mere anger. It will not be undercut by the force of grief beneath it. It also cannot be overcome by fear. These things only stand to strengthen the foundations of our oppressors. Distill them instead into raw purpose. With that, we may be able to topple the tower. For with purpose, we move as one being, exerting our will against the walls of our oppressors. With purpose, we will bring about the Fall so that we may begin anew among the ashes that remain."

John stood in silence as a dry wind swept dust around them. He waited, looking from face to face, trying to judge how his words had landed. The faces that stared back at him appeared poised at the edge of applause. What else could he say to them? What more did they need to release him from this position?

In the span of a few moments, he landed on what he must say. "In Samson's final moments, he left us with a phrase we all know. They are somehow made stronger when said by a man facing his own death. I'm sure some of you heard them, but I will repeat them now."

John paused now, this time intentionally. This part was a lie, of course. The words he was about to say had been radioed out by Jim, but they were stronger when put at the end of Samson's life.

"Fall with grace," John said.

With no further provocation, the crowd began to chant. They started with the first part of the well-known phrase. "Someday we will all fall." Then, after a beat, they followed in resounding unison, "Fall with grace."

~

The camp was quiet now, as preparations for the departure in the morning began to wind down. Many people were off getting whatever sleep they could. Those trained in piloting the mechs, who had been learning by rigorous trial and error how real mechs differed from simulations, badly needed the rest. Those left awake were doing the menial but vital work of securing and double-checking that everything was ready to go. Some loading and organization was still happening at each of the three command mechs, which carried most of the supplies for their force.

Rather than sleep inside the belly of the command mech, Alison was lying awake on her bedroll on a patch of cold dirt near the embers of a small campfire. She had been dismissed from any loading duties due to her service earlier in the day. She'd been pestered beyond her tolerance to recount the battle as she'd seen it from her vantage point above it all. Eventually she had shortened it until those asking had lost interest. She had made sure to amend the part where Jim was the one who radioed out the "Fall with grace" call, of course, not wanting to undermine John's account.

She watched as the work near Command Three continued in the dim light of a few lanterns. The wind occasionally blew through camp, picking up ash from the numerous campfires used to heat water or cook rations. The smell of it reminded her of nights she'd spent alone in the desert between one waypoint or another. She found her mind wandering the same way it had during many of her missions. She thought about Eva and her family. Alison hoped they were all asleep in the old house as it creaked in the wind with familiar pops and groans. If she closed her eyes and listened hard enough, she was able to believe she could hear her father snoring loudly. She and her mother had always given him a hard time when she was growing up, comparing him to a bear or, on particularly bad nights, a diesel truck engine.

As they always had, these thoughts began to carry her off to sleep. She heard the sound of boots on the metal ramp leading down from the cargo desk at Command Three and opened her eyes. As she looked at the stars hanging above her, her heart began to race. She turned her head toward the figure approaching from across the sand.

"Alison, are you awake?" Jim asked as he crouched down next to her. "You need to come with me. There's something happening."

She propped herself up on her elbows and looked up into the deeply shadowed face next to her. His shape was merely a shadow blotting out stars, but she could read the tension in his voice without seeing his face. Together, they headed toward Command Three. They entered from the cargo ramp and worked their way up toward the sounds of arguing voices on the Command Deck.

"We can't let an opportunity like this slip away," one of the voices said angrily. The tone was new, but it was definitely Katherine's voice. "The information we could get if we caught one is worth the risk."

"We're leaving tomorrow morning," another voice, John's, retorted. "We don't have time to send another team out there. We have to get moving. We can't afford this."

"I am the commanding officer here, John." Katherine said. "We're sending a team in, and we have to look united, or this whole thing will fall apart. You may have rallied them with more of your rhetoric, but I have command here."

As Jim and Alison approached the last few stairs to the command deck, Jim put out an arm to stop her. He held a finger to his lips. Together, they stood in the shadowed corridor, allowing the argument to continue.

"I don't understand what you think you're going to accomplish by sending this many people in there," John said. "Our orders are to make it to our next rendezvous, right? As far as I can tell, that's the only priority here. It has the added benefit of getting us the hell away from whatever force is tracking behind us."

"Exactly, John," Katherine said, her voice bordering on condescension. "Whatever the hell is following us. We could be running from ghosts, for all we know, or there could be a whole company of mechs back there. Wouldn't it be better to know what we're dealing with? I'm sure Central Command would want this information."

When John didn't respond, Jim waited a few moments, then nudged Alison to proceed with him into the room. When they entered, John was standing over the map display in the middle of the room, and Katherine was looking out through the front window into the night. The room was empty otherwise, and lit only by the light emanating from the consoles and map display. Alison and Jim stepped up to the map before the other two realized they were there.

"Hello, John," Jim said. "I've brought Alison. Do you want to read her in?"

John looked up from the map, locked eyes with Alison. She could feel the paternal responsibility he felt for her for her in that glance. She'd never given him the slightest indication she needed it, but in that concern, she could tell that something was very wrong.

"Your family is fine as it stands now," John said, keeping his eyes locked on hers. "We've received information from someone at your family's home that there are three enemy soldiers there right now. Someone on a secure radio frequency in our sweep range let us know about an hour ago. The soldiers apparently aided in the return of your sister and are staying there tonight before they head back. We don't have a lot more information than that."

"I don't understand," Alison said, choosing her words slowly and carefully. "Why are you telling me this? You called me up here to tell me my family is safe and sound?"

"No," Katherine said from behind them. She'd left the window and was standing a few paces from the map table. "We've called you up here to tell you they may not be safe. We're sending in a team to attempt to secure at least one of the soldiers staying with your family. We can't guarantee things are going to go calmly. We're going to try our best, but a lot of this depends on how the soldiers themselves react."

"You can't do this," Alison said, her hands balling into fists. "John, talk to her. You can't go in there. If they were in danger, they would have said so."

"I understand," Katherine said. "From what we've been told, the soldiers will be leaving in the morning. This is a tight window of opportunity, and we've decided to take it. The information we could gain from this could be incredibly valuable."

"Why the hell even tell me if you've already decided?" Alison asked. "What fucking point is there? What if I try to stop you?"

"We were hoping you would help," Jim said from beside her. "Nobody knows this terrain as well as you. Them being inside your family home means we have the ultimate home field advantage if you agree to be part of our team."

"We have to let them know what's happening," Alison said. She inhaled deeply, warding off the sudden urge to scream. "We have to get them out of there before you do this."

"We can't," John said. "If we're going to do this, we can't arouse suspicion. And we are doing it." He said these last words as if he was telling himself as well as Alison.

Alison couldn't seem to think more than a few words ahead of the situation, and took a moment to collect her thoughts. "I'll go. If you're going, I will need to be there."

"Good," Katherine said, her voice cool and controlled. She returned to her position at the window. "Jim and everyone else will be relying on you for your help."

Alison resented how calm everyone was, and how much of her own emotions she had to contain just to remain in the conversation.

"We really do need you for this to go smoothly," Jim said. He placed a hand on her shoulder.

Alison shrugged it off and took a step away. "I never thought this would..." She placed both her hands flat on the broad map table, taking another moment to compose her words. "I never thought this would come so close to home. At least, not this quickly. I thought by the time any of this started to affect them, it would all have started to even out. What would you do if this was your family?"

She asked the question to the table and didn't expect a response. The room was nearly silent as her words hung in the air around them. The only sounds were a low droning from the computer terminals and the soft static hiss from the communications console. When a response didn't come, Alison took her palms from the table and stood up straight.

"Who called the information in?" she asked. "Was it Brian?"

"The man said he was your father. We didn't get a name," John said. "The message was intended for you, really. He took more risk than he knows in sending it out. It was an old encryption pad. It's entirely possible the government forces may have intercepted it."

"I don't think so," Alison said. "If it's the one I gave him, it's one I made. Registered it and never used it, so it would stay active. I needed a way for him to contact me if he ever needed to. What did he say, exactly?"

"It was brief," John said. "He said that Eva is safe and that the three government soldiers had brought her back. He said the soldiers would be gone by tomorrow morning, and not to worry."

The fact that Jack had felt the need to let her know Eva was safe meant she hadn't been at some point. This hurt her somewhere deep. Alison felt like she was failing Eva by being out here now.

"My father meant that message for me." She looked at Katherine, knowing she was the one with power. "You have no right to use this information and put them in danger."

"This is a war," Katherine said without turning around. "Information carries value. You should know this. Your entire purpose in this organization is the transfer of information. To let this slip by would be a gross miscalculation. You do not have to go in with our team, but know they will be leaving within the hour."

Alison didn't respond or even wait for a dismissal. She turned on her heel and headed out of the room. Jim hurried after her, staying a few paces back as she made her way down the stairs and back out into the cool night air.

"Alison, wait." He grabbed her arm, bringing her in stride with him. "I know you don't like this, but she's right. We can't let an opportunity like this go."

"I know," Alison said, allowing herself to stop moving. "I know. That's what makes this so hard. And I'll go with your team. Just give me a few goddamn minutes, okay?"

"Sure," Jim said. He held up his hands and backed away. "We'll be gathering up at the eastern edge of camp. I'll save a spot for you in my truck."

CHAPTER 14

The team consisted of three trucks loaded with the best-trained tacticians and soldiers in their group. A number of them had even defected from various military or corporate security organizations. Jim and Alison sat in the front of the lead truck and navigated without lights toward her childhood home.

"You'll need to follow a dirt road when we get closer," Alison said. "Sound carries in the area. I know from listening for coyotes as a kid. When anyone heard one, we'd call for my dad, and he'd come out with his shotgun and fire into the air. He used to say it was easier to scare the lot of them than aim for one and miss."

"Where is the road we need to take?" Jim asked. "And how far away do we need to leave the trucks?"

"I'm sorry," Alison said. "I keep getting caught up thinking about them. I'm worried."

"We understand, and we're going to do our best." He tapped the paper map in front of her softly.

"It's about two miles up." Alison pointed to a blank area on the map. "It's not an official road, of course. My father and anyone else living out here technically aren't supposed to even be here. But the officials who patrol out here look the other way as long as we cut them in on our crop.

"Everyone in the area is used to the sounds of a group like ours," she said as they approached the point she'd indicated on the map. "In a way, I think that will be an advantage. As long as the government wasn't knocking down your door, you went about life as normal. So, even if someone does see us, they're more likely to stay shuttered in their houses than start an assault."

"Is this the spot?" Jim asked as they approached a small tributary road. "It doesn't look like anyone even lives out here. There's a major road up ahead we would probably have a lot more luck with."

"That road takes you above the valley," Alison said dismissively. "You'd send any sound you made echoing down on my family's land. No, this road will keep us in some low trees until we're close to the house."

This satisfied Jim, and stopped the truck and cut the engine. He got out and signaled the drivers of the other two vehicles to do the same. When all the engines were off, the night sounds came flooding into the vehicle, along with a cloud of fine dust from the other trucks. She'd been here so recently, she thought, but the sounds and smells still brought a surge of emotions over her. Normally, she'd have taken the main road in and driven directly up to their home. She would have been in a rush to cover the final miles, to see Eva. To hold her daughter in her arms.

Now, however, they were taking the little-used road she'd always thought of as their escape road. Her father had always told her to take this road and stick to the shadows if government forces came for them. Now the government forces were already there. Based on the message her father had sent, the soldiers wouldn't be expecting them, but they were still soldiers. Their training would keep them on edge, especially out here in unknown territory.

After everyone but the drivers had exited the trucks, three groups were separated out and began to make their way down the road. Jim and Alison took up position at the rear of the first group so she could relay information about the various bends in the road ahead. When they got closer, she began to instinctively use hand signals she'd learned as part of her initial training with the Harbingers of the Fall. She signaled to Jim that the house was a half-mile away and that there were no more turns. Jim nodded and turned to his soldiers. He used signals Alison was unfamiliar with to instruct them, and without reply, they fanned out and pushed their way into the thick woods that surround her family home.

Alison looked at Jim, hoping for clarification on her role. He shook his head and held out his hand, telling her to wait there. When the second group arrived, he gave them another set of commands, and they began pushing into the woods as well. Alison, getting frustrated at not understanding the plan, approached Jim and spoke to him in a low whisper.

"I want to know what the hell they're doing, Jim." She looked at him angrily. "This is my family. I have a right to know."

"I have the first two teams surrounding the house, cutting off their angles of escape as best we can." He looked over Alison's shoulder where the third group was approaching. "You and I will head up the rest of the way to the house, behind this last group. If everything goes well, we'll have those soldiers extracted from the house before they even know what's happening."

Alison nodded, understanding the risk they were taking in talking, even this far away. The group Jim had assembled really did seem to be skilled. Jim himself was surprisingly adept in this capacity as a commander. She would have to ask him what he did before he joined the Harbingers when they got out of here, she thought.

When they reached the edge of the woods surrounding her home, Alison could see the shadowy form of it. All the lights were off inside, and the moon was low on the horizon. A porch lamp cast a semicircle of light out into the backyard as a thin wisp of smoke trailed from the brick chimney. The smell of burning wood lingered in the clearing as she scanned the yard, making sure her father wasn't asleep on the porch. She strained her eyes and did spot movement. Someone was sitting on the bench swing anchored to the old cottonwood tree in the backyard. She watched for a moment, then pointed the figure out to Jim.

"That's my father," she whispered. "I think. I mean, it looks like him."

The sound of the back door opening and approaching footsteps caused Alison to jump. She watched as a figure approach her father slowly. Her heart began to race when she spotted a gun in the unknown figure's hand. Her father—she could see him clearly now—had his shotgun laid across his lap. Immobilized by fear, she took a breath in and held it.

The man behind her father, who was wearing a government uniform, said something. Her father lifted his shotgun and tossed it into the grass at his feet. Alison began to shake and realized she hadn't taken a breath in too long. Her thoughts became preoccupied with how to quietly exhale and get another gulp of air inside her. By the time she was able to focus her attention again, the unknown man had her father's gun in his hands. The two seemed to have had some kind of brief argument, and the soldier started to move back toward the house. He was moving quickly, casting glances toward the tree line as he fled. Alison realized her father must have warned the man.

The soldier aimed her father's shotgun up into the sky and fired off a single blast. The sound and light cracked the night. Suddenly, new flashes of light began going off in the woods all around her. It took her a moment to realize the flashes were coming from gunfire. Her first instinct was to leap out of cover, but Jim placed a firm hand on her shoulder to keep her in place. She looked away from the house and saw her father, sitting on his swing, motionless. Had he been hit in this barrage? The soldier had made it inside the house, and for a few moments, there was silence again. Alison could see the hazy shapes of her comrades working their way out of the woods and toward the house.

She managed to push Jim's hand from her shoulder and stepped out of the woods herself, feeling helpless to stop the encroaching shadows. The gun her father had given her was still in her pack, but to crouch down now and take it out would take too long. She cursed herself silently for not having thought about it earlier.

The silence was broken by a new sound, and Alison was running before she knew what was happening. Eva was crying from inside the house, and her panicked cries were all Alison could hear. She was already halfway across the yard when someone hit her from behind. She landed, sprawling, in the high grass.

A hand came over her mouth as the people she'd been traveling with passed swiftly over her. From this vantage point, they looked like dark giants advancing on her family home. She tried to scream for them to stop but couldn't get a sound past the hand covering her mouth.

"You have to be quiet, Alison," Jim said firmly. He held her tight as the forces continued their advance on the house. "You have to be quiet."

She began to cry, regretting having agreed to be here. A team smashed a window and tossed something into the dark room within. She remembered sneaking out of that window when she was younger, and her mind went foggy as she struggled to scream or breathe. She had snuck out so many times her father had nailed it shut from the outside. Now, smoke was the only thing pushing its way out.

Sounds that terrified her were coming from inside the house. She managed scramble onto her knees before Jim had hold of her again, and she knelt in the grass. Flashes of gunfire lit up different parts of her house as people moved through it. After too long, the sound of a truck joined the rising cacophony of sound. New, frantic, orders were being called all around her. From her position in the backyard, she could only guess at what was happening at the front of the house.

She heard someone yell to move the trucks up to the house. The soldiers were escaping. She noticed Jim had left her only by the sudden coldness that replaced where he had been. An explosion went off inside the house, and she simply sank back onto her heels, unable to process the scene unfolding in front of her. She stood up, and a second sharp gulp of fire ripped open a hole in what used to be her bedroom wall. She staggered back as another series of explosions went off, and the house became a blooming blur of orange and yellow flames before her eyes. She struggled against the weight of her body and felt herself walking, then running the final yards toward her home. She made it to the back door and could feel the heat inside before another blast knocked her off her feet, back into the yard. She felt her weight lessen suddenly as someone lifted her from under her arms and dragged her away from the house. Whoever had moved her back deposited her there and sprinted off to accomplish another task somewhere. Orders flew through the air around her.

Alison rolled over, spitting blood into the grass. When she looked up, she could see her father lying limp on the ground beneath his swing. Again, she felt the weightlessness of being carried and turned her head to look at the house. She watched it for as long as she could as she was pulled, against her will, into one of the trucks. The fire raging inside the home illuminated the scene in flickering orange tones. The house was completely destroyed. She watched as people were dragged into the other trucks. The first two spun their tires and then flew out into the darkness beyond, trying catch up to the fleeing government soldiers.

As all of this happened, Alison struggled to free herself from the arms keeping her inside the last truck. Someone shouted that they had to go. The doors shut on the scene in front of her, and she was blanketed by sudden darkness. For a few moments she continued to struggle, but eventually, darkness reached into her mind, and she lost consciousness.

~

John had watched the team head out: three trucks and some of their best soldiers. In the end, he hadn't been able to argue with Katherine, or her logic. For the most part, she was right. It would be better to know who was chasing them. It might even make sense to turn around and face them head-on if the force could be easily overmatched.

His main reservation had been the endangerment of Alison's family. He'd seen similar operations go badly too many times to truthfully tell Alison everything would work out. He hadn't even gotten the chance to lie to her before they'd left. But even if this plan didn't work, it was objectively worth the risk from a detached and distant enough perspective.

He sat in front of the comms panel on the command deck, drumming his fingers along the stationery pad there as he waited for anything to come through. Most everyone would be asleep by now, except for the few essential lookouts and those finishing some of the more labor-intensive tasks required to gear up for the next long haul. Maintenance was needed on some of the mechs, this one included. Everyone he'd spoken with had assured him everything would be buttoned up by sunrise.

The team out in the field hadn't radioed in any news, but that wasn't surprising. They were maintaining radio silence until they began their journey back, to minimize the possibility of being tracked. John had been outside earlier when he'd heard what sounded like a series of small explosions far off in the distance. That had prompted him to go inside and take over at the communications terminal. Every errant crackle of static on the radio caused him to jump with alarm. The team should have been getting back soon. It had been too long.

"Have you gotten any sleep, John?" Katherine asked, startling him. John wasn't sure when Katherine had joined him on the deck. It was possible that she'd been there for a while, listening to the radio with him.

"No. I couldn't," he said, rubbing at his eyes. "They should be back by now, shouldn't they?"

"No telling. Anything could have happened to delay them. Hell, they could be lost for all we know, John. You get some rest, and I'll watch the comms."

He considered telling her he couldn't leave but knew that he needed to rest before they set out at sunrise. "Okay, but please wake me as soon as you've heard anything. I'll be in a bunk downstairs."

"Go to bed, John," Katherine said.

He stood up, and she took his seat. John didn't look back as he walked out of the room, not wanting to face the concerned expression she must have been wearing. She would either come and get him, or she wouldn't. Nothing he could do right now would be of any help to Alison or the rest of the team. He could best serve them by being rested and ready to go once they returned.

When he reached the bunk rooms downstairs, he managed to find an empty bed and climbed in. There would eventually have to be some sort of official schedule and assignment of bunk space. Up to this point, things had gone too fast for that. As his eyes adjusted, he found himself staring up at the underside of the bunk above him like he had done recently. He reached up and ran his fingertips across a series of new etchings he found there. After having the bottoms of the bunks sanded smooth to erase the enemy soldiers', the new crew had apparently begun to fill in with their own inscriptions. Instead of ranks, they'd put their names and towns of origin. And, taking the place of the government propaganda slogans, he now saw phrases pulled directly from writings he had supplied to the cause. The selections of crude drawings, however, were nearly the same. How much had really changed, he wondered. This machine would still be used to crush other human beings.

John sighed and dropped his arm back to his side. He realized he wouldn't be able to sleep and swung his legs out into the narrow aisle between the bunks. His left leg spasmed with a familiar jolt of pain. No matter how long he struggled with the leg, it always reminded him of his inherent feebleness.

He massaged the offending leg and allowed his mind to wander back to the day he'd first received this lasting injury. It had been an unusually sunny day for the kind of operation they were going to be running. His team had been deployed, with a full complement of armored units, into an enemy-controlled city. Was it bad that he didn't even remember which city? No, he decided. The injury and the resulting trauma were enough for him to accept some memory loss of the event. And, really, what was the difference between one raid and another? He often found when running memories back during moments like this that he was unable to recall the details of who, and why, he'd been sent to kill.

His leg spasmed again, bringing him momentarily back into the present—back to the soft snores of the sleeping rebels around him. John closed his eyes, allowing his mind to slide back into his train of thought. The sun had been high, without a cloud in the sky. A light breeze had rustled the leaves of the broad elms around them. He remembered thinking that in another time, it would have been a great day to fly a kite.

Instead, he had ordered his team to load up in their mechs and spread out. They were going to slowly encircle n a small camp of rebel soldiers and squeeze until the rebels either surrendered or were all dead. He'd taken up his post at the center of the curve as his forces had advanced. When small arms fire had begun, he'd given the weapons-free order. Unlike most of the sweeps he'd been on, the rebel forces hadn't immediately turned tail. They'd hunkered down in hastily dug trenches. That hadn't worried John, of course. Even one of their light reconnaissance mechs could have easily stepped over a trench that wide. What had bothered John was that they hadn't immediately tried to run away. He'd developed an uneasy sense that the rebels were guarding something important.

John had been piloting a Lupine class mech for the operation, a four-legged unit designed for agility and stability. There was no point in bringing a Neith class command mech for a simple rebel encampment. He'd radioed to his semicircle of forces to be careful and had continued to press forward. When the enemy had stopped returning fire, John had ordered his auxiliary forces, those tasked with manual reloads and navigation duties, to disembark and clear the small cluster of wooden structures the old-fashioned way. If there really was something of value there, John wouldn't have wanted to be responsible for blowing it to hell before he knew what it was. He'd also disembarked his mech and turned over the controls to his copilot.

It had felt good to cover ground on his own two feet, to use hand signals and take cover behind the now burning vehicles and supply crates of the rebel camp. It had reminded him of his better days in his urban tactical unit. He'd signaled for a trio of soldiers to advance on the first wooden shack and watched as they'd moved in formation through tall grass toward the door. He'd been struck again by the surreal nature of the high sun. It had made the whole thing seem like a training operation rather than an actual live-fire scenario.

That had changed suddenly when part of his advancing formation was obliterated in an ear-splitting explosion. That's why the rebel forces hadn't retreated, he realized. The entire area had been mined to ward against advancing forces.

John, shocked but still in a combat-ready frame of mind, had immediately signaled for everyone in his advancing party to halt. A man had emerged from one of the shacks then. The sudden shifts as his men had turned to train their weapons on the man had made John wince, expecting the motion to trip another mine. John's continued hand signal had seemed to reassure them, and no one had moved. The rebel man had put his hands up, and he had appeared unarmed. Of course, John hadn't approached to make an arrest, for fear of setting off one of the mines, but he hadn't expected the man would be able to approach either.

They'd stared at each other for what seemed a long time across the unknown field of mines. The man and anyone else in the camp, if taken alive, could have been holding a trove of valuable information about the rebel forces in other places around the country. More importantly, bringing in a rebel alive would have done wonders for John's reputation. It could have even gotten him promoted.

Looking down, John had been able to see the faint paths in the tall grass that must have been the safe ways in and out of the minefield. The grass had been parted slightly in ways that seemed unnatural to the terrain, so he'd ordered his men to follow those paths to advance. Still unsure of whether or not the man was alone, he'd kept his eyes up when he could, looking for movement.

He'd ordered the man to kneel as they got close to him. He'd obeyed quickly, but John had noticed the look on his face too late. The man had mouthed something to John from across the high grass. It might have been a curse, but John had always thought it was an apology of sorts. Maybe he'd been saying he had no choice. And wasn't that the truth? Did anyone really have a choice in these things? The man had revealed some sort of detonator in one of his hands. Before John had been able to react, the man had pressed the button.

The mines all around them had lit up like a carpet of fire, sending dark earth erupting into the sky. All but one of his advancing soldiers had died almost instantly. He himself had been blown backward. He remembered the feeling of his limbs waving uselessly in the air as his body had flown in a graceful arc, then the sudden smack as his head had connected with something. Later, they'd told him he'd been out for more than an hour. To him, it hadn't felt like more than an eye blink. He'd woken inside the Ursudae class mech, the only unit they'd had with any sort of space for lying down. He remembered a searing pain in his left leg. He had tried to sit up and had felt a cascade of pain ripple down his back. He'd clutched at the vest of the soldier tending to his wounds, and then slipped back into a gray fog.

Over the next few months, John had rehabbed in one of the most prestigious medical institutions in the country. Apparently, his decision not to raze the camp, not to burn it to the ground, had secured some of the most valuable information on the rebel forces to date. Intelligence experts had said the information recovered detailed a far-reaching network of camps spread across the territory. Each day, as he'd learned to use his leg again, John had watched the state news reports on television as the rebel camps had fallen like dominoes. He'd been congratulated by countless faces in suits with strong handshakes and trailing wakes of photographers.

It was then that he'd begun to sour completely at the idea of Stability. What did Stability mean but the continued success of those with power over those without it? He had started writing his first manifesto in his hospital room and had grinned when he'd been asked to teach at the newly built United Entities Mechanized Warfare Academy deep in the desert.

John opened his eyes again, still sitting at the edge of the bunk, the names of his new crew now etched into the metal. The pain in his leg had subsided to a dull ache and protested only minimally as he forced himself to stand. The sound of running feet reached him long before a young woman burst into the bunk room. She looked at his face, and he could read her message even before she spoke.

"Something is happening with the team," she said. "Katherine asked me to come get you."

John walked toward her slowly, attempting to mask the pain in his leg. She winced as if expecting him to bark orders at her, but John simply brushed past her without a word and headed for the stairs.

CHAPTER 15

Alison opened her eyes. She was still in the truck. It was stopped somewhere in the city, somewhere with tall buildings. The arms that had held her down were gone now, so she scrambled into a sitting position.

"Hey, calm down," a voice that must belong to the driver called to her from the front of the truck. "It's going to be okay. You passed out."

"Where is everyone else?" she asked. "Where are we? I need to go back."

"We think we've found them, or another group of them anyway." The voice came to her as if through water. "We thought we'd lost them, but we picked up on some heat signatures back at Samson's downed mech. The scum must be scavenging it for parts."

"Let me out," Alison said coldly. "I need to get out."

"I can't do that," he said. "I've got orders, you know. They'll be back soon."

Alison started to argue then noticed that the doors weren't locked. Her comrades hadn't expected her to wake up, much less run out into the night. She felt behind her and sighed with relief when she felt the familiar bulk of her pack. Working quickly, she rummaged inside for the gun her father had given her. The drawstring bag of rounds was there too. She loaded the gun slowly, trying to mask the sounds with an occasional grunt or by shifting her weight. She remembered her father's hands as they'd guided her when she was a child. His strong fingers showing hers where the various simple mechanisms were. Soon, the gun was fully loaded with six shells.

She shouldered her pack and hefted the gun in her hand. It was much heavier than the .22 caliber pistols she'd used as a child. The idea was the same, that's what her father had told her—just more powerful. She tucked it into her jeans behind her and reached for the door handle. In one fluid motion, she used it to hoist herself up and then opened the door. She was off and running before the man in the driver's seat knew she was gone. She made it around the corner and ducked into a deep shadow.

Unsure of where to go next, she stopped and listened to the sounds of the empty streets around her. The hushed calls of the driver trying to find her betrayed a sense of caution, and she tried to tune them out. She looked around, remembering this intersection from the countless times she'd traveled through the city. The same familiar surfaces were now coated with a fine layer of dust. A faint haze of smoke passed in the air around her, carried up by the soft breeze in this concrete canyon. She remembered the driver had said they were near Samson's downed mech, so she followed the smoke.

The sound of her footfalls was unnerving. The buildings took the sound and bent it back toward her in ways that made her feel as if someone was following her. The driver wouldn't be following her, she thought. He wouldn't have abandoned the vehicle for long. No, he was probably back in the truck trying to signal the others to let them know what had happened.

Still, she knew she should slow down. It wouldn't do to alert anyone to her approach. She slowed down and made her way to the crumpled remains of a building, silent in the moonlight. She heard the sound of someone struggling just around the next building, so she peeked carefully around the corner and saw a soldier.

He was working to remove a large metal ammunition box from what looked like the arm of a mech.

"Fuck off!" he yelled when the box didn't come loose. This must have been where Samson's mech had started to go down. Alison heard a sound coming from further down the road and saw the main heap of Samson's mech, tangled beneath the weight of a collapsed building.

"It's fine," the soldier closest to her yelled out toward the main wreckage. "I'm fine. This goddamn box won't come off, is all."

So, there were others here too, Alison thought. It wouldn't do to alert everyone to her presence, so she picked up a short metal pipe and hefted it like a club. It would do nicely. While the soldier was busy broadcasting his location to anyone within range, she managed to cover the few yards from her shadow to where he was standing. As he turned back to the ammunition box, she wound up and struck him hard across the ribs before he had time to turn around and see her. His body hit the pavement, and he gasped for air. Her adrenaline approached a full roar as she stood over him, watching fear and confusion wash across his face.

He reached for his pistol, but she brought the pipe down on him again. He must have regained some of his breath because he was able to cry out in pain. She dropped the pipe and drew out her revolver. She watched as a new wave of fear seemed to wash through him.

"Okay, okay," the soldier said as she took aim at his head. He scrambled backward and put his hands out in front of him. "I've got my hands up. What the hell do you want?"

Alison pulled the hammer back on her revolver, relishing the crisp mechanical sound it made. Suddenly, she heard shots being fired from near the wrecked mech down the street. The flashes of light that accompanied the sounds distracted her momentarily, and then she was on the ground. Her finger pulled tight on the trigger, and her shot ricocheted off the metal arm. In mere seconds, the soldier had knocked her down and worked his way past her to the other side of the mech's arm.

"Put the fucking gun down and no one has to be hurt here!" he yelled at her from cover. "This isn't going to end well. I can fucking promise you that."

No, it won't, she thought. She lurched around the side of the arm with her gun raised and was met by a mirror of motion as he levelled his own weapon at her. In this moment, she was able to see him clearly for the first time. He wasn't what she had expected. He was no older than she was, and wearing the uniform of a cadet, like the ones she'd seen at bonfire parties in the desert. His face was set in anger, but his eyes still betrayed a deep sense of uncertainty. She watched as he sized her up, probably noting the slight tremor in her hands. Alison hoped he mistook the tremor for fear.

"Hey, it's okay," the soldier said in a soft, exaggerated parody of calm. "You don't have to do this. I don't know if you're with the Harbingers or if you're just pissed off, but just put the gun down and we'll figure this out."

"You don't understand!" she yelled, shaking the gun at him for emphasis. Why couldn't she just pull the trigger? Her eyes betrayed her, beginning to well up with tears. For a moment, she lowered her weapon and blinked away the annoyances. "You've had it all. The care, the money. All the shit you could ever want was yours. But us? No. No, we haven't earned our place among the elite."

She adjusted her grip on the gun, regaining her composure. "You people murdered my fucking family, and I'm supposed to understand? Stability? Recovery? Well, we don't want recovery. We don't want Stability. We want all of this to fucking stop."

"I do understand," the soldier said. "But if you shoot me, your life is over. The rest of my squad is on the way and that..." He gestured at her gun. "That'll draw them in firing."

"You think I care? You do, don't you. That is a fucking mistake." She extended her weapon in the way her father had taught her: one arm straight out with the other bent slightly for support. The thought of her father again brought unwanted tears. She wiped at them furiously, and as she did, the man made a sudden move. She got off a shot, but he was already gone. He leapt forward and tackled her to the ground. Her head whipped backward against a rock as she hit the pavement. Alison was able to squeeze off one last round, but then her hands became unresponsive. She wasn't unconscious, but her head had hit the ground pretty hard, and she was finding it hard to focus or move with purpose.

The man stood and looked down at her. A surge of anger flowed through her. She tried to get back up only to find her arms were already bound behind her back. The sound of footsteps approaching brought on a new sense of hope; maybe her comrades had taken out whoever was at the main wreckage and would be able to take this asshole down as well.

"Turner! It's me!" the man above her yelled, dashing her hopes. "I've got a woman here. She's secured. I'll stay with her. You guys get the truck and pick us up on the way back, and then let's get the fuck out of here."

So, she was a captive now? She watched them angrily from the ground, thinking of all the ways she would hurt them if only she had her hands free.

"Just leave her here, Mark. We don't have room for one of these fucking people," the soldier, Turner, said. "Or just put a bullet in her. She clearly tried to do a number on you."

"Turner, if there's anyone else watching us, she's our best chance of getting out of here," the first soldier, Mark, said with authority.

"Fine. Let's get as much of this ammunition as we can back to the truck," Turner said, doing nothing to hide his contempt. He turned to Mark. "Make sure no one else fucking surprises you out here."

"Thank you, Turner," Mark said. Then he lowered his voice, as if Alison wouldn't hear them. "She might also have information we can use."

When the truck pulled up, she fought them with every muscle as they picked her up and forced her into the enclosed rear cargo area. Once she was shut in darkness, she stopped struggling. It would be better to listen than to waste energy. She squirmed as best as she could toward the cab of the truck and pressed her ear against the cool metal.

"Say again, home base. Repeat, say again," someone said into a radio in the front of the vehicle.

"Thank God you're alive," a woman said on the other end. "Get back here now. Zak and the others were attacked out at that family's home."

So, this was another group of soldiers, Alison thought. How many of these privvies were out in her town?

"Fuck, Brooke. Is everyone alright?" Mark asked. "Did they make it back?"

"They're fine," the woman said. "Everyone is home and accounted for except for you guys. Just get back."

"We got some heat here too," Mark said. "It could be the same guys."

Alison clenched her teeth, resisting the urge to yell at them. She wanted to tell them that they had no idea who they were dealing with, that they had three command mechs and more firepower than they could imagine. Instead, she stayed silent and listened.

Mark continued, "Everything looks quiet, but we're bringing a prisoner with us."

"Say again, Mark?" The woman on the radio sounded alarmed. "They got to you too?"

"Turner and the others scared off the main bunch before they got close enough to do any real damage. But listen, we've got a prisoner with us. She got the drop on me, but I took care of it. We're bringing her back with us."

There was a silence. Alison wondered if Brooke was his commanding officer. Perhaps she would instruct them to kill her before they went back.

"Mark, tell me she's not pretty," the voice said instead. "Because I swear to god, if this bitch tried to kill you, she had better not be prettier than me."

"I have no idea, Brooke," Mark said. "I was sort of more focused on the gun in her hand than if I'd leave you for her."

Alison fumed with a renewed surge of anger that they could be so carelessly casual about her capture and the deaths of her entire family. She settled in as comfortably as she could on the metal floor of the cargo space. The truck carried her away, and she fought her tears for as long as she could. Eventually, she found them impossible to resist and as quietly as she could, she began to sob. She whispered Eva's name over and over. She did this for as long as she could before darkness and the wound at the back of her head conspired to pull her into sleep.

CHAPTER 16

The truck came to a sudden stop, and Alison used the wall of the cargo area to get into a sitting position. When the rear door opened, she contemplated kicking whoever was behind it. Instead, she remained calm and began taking mental notes about their setup. They hadn't even bothered to blindfold her. The cadet named Turner led her by the arm as two other cadets started checking Mark for injuries. She smiled to herself, remembering how it had felt when she'd swung the pipe into his ribs.

"I'm fine," Mark said. "Just get her over to the medical tent. She hit her head pretty hard. And keep her under guard."

Her brief moment of enjoyment was cut short as a woman ran up to Mark. Alison fought the urge to hurl every insult she could think of at them as they embraced. Mercifully, Turner pushed her on toward a tent near the edge of the camp they'd set up in a park. If it weren't for the ancient swing set and a pair of old worn wooden picnic tables, she'd have assumed it was just a slightly greener patch of land. As she walked across the heavily trampled grass, her head began to pound in a way she didn't think was merely a headache. Each step sent a wave of pain through her head that ended just behind her eyes.

Turner deposited her with another soldier at the tent who began taking a look at her head wound. Alison didn't believe the soldier really cared if the job was done well, but the burning sensation she felt meant something antiseptic had been applied to the back of her head at least. She glanced at a small box labeled with a prescription symbol but looked away when Turner eyed her suspiciously. The plastic cuffs binding her hands together had begun to rub the skin raw in a clean line, but she said nothing.

She wasn't sure when she decided to stop speaking, even to scream obscenities at these people, but it was already serving her well. They were more open with information around her than she ever could have hoped. Simply listening was gaining her more of an advantage than they understood.

The snippets of conversation she'd heard in the truck before she blacked out had told her their force was almost exclusively composed of cadets from the school. The only person with any practical experience in a battle environment was a pilot, who was also laid up on a cot nearby. The only other patient, a kid with vacant eyes in the corner, could also have seen battle at some point.

From the brief moments she'd spent outside of the truck she also knew what the strength of their force was. Unless they had units out on patrol or still coming in, they only had seven mechs and a handful of light and midrange trucks to work with. If she could get this information to her comrades, they could turn around and crush these kids into dust before they even got off a reasonable counterattack. She would continue to maintain her silence until she found a way to get away. Maybe she would even be able to take a few of them out in the process. She could figure out which of them had been at her family home and make them pay for what had happened.

Before she knew what was happening, tears began to spill from her eyes again, and with her hands bound behind her back she was unable to wipe them away. By focusing her attention on the activity closer to the center of camp, she managed to make them stop. She watched, through the open flap of the tent, as the young soldiers gathered under their single command mech. Someone was standing on a truck and making some grandiose speech she couldn't quite hear. After the crowd dispersed, a thin cadet with a mohawk came and led her out to a truck.

"Just sit here and don't do anything," He said as he pushed her into the cargo space. The soldier then sat on the tailgate and started cleaning his rifle, occasionally looking back to make sure she wasn't doing anything suspicious.

"They got you on guard duty, eh?" the cadet who'd bandaged her head called over to the mohawk man on the tailgate.

"Yeah, I'm stuck with her for a while." He cast a glance back at Alison and pushed off the tailgate, making sure to take his rifle with him. He walked a few paces away, apparently thinking that would be good enough. "Any idea how long we've got? The way this rebel chick keeps looking around is giving me the creeps. Like she knows something we don't."

"She absolutely knows something we don't. That's the only reason she's not out in the desert with a hole in her head. Anyway, we've got about another hour or so and we should be pushing off."

"Still no word from command?" Mohawk man said this in a low whisper, but Alison was still able to hear it. "We're just chasing after these guys and hoping for the best?"

"Sounds like it," the medic said. "But I'm not sure what else we could do. I have to get the med tent packed up. You keep an eye on her though. She's not as banged up as she looks."

Alison appreciated the assessment, but she absolutely felt banged up. She'd suffered two head wounds in a very short timeframe. She didn't know much about head trauma but understood that it wasn't good to add them up. Alison closed her eyes and thought back over the last few hours. With her eyes closed, her mind sank into a wavering haze of grief and anger. She felt herself slipping back into sleep and fought to keep clarity. She wanted to remember everything, however painful, and there was something she couldn't seem to recall on the fringes of her frantic memory.

The mohawk man got into the cargo area with her and pulled the tailgate up, bringing her out of her daze. She heard the sounds of seven mech engines firing, and then the truck began speeding into the night, carrying her away from the city she'd once called home. Alison watched through the open rear window as the ghosts of trees flashed by in the darkness. Soon, they were clear of even these, and all she could see were the faint impressions of stars above an inky horizon. Her restraints allowed her enough range to lean her head back against the side of the cargo space, and so she did. She allowed the soft hum of the electric engine and the rumble of the tires as they bumped along the desert to coax her into sleep.

~

John made it to the command deck and saw Jim and Katherine talking closely by the dark viewing window. "Give me an update." His eyes flitted between the two of them. "What happened?"

Katherine looked worried momentarily, but she stepped away from Jim and gestured for him to explain.

"We couldn't secure the targets," Jim said. "It's like they knew we were coming. We had just gotten into formation when they fired a shot. We opened fire and...everything just went completely off the rails."

"What happened?" John asked, in two measured breaths.

"I don't know. I mean, it all happened so fast." Jim pressed his fingers against his closed eyelids for a moment, then continued. "We opened fire, and then they were running out the front door toward their truck. I ordered our men not to shoot to kill. We needed at least one of these guys alive, right? They were moving so fast, and they were taking our guys down before we even had our trucks in position to follow. They took out the whole house. I'm not sure anyone made it out of there. We had two of our own still inside when it went up."

"What do you mean you don't know?" John asked, taking a few steps toward Jim.

"I was trying to get the trucks up as soon as I could to chase the guys down," Jim said. "I didn't have time to look around before we left, but the house was basically gone. It just burned so quickly."

"Where is Alison?" John asked coldly.

"I know she was with us when we went after them," Jim said. "Then, you know, we found the soldiers down by Samson's mech: three guys pulling out the unspent ammunition canisters. Alison was out cold when we left the farmhouse, so we left her with a driver and went in to try another extraction. They must have heard us coming, because we weren't able to take them the second time either. They got Crawford and Simms before we had to retreat. I don't know where she went, but she was gone by the time we made it back to the trucks."

"Your driver just let her go?"

"What was he supposed to do?" Jim asked. "Run through the streets calling her name? Maybe she went after the guys herself. I don't know what the hell she was thinking."

"You know exactly what she was thinking," John said. "Her entire family was inside that goddamned house."

"She did say something about going back." Jim nodded. "The driver did say that, so maybe that is where she went. But she had her gun with her too, so I don't know. I didn't have the resources to go out and find her, John. I had to get us back here."

"It was the right call, John," Katherine said. "There was no way to know where she went. We'd lost enough men already."

For a long time, John said nothing. The way they were talking to him, it was as if they thought there was nothing to be done. John's mind began to shuffle through memories like cards in a deck. His first draw from this deck was a memory of Alison's face, the moment they'd said her family was in danger. In her eyes, he'd seen a mirror of his own on the day he'd opened a letter informing him his family was gone. Another memory flashed by. He was in front of a small boy, weeping at a breakfast table, in front of a shattered cereal bowl. These memories and the shared threads of grief wound up inside him. He made a decision.

Without a word, he turned and left the command deck. He took the stairs down two decks to the cargo bay. His personal affects, what little he had been able to pull together from the gear on board the mech, were in a locker on one wall. He was strapping his holster to his waist when he heard footsteps on the metal floor behind him.

"I'm leaving," John said with a flat and final tone.

"I had a number of orders to carry out at that school, and retrieving you was one of them," Katherine said.

"I'm sorry to disappoint you, Katherine, but you're not going to be able to keep me here," John's hand dropped subconsciously down to his sidearm. "If we left anyone alive back at that house, I need to know. I owe it to her. We owe it to her."

She took a few steps toward him. "I'm not going to stop you, John. But think about what you're doing. You're the voice of this movement. What is it going to look like if I show up at Central Command, and the man whose words these people know by heart has refused to come? Hell, what am I supposed to tell the people we're dragging across this godforsaken desert right now?"

"Tell them we went back to find our fallen comrades," Jim said from the stairwell, surprising both John and Katherine. "You can't go out there alone. Who the hell knows what you'll come across?"

"I'm going alone," John said. "You said it. We've lost too many people already. Just..." He paused to think. "Give me a truck, one of the lighter ones, and enough supplies for a few days. I'll find anything else I need along the way. Tell whoever wants me out at Central Command that I've gone to clean up my own mess."

"John." Katherine closed the final few steps to him. "You can't blame yourself for any of this. It was my decision to send a team out there, but you know we really had no choice."

"I don't believe that anymore," John said. "I've made the same choice too many times to ignore the fact that it always turns out the same way. Someone suffers at the expense of someone else's grand idea of what is right. That might be how the world works, but it doesn't mean I can't at least try to fix what I've broken."

Katherine looked back at Jim, and he nodded. John could see that the two of them worked well together. He knew they could handle this small fleet without him. They'd been doing it largely without him anyway. John had always been a secondary objective here.

"Take what you need," Katherine said. "You're dismissed. But promise me you'll be careful. If you don't find anything, I want you to meet us at our rendezvous point."

"We actually have a rendezvous point now?" John asked, looking up from his preparations.

"Just got confirmation on what we suspected," Jim said. "We are headed for Ember Springs. There's a complex nearby called the Hollows. You won't need to know anything more specific than that. When you get in the area, someone should spot you and bring you in. You're now one of a select few people who know the location of Central Command."

"Thank you," John said. He looked at Jim, then back to Katherine. "I just have to make sure. I need to see this through."

"We're leaving before daybreak," she said. "Gather what you need and get out as soon as you can. I don't want anyone to see you leave."

John turned away from her and busied himself with the straps of his ballistic vest. He listened to their footsteps as she and Jim walked back to the stairwell and up toward the Command Deck.

~

The eastern sky had just begun to blush with the coming dawn as John loaded a five-gallon tank of water into the back of a light truck. He'd selected one that had already seen its best days. Before too long, they would have had to leave it behind anyway. It ran on a battery like the others but also had an old-fashioned gasoline backup engine. The only people who would miss it were the ones who'd evidently been using it to play cards in occasionally.

John cleaned out the accumulated beer cans and liquor bottles from the enclosed bed of the truck, then gathered the cards that were scattered around. He put the deck on a crate outside and placed a rock on top to stop it from being taken by the wind. He kept a pack of cigarettes he found among the trash as payment for his work. None of the alcohol bottles were full, and John wondered for a moment where they'd been keeping it.

Stepping up into the driver's seat, he remembered all the times he'd driven a truck like this one out into the desert back at the Academy. Those nights felt so far away now. It was hard to believe the last one had occurred only a few days ago. John pressed a button on a screen to the right of the steering wheel, and the engine started. The battery read fifty percent, but a warning on the dash indicated that service was necessary to maintain optimal efficiency. Even though the fuel tank was full, he'd loaded a twenty-gallon container, just in case. This, they also wouldn't miss. Only a few vehicles in their fleet used it, most of them in a backup capacity like this truck.

The camp would soon be up and moving on. John needed to be gone before that happened. He didn't touch the headlights as he put the truck in drive. Some people were already awake, and he didn't want to draw attention to himself. The moon would provide enough light for him to get out of camp.

As he drove out along their trampled back trail, he realized that Katherine must have already informed the lookouts that a truck would be leaving camp, because no one radioed his vehicle to verify his cause for leaving. He could see the resting expanse of the city on the horizon. Beyond the urban sprawl, he noted a column of smoke that must mark the place of Alison's family home, or whatever was left of it. Behind him, he heard a low rumble, like distant thunder, as the command mechs began to cycle up their main engines.

CHAPTER 17

By the time they finally brought their small convoy to a halt, Alison's head felt a little better. Her arms and legs, however, ached from restricted movement. They still must not have known what to do with her, so they left her in the truck for some time. She listened as tents were set up and could smell food being cooked on a campfire somewhere close. Finally, one of the soldiers staffing the medical tent pulled her out and brought her over to it. Mercifully—or maybe because it was easier than carrying her— they cut her ankle restraints, granting access to her legs. Her arms were brought around to her front as well. She sat in the dirt that served as the floor of the medical tent. In yet another improvement to her conditions, the entrance flap had been pulled open on one side to let in the desert air. The pleasant aroma of creosote flowed into the tent, telling of a coming shift in the weather.

They hadn't begun asking her questions yet, but they would. She wasn't sure what lengths they might go to when she didn't answer. In all likelihood, she wouldn't have the answers they were looking for anyway. She didn't know the ultimate destination; nobody really seemed to. If they had, they'd kept it successfully quiet. That was one of the many things the Harbingers of the Fall did well, she had come to realize: compartmentalization of information. No one knew more than they had to, and she hadn't needed to know much these last few days.

She did know about the general size and strength of the stolen fleet. She knew who was currently in charge, and she knew the names of some important people who had turned against the United Entities and joined the Harbingers. It might have been satisfying to tell them some of these things and watch their faces as they felt the betrayal sink in. But no. Any information she gave them would be too much.

She sat in the dirt, awaiting the inevitable duo of strong men to arrive and carry her off to some smaller tent where the interrogation would begin. But it didn't happen. Instead, she occupied herself by gathering up stones she could reach and sorting out the smooth ones. These she kept, and the rough ones she tossed idly behind her. The soldier tasked with watching her eyed this activity suspiciously. He eventually lost interest and occupied himself with the purposeless task of chambering a round into his rifle and then ejecting it, over and over again.

When Alison had forty-eight stones she liked, she laid them down in the dirt in two rows. Each one with six piles of four stones. She'd created a makeshift mancala game, like the one she'd played as a child. In the house, there had been a skinny cabinet recessed into one wall of the living room stocked with a number of old games.

The wooden board and glass beads had come out occasionally throughout her life, most often on days when her mother was scheduled to work a later shift. Alison would quietly retrieve the game, put it on the scuffed coffee table, and begin to set the pieces. Her mother would join her after she had donned her factory uniform, and they would play until she had to leave. They talked while they played, usually about nothing serious. But occasionally they had strayed into heavier topics. As Alison had grown older, the tradition had become less frequent. Whenever they did find time to play, it always seemed to signify that one of them had something to talk about.

Alison looked down at her makeshift board, chose one of the piles, and moved the stones along, depositing one stone in each of the following piles.

The last time she'd played this game with her mother had been before Alison first left for the Harbingers of the Fall. Alison had let a series of nearly incoherent words fall out all at once, but Sandy hadn't missed a beat. She'd just continued dropping her stones into their places, each one making a sharp tick as it landed. When she'd finished her turn, Sandy had looked across the room at Eva, who had only been a year old then. Alison had feared her mother would press her to explain why she had to leave.

But Sandy hadn't pressed her on it. Perhaps she'd known that Alison had already run through the reasons for her decision hundreds of times. And Alison had. She'd agonized over the decision from the moment she'd discovered she was pregnant. Given the turmoil and outright horror in the world, it had been only through luck that their family had remained as intact as it was. Vicious diseases had rolled through the region like clockwork year after year, with the Enclaves restricting the supply of medicine. Every year their community lost people when they weren't selected for what was officially called Controlled Care Dispersal but was essentially a lottery. Alison couldn't stand by and let luck mean the difference between life and death for her family, for her daughter. She couldn't watch Eva go off to the state sponsored schools and be swept into the propaganda, as almost everyone was. Alison couldn't bear to watch Eva be told that her only place in the world would be to support Stability, the grand and greedy god of the ruling class.

She had wanted to make a difference for Eva, to give her the opportunity to live in a world where she wasn't expected to be part of a tourniquet generation; doing nothing but holding on tight and doing exactly as told until the damage from the Decline was completely repaired. In the best-case scenario for Eva, she could have tested well and been absorbed directly into an Enclave and never seen her family again. No, Alison couldn't have sat idly by and watched any of those things happen. Her mother had known that, so they had finished their game in silence.

Now, in front of her makeshift mancala board, Alison allowed bitter tears to roll down her face and fall into the dust. What had her decision done for Eva now? If she'd stayed behind instead of joining the Harbingers, would Eva still be alive? Maybe not, but perhaps Alison would have been able to do something, to offer some sort of comfort in those final moments. The sound of Eva's screams echoed inside her, reaching out through time in a way Alison knew would become all too familiar as she lived on without her.

Alison reached out and selected another pile of stones, taking the turn for some invisible person across from her, and played a game she would never be able to share with Eva.

John had made good time bumping along the trampled desert path their mechs and trucks had cut into the landscape. Once Katherine and the others began to approach their final destination, they would have to consider diverting their force into smaller and smaller groups so their paths wouldn't be so easily read. But that wasn't his problem anymore. Katherine and Jim were more than qualified to think of that themselves. He had his own problems lying in wait ahead of him. He had no idea how close on their heels the tailing soldiers might be. Even a simple roadside explosive device would have been enough to end his mission before it even began. The chaos the Harbingers had stirred up was in many ways just as dangerous to him as to any of his enemies.

When he reached the city outskirts, he broke away from the trampled path made by those he'd left behind. Sometime in the day ahead, their pursuers would come along that beaten path, and he didn't want to be on it when they did.

As the sun cleared the mountains of this valley, he could still see what he believed was the thin column of smoke from the burning house. There were a number of small fires burning all around him, but this one was in the right direction. The smoke had begun to turn white, indicating someone had either tried to extinguish the flames, or that all the combustible materials had been used up. Either way, he needed to get a solid bearing on its location before it completely dissipated.

Weaving through the streets became increasingly hard as he approached what must have been the financial district of

Tonopah. There were no banks actually still using the towering structures. After the Decline, the surviving financial institutions had migrated into the Enclaves. And so, these buildings were largely abandoned. John thought it was surprising these places were still called cities at this point. Small government-run neighborhoods were the real survivors when it came to post-Decline civilization, outside of the Enclaves, of course.

And then there were the smaller communities, like Alison's, that managed to forge an existence outside of standard protocols. Small communities could watch out for one another in a way densely packed cities just weren't engineered for. Those who did remain in the cities subsisted on meager rations and worked their assigned duties. Of course, everyone in the outskirt communities had mandated duties as well, but it was well known that illegal family farms operated sporadically in those areas. They continued to exist because the neighbors, who were the only ones who could really report these kinds of transgressions, tended to benefit from the farms themselves. In exchange for their silence, a basket or, more likely, a plastic bag of whatever was in season would occasionally turn up on their doorstep.

Most of this he'd gathered from Alison during their discussions along the ridge. She'd always been open with him about what it was like out in the 'real world,' as she'd frequently referred to it. Her family had operated one of the small illegal farms in their area. Alison's father had also managed to maintain his position at one of the heavily guarded government farms in the area. He'd worked both jobs every day and never complained, Alison had told him one night with begrudging pride in her voice.

John had asked her once how they managed to get seeds out of the agriculture compound in order to have their own crops. She'd laughed and told him that there were still some seeds that would grow and then yield viable seeds for planting the following year. Her father had treated them like gold, of course. Occasionally, he would take a trip somewhere, Alison had said, and he'd take his box of seeds with him. When he'd return, he'd have a few less of one and more of another. Illegal seed trading, punishable by death or simple disappearance, was just a part of life for people outside the Enclaves. John admired them, and sometimes wished that he had found his way into one of those communities instead of his tower at the school.

As with everything else, the government had an official reason they controlled agriculture to the extent they did. Engineered strains of poisonous and destructive crops had become wildly common just before the decline. It seemed that just as worldwide digital technology had begun to rot away from the inside, so had the ecology of the world's food production infrastructure. Destabilization had spiked in other sectors as well. Medical antibiotics had become less and less effective until the waves of sickness that passed through cities had become terrifyingly lethal. People had fled the densely populated areas like ants leaving the nest during a rainstorm.

Of course, most of this had happened long before Alison's time. John himself had been young when the Decline had officially begun. He'd been lucky enough to grow up in a wealthy family and had become ensconced in the ever-thickening shield between the Enclaves and the 'real world.' When he'd come of age, he'd been assigned to the security forces. By that time, even those as lucky as him still had to earn their keep. It benefitted the government and the various corporate survivors to keep their security and military forces in good health and in safe housing. If they couldn't buy loyalty, at least they could buy obedience.

John hadn't thought of it that way when he was younger, of course. Life inside the Enclaves was all he had known. He'd fervently supported the line of 'Stability Over Self' for longer that he cared to admit to most people. And, in a way, part of him had never been able to completely shake it. The measures the United Entities put in place when they unified did have a sort of elegant and effective nature when viewed clinically. It was only when you got up close that the ideas broke down. Up close was where you saw children die of diseases that could be treated, when entire communities starved because of logistical decisions made hundreds of miles away. When you got close, it looked a lot more like systemic oppression. Perhaps it all amounted to the same thing, he thought.

While he'd been lost in thought, John had failed to realize that the column of smoke he'd been following was now completely obscured by the tall buildings around him.

"Shit," he said. "Son of a bitch."

John stopped the truck in the center of the street, straddling the center yellow line to keep himself as far from stalled cars and any potential explosive devices as possible. He looked out through his windshield and found the direction of the sunrise easily. Ahead of him was an intersection bathed in light coming in from the east. He took his foot off the brake and allowed his truck to roll slowly into the lighted intersection.

As the crisp rays of dawn spilled into the cab of his truck, John put the car in park. He switched off the engine. The warmth of the light and the stillness calmed John's mind in a way he hadn't realized he needed.

He opened his door and stepped out into the street, keenly aware of how open this left him to attack, but not caring at the moment. All around him, buildings towered like monuments to long-forgotten gods. Their exteriors, once adorned with thousands of yards of glass and other embellishments, now showed their fragile skeletons of steel. Gaping holes in some of them peered down like empty eye sockets.

John patted his pockets and withdrew the half-empty pack of cigarettes he'd found in the back of the truck as he'd left the camp. He turned away from the shadows and felt the light as it crept across his face. When he was facing the sun, low and bright on the horizon, John meditated on how a distant civilization would remark on the perfect grid of this city: indeed, the many thousands of perfect grids of cities across the globe. How on particular days, often equinoxes, but not always, the sun would shine perfectly down the rows of these massive steel structures as the sun rose or set.

He wondered what these distant people would make of this, and it gave him the queer sensation of shrinking, of becoming smaller in this universe than he could imagine. It became clear to him, in this intersection, that he was only a small part of the grand and spiraling dance of time. He'd be hard-pressed to explain the feeling, even to himself, if he ever remarked on this moment again. The world seemed to have simply stopped in regard to his movements for a while. He leaned against the driver's side door and breathed in deeply, enjoying the cool air not yet heated by the sun. On the breeze, he could smell plant life. Not all of it was pleasant, of course; there must have been rot and decay throughout these huge edifices. But it was reassuring, in a way, that the forces of nature had made their way this deep into the forest of metal and concrete.

He remembered the pack of cigarettes in his hand but found that while the urge to light one was there, the will wasn't.

He spied a thin wisp of smoke as he peered up the street, directly in line with the sun. It must be the farmhouse. He believed this without much logic or reason behind it other than that Alison had said her home was on the east edge of the city. He opened the door to the truck and got back in. In just the few moments the truck had spent in the morning sun the cab had warmed up considerably. He headed off in the direction of the smoke in the distance.

CHAPTER 18

As the worst of her surge of guilt and grief finally passed, Alison managed to compose herself. Her tears had left tracks of clean skin in the fine dust that had settled like a mask on her face. She leaned her cheek onto one shoulder and used it to wipe at the moisture there, then leaned in the other direction to do the same on that side. Hopefully, this obscured any evidence of her recent weakness. They would not break her.

"Hey, go get some rest," someone said as they walked into the tent. The mohawk man dropped the round he'd been chambering into the dust and immediately went searching for it. "Mark wants me on shift tonight. Gotta be useful, you know."

"You sure, Zak?" The man found the errant round and slid it back into the chamber of his rifle.

"Sure. Go get some sleep," the new soldier, Zak, said.

Alison made no indication that she had any interest in the changing of the guard, but she filed away a few bits of information for herself all the same. Mark, the man who'd captured her, apparently held a leadership role with this group. He was probably the one she'd seen standing and speaking grandiosely from the top of a truck earlier.

Zak was a bit on the short side for a military type and looked like he would have been more at home in a research installation somewhere. He leaned against the truck that held up one side of the medical tent and she could feel his eyes on her. The tent was more of a canvas walled jail at this point, since most of the patients had been treated and released. The only two people remaining were Alison and the curiously quiet soldier who rocked back and forth on his bedroll, and neither of them needed any particular care. She continued playing her one-sided game of mancala, picking up one pile of rocks and dropping one into the next hole until they'd all been used up. If she finished at one end or another, she picked another pile on that side. But, if she finished on a pile instead, she moved to the other side. It was a simple rhythmic game that helped pass the time quickly.

"Who's winning?" he asked her.

Alison narrowed her eyes at the question. It was the first thing anyone had asked her that hadn't made her immediately angry; it had even been a little funny. She continued her movements without responding. The man crouched down, watching her hands as she played, and then he looked up into her face. She worried about whether or not he could tell that she'd been crying recently.

"Can I play?" he asked. Almost without thinking, she dropped the rest of the rocks in her hand and waved at the improvised board. She could play a game with this man, she thought. It might cut the boredom, at least for a moment.

The soldier distributed the piles of rocks into the twelve divots in the dirt. Alison hadn't dug the divots, exactly. She had just moved the piles of rocks so many times they'd begun to wear down into the earth with each game.

Once the correct number of rocks was in each of the piles, he made the first move. As they played, Alison allowed her knees to first lower, then come all the way down into a cross-legged position. She had actually started to think about who might win this game. The realization that her mind had slipped so far from its dual track of sorrow and hatred startled her.

"Who taught you to play?" Zak asked, as Alison made a selection and moved her stones. She didn't respond, but simply continued her move in silence. Her silence didn't stop Zak from talking, however. "I used to play this all the time when I was a kid. Come to think of it, my mom must have taught me how to play."

Alison kicked out instinctively before she could stop herself. The mention of his mother had plucked at a raw thread inside her, and the pain that pulled at her heart had been too much to hold back. The stones of the game scattered, and a puff of dust drifted away in a soft breeze. The man sat, frozen in surprise, but he eventually gathered up the scattered pieces, even replacing the ones he couldn't find with new ones from further out. Alison tucked her leg back in and allowed him to reset the game board. He scooped dirt out of the holes she'd collapsed with her kick, and soon had everything back in place.

"She taught me just before she died. Or close enough," Zak said, continuing the conversation despite her outburst. "Everyone would always ask me what I wanted to do after it happened, and I'd always choose playing mancala or checkers. This one helped more, though. It's more methodical. There's less thinking involved."

Alison didn't look up after he paused for her reply. She simply continued to stare at the game board. If he wanted to talk, he could talk.

"We were having breakfast when it happened," Zak said. "Some of your kind, rebels of some sort, were apparently living next door." He waved a hand absently at the canvas wall of the tent, indicating how close they'd apparently been. "And when the government came to shut them down, the rebels just started shooting. It seems like they fired randomly. This line of bullets kind of ripped through our kitchen wall, you know? It went on for forever, or it felt like it did. Eventually someone came and pulled me out, and I was put into the care of the state."

"So, I was in and out of various foster homes," Zak said. He laughed and made an opening move in the game. "That's the most cliché thing I say about myself, you know. 'In and out of various foster homes.' It doesn't help anyone understand, but it gives them a place to nod and say they're sorry. Nothing can really sum up a stretch of time where you're plugged in and out of people's lives like a second-hand appliance."

"What makes you think they did it?" Alison asked, surprising even herself. She reached out to make her own move on the board, hoping he didn't notice her bound hands shaking.

"What do you mean?" Zak asked. Alison heard a change in tone he couldn't have intended. Until now, he'd been putting on a show of being calm and collected.

"You said the rebels just fired randomly into your apartment," she said. "I'm asking why you think it had to be the rebels."

It was true, she thought. Nothing in his story concretely put the gun that killed his family in the hands of the rebels next door.

"I'm not sure," Zak said, that cautious tone becoming one of distress. "It's what the reports all said when they finished the investigation."

"Of course, that's what they said," she replied shortly.

"At any rate, it doesn't matter." His tone was darker now, and she could tell he didn't want to dwell in this for long. "If they hadn't been there, the government wouldn't have showed up. If they hadn't started shooting, no one would have been shot."

"Did you ever think that if the government hadn't showed up, no one would have had to shoot?" Alison asked. She wasn't sure exactly where she was going with her line of questioning but pressed anyway. She wasn't going to erase a lifetime of indoctrination in a single conversation, but working on this seed of doubt felt like a good move.

"No, because that's not an option here," Zak said. It was his turn in their game, but he was clearly frustrated and didn't seem to notice. "It was their job to show up and take those guys in. It's the job of the government and the security forces to make sure dangerous people don't cause harm to citizens."

"No," she said. "It's not. It's their job to make sure the right people do the harm."

Zak was silent. She could tell when he closed his eyes that he had a thousand preprogrammed counterarguments fighting in his mind. What she'd said must have actually caught in the gears of that machine, because he said nothing in response. Instead, he reached down, selected a pile of rocks, and moved them along until he had to stop, and yield play back to her.

~

The final gray wisps of smoke died out before John could reach them. His heading hadn't changed as he reached the edge of the city, however. He hoped that if he headed in the same direction he would stumble across the house, or someone who might know where to find it.

John crested a small hill on a cracked asphalt road and saw a number of small buildings spread across a low valley. Like a spilled container of ink, there was a small forest in the valley. It ran up to some of the houses and completely encircled others. The city disappeared completely out of view by the time he reached the first cluster of buildings. In another time, these scattered homes would have been surrounded by rows of whatever crops were in demand. Now, they sat like lonely islands in the center of overgrown fields of tall grass, weeds, and wildflowers. A few of them had dim lights in some of their windows, a good sign that he might be able to talk to someone. What he didn't see was anything indicating the direction of the battle the previous night.

As he descended the hill into the valley, he crossed an ancient cattle guard set across the road. It was a useless artifact, since there were no more cattle to keep confined. The paved road continued for a few yards, then was abruptly replaced by a well-kept but still decidedly dirt road.

John slowed his truck down, enjoying the way the road felt beneath his tires. He looked into his rear-view mirror and took in the scene there. He could see why those who lived out here would choose to do so. The hill was just enough to obscure all but the tallest buildings of the city from view. The people who lived in this valley must have traveled quite a distance in order to retrieve their allotments on ration days. Everyone in these homes would also have an official government posting they were responsible for. Most were probably posted at the government-operated farms scattered even further from the city. Near each of those installations were government housing compounds they could have stayed in. But maybe being able to pretend they were alone out here was worth the extra work.

As he approached the first of the homes, he slowed down further, scanning the yard and windows for movement. Another advantage to living out here, he thought, was that everyone in the area likely knew he was there by now. The sound of his truck would have carried through the valley the moment he'd crested the hill. When he got closer to the first house, he saw the curtains in an upper window of the home draw together slowly.

He stopped the truck in front of an ancient metal mailbox on a wooden post and shut off the engine. The front yard was unkempt, and the weeds had grown into a forest that obscured his view of the large window at the front of the house. He could see toys and an occasional piece of machinery through the untamed chaos. As he exited the cab, he felt eyes on him. He waved toward the house in a way he hoped was reassuring, and opened the chain-link gate, reaching over it to do so. He spied what must be an old gasoline-powered car hiding in the shadow cast by the house. He didn't slow his pace to investigate it further, but it looked like it might still work. It was concealed, to make anyone passing by believe it to be just one more piece of detritus in the sea of weeds.

John approached the wooden porch, where an ancient pair of rocking chairs sat facing the road. As he mounted the steps, the boards creaked beneath his weight. Whoever was behind the front door, for someone must be there by now, could have had a rifle or shotgun in hand. Though they were illegal, people in areas like this still had access to a few family heirloom firearms. If John was right that the recent battle was somewhere close by, everyone in the valley would be on edge. Even if something like that hadn't happened recently, a man approaching in what was unmistakably a government truck, however old and defaced it might be, would be cause for alarm.

He stopped at the front door, a large blue one his wife would have approved of, and contemplated what he would say if anyone answered. Before he could think of a proper introduction, or even knock on the door, it opened to reveal a man in a dirty set of working pants and an equally soiled shirt. He wasn't holding a weapon, but that didn't mean someone further inside wasn't. It would mean an immediate arrest, at the very least, if he had opened the door on a government official with a firearm in hand.

Instead, the man smiled a broad caricature smile. "Hello sir." He stood very still, clearly not wanting to alarm John. "What is it I can do for you this morning?"

"I need, uh…" John fumbled through his options. He could have told the man he was with the military and saw how much that authority would get him. He could have told the truth, but the man might have believed it to be a trick. John decided to go with something approaching the truth, "I'm not here to search your home, or even ask you for anything more than directions."

The man didn't move or drop the wide smile, but John thought he could see confusion in his eyes.

"There was a fire recently," John said. He left out the part about the gunfire and explosions. "A house in this valley, or perhaps another close by, burned down. I'm looking for it."

It wasn't a question, exactly, but the man took his smile down a few notches, apparently thinking through his own options. The community must have been a close one, and talking to the authorities was something they'd probably discourage. Informing on a neighbor was as likely to get the informant exposed as it was to get them off the hook. Everyone in these rural communities knew something about everyone else that could get them arrested.

The man hesitated a few more moments, then settled on an approach. "You're probably looking for the Harrow place," he said, evidently deciding that telling a government man the location of a burned farmhouse wasn't likely to incur the wrath of any of his neighbors. They'd probably be happy just to see John go about whatever business he had there and leave the area. "You're right about it being close by, but you've still got a couple miles. Keep to this road and make a right when you reach the Farson place. It's the green house with a godawful stone bear in the yard. Keep that way until you pass over another cattle guard and make your first right into the trees. It's a small road so make sure you're paying attention. That'll take you to it, the Harrow farm, or whatever is left of it."

"Thank you, sir," John said, and he stepped back. He could see the man relax visibly as he turned away and headed back down the porch to his truck. By the time he'd opened his door and climbed back into the cab, the man had closed his front door and the home resumed its surreal, vacant look.

John followed the directions the smiling man had laid out for him. He liked the craftsmanship on the large stone bear in front of the green house. John believed he saw a face in an upper window of the home. He didn't have time to dwell on it, and he quickly came upon the small road leading to the Harrow farm.

As he made his way toward Alison's family home, he felt like he was entering an enemy camp. Most families here were, at the very least, mildly anti-government. With the recent events in the city and at the Harrow place, it was entirely possible the local residents might be emboldened and see him as an easy target. Probably the only thing that had kept someone from firing off a shot from one of the upper windows of the homes he had passed was that both his uniform and vehicle had been stripped of insignia. It was the sort of thing a lone government soldier would be smart to do, but it was also the first thing he and the rebels in his party had done when they'd stopped to rest.

As he passed over the second cattle guard, the road began to slope down. The clear smell of smoke hit him without warning.

The denser concentration of trees must have trapped some of it down low. Shafts of early morning light cut through the thin smoke in front of him like barriers in the road ahead. Something was still smoldering or on fire up ahead.

Looking down the long gravel drive, he saw the vague shape of what was once a home. The lane was lined on either side with old aspen trees. The ones at the end closest to the house were singed, still letting off tendrils of white smoke. John came upon a mailbox, snapped from its post, lying in the road six feet from where it should be. He got out of his truck and approached the mailbox for reasons he couldn't quite explain. He picked it up and examined it. "Harrow Farm" was written on the side of it in flowing white script. He dragged it off the dirt road and leaned it upright against a tree.

John stood for a long time, looking through the smoke-choked driveway, taking in the dark smoldering hulk of the home. He contemplated getting into his truck and driving the final distance, but felt it would somehow disrespect the site. He also had the strong urge to turn back and leave the home unexamined.

After a few more moments of indecision, he found himself walking up the lane. His hand fell to his holster and rested on his sidearm. The gravel shifted beneath his feet, and he noted the deep tread marks of recent vehicle traffic. First, the government soldiers would have torn out of there as fast as they could, and then Jim would have followed with his team in their three vehicles. What John didn't see were signs of anyone else returning to put the fire out. The air was dry and had none of the smell of wet wood burning, so the fire must have been left unchecked.

It was probably just as well. The house had been located in a field already cleared of most vegetation.

The remnants of a sprawling cottonwood tree in the backyard still had a bench swing holding onto one charred branch. Below the swing, John could see the shape of a collapsed body. While he stared out at the house and the body beneath the tree, he tripped over something else directly in his path. He fell to his knees beside the body of a man lying face down in the dirt. How hadn't he seen it before? John moved away from the body and looked up at the pale sky. After he'd calmed his nerves, he managed to stand back up. He approached the body he'd tripped over and crouched down beside it. Getting his fingers beneath one of the arms, he rolled the body onto its back. Based on stories Alison had told him over the years, this was most likely Brian. He'd been a member of the Harbingers of the Fall himself, embedded in the GovNET bureaucracy somewhere. In another life, Brian and Alison would have been married. They'd have loved Eva and lived a quiet life of insignificance as the world continued to sour around them. Perhaps that would have been better, John thought.

He stood up and walked past the softly crackling remains of the house to where the bench swing still hung from the tree. This would have been the backyard. The man on the ground beneath the swing was older, Alison's father, then. John didn't bother with a closer examination, and turned back to face what remained of the home. Soft white wisps of smoke escaped the pile of blackened beams, threatening to flare back up into a flame.

John walked toward the back of the home and stood in the frame of what would have been a back door. He took a tentative step into the rubble. When his arm brushed against one wall, he found that much of this area was still hot enough to singe his clothing. He stepped back out of the doorway and instead walked the perimeter of the building looking for, but not wanting to see, the shapes of the two remaining people unaccounted for.

CHAPTER 19

Alison took her seat in the spot she'd begun to think of as her own. In the covered storage bed of what served as their makeshift medical truck, she'd found a place between two large crates of supplies. Any time someone wasn't explicitly posted to watch her, her hands were restrained. She assumed it was so she couldn't go snooping around in the boxes and containers, but she had learned what was in most of them by simply paying attention. These people, most of them anyway, had already begun to look past her. They ignored her presence, possibly because she made them uncomfortable. When they moved her in and out of the truck, it was almost like they were moving yet another crate of supplies.

They'd been rolling along the desert for hours now, and it came as a serious relief when she felt the truck stopping. They weren't done for the day, of course. Everyone would use the restroom and then get back into the truck, unless she said she needed to get out herself. She'd decided recently that suffering the indignity of talking to her captors occasionally was worth the reward of not soiling herself.

When the truck came to a complete stop, she caught the eyes of the soldier positioned in the back with her. She was lucky, and he seemed to understand what it meant. It was clear that he didn't want to talk any more than she did, so the process was carried out with the bare minimum of communication. Outside, she had very little in the way of privacy, but anyone else was trying to get back inside their vehicle or mech as fast as they could. Those in the command mech, and those lucky enough to have onboard restrooms, kept watch. Others had probably figured out how to piss into a water bottle by then. Alison would have done that herself, but her restraints tended to interfere with a complex task like that.

As she urinated behind the truck, she caught a bit of conversation between her usual guard and one of the soldiers positioned up in the main cab of the truck. Her guard, the stocky man with his single straight row of hair poking up from the center of his head, was obviously starved for interaction.

"Big storm coming up ahead," the soldier from up front said. "Not sure how long we're going to be able to stay in contact with the recon team out front. I bet Mark is freaking the fuck out."

"I'm sure he is," the mohawk man said, laughing too loudly. "It'd be a hell of a waste to lose a piece of ass like that."

"Sure, yeah," the other man said. Clearly, mohawk man's relegation to guard duty wasn't by accident. "You'd better get the prisoner loaded back up before the convoy leaves without us."

Alison heard the footsteps of her guard approaching. She quickly stood and pulled her jeans back up. As he came around the truck, she could tell he was disappointed that she'd already finished her business.

A light rain began to fall around them, and the sound of it hitting the dry sand was like a deep sigh from the Earth itself. A sudden gust of wind carried the particularly potent smell of wet creosote, and Alison was temporarily carried away by it. In her mind, she was far away from the man watching her struggle with her restraints to button her pants. Instead, she was lying in her bed at home with her window open.

The eaves of her house had shielded her from most of the rain, but a fine mist still found its way into her bedroom and onto her face and neck. The drops that hit her pillow made soft popping sounds next to her ears. She'd have to close the window soon; it wouldn't do to let her whole bed become soaked. But for now, she could enjoy the scents of the aspen trees and the creosote bushes.

A rough hand grabbed her by the arm and pushed her toward the open back end of the truck. She shook her head, coming back into the present. Just as she was about to hoist herself into the bed of the truck, she heard the groaning sound of the command mech's eight massive legs as they began to lower the center module to the ground. She turned to look and saw that the cargo door at the bottom of the module was already open. Someone was waving toward her. More precisely, they were waving at the soldiers around the medical section of the convoy. Someone must be hurt, she thought with unwelcome concern. She pushed back on this feeling with disgust and self-corrected it to one of mere interest.

Before the module was completely lowered, a man jumped the few remaining feet to the ground. He turned back to the mech and held out his arms. Someone else lowered the limp body of another soldier into them.

Before Alison could finish getting into the truck, soldiers were around her. They shoved her roughly aside as they clambered into the back of the truck for supplies. Her guard withdrew a new restraint from a pocket of his jacket, and he pulled Alison around the side of the truck again. He secured her wrist restraints, thin plastic and metal things that dug into her skin if she twisted too sharply, directly to a handle on the side of the truck. The handle would have been used if someone was riding on the outside of the truck, and the angle it provided allowed her to watch some of what was happening.

As the wounded soldier was carried over, commands were issued from people she couldn't see.

The people she could see were stacking supply crates, looking through them for what was being ordered. From what she could tell, someone had sustained an injury and had lost a lot of blood. Gauze, alcohol, sutures, ice packs, and all kinds of things were called for and found in the supply crates.

As Alison watched, her heart jumped. One of the crates was tilted toward her, and she could see her pack at the bottom. It was surrounded by an assortment of other random objects. The crate was apparently a catch-all for things that didn't have another place.

She watched as the plastic crate was sealed back up and put aside. Taking mental notes on every scratch, defect, and feature, she committed the bin to memory. She would be moved out of view of the crate at some point, and if she was ever going to get her property back, she would need to be able to identify this crate from among a dozen others very quickly. On one side, she noted a scratch that looked like a crude number seven.

While Alison stared at the crate containing all her remaining possessions, work continued on whoever had been injured. Without making herself too obvious, she leaned out, away from the truck to get a better view, and saw Zak being tended to. She didn't feel worry, exactly, but did feel a certain confused sense of interest in his fate. She watched as his face, covered in sticky blood, was washed. They had apparently found a wound at the back of his head and begun to clean and prep it for stitches.

As all of this happened, Alison noted that the rest of the convoy had begun to set up camp for the night. They could make more ground today; she was sure of it. Even this injured man wouldn't have been enough to stop them from moving on.

A distant rumble of thunder washed over the desert, and she looked out in the direction they had been traveling. The light rain was turning into a serious storm up ahead, and what she could see of it along the horizon was a deep inky blackness punctuated only by flashes of lightning. She looked over toward the command mech and saw a man pacing back and forth along the observation deck on the roof of the massive machine. From here, she couldn't quite see who it was, but she had a guess. It was Mark, the soldier who had somehow become the leader of this group, and he looked agitated. His glances toward the horizon betrayed his urge to continue forward, or perhaps just a need to know what was out there. The storm was probably interfering with any effort to stay in contact with the reconnaissance team mohawk man had talked to the driver about.

She watched Mark pace along the railing again. Then a large flap of canvas obscured her view as the medical tent was set up around their new patient. Alison realized that she had been forgotten, and also that the rain was coming down even harder. Her clothes were beginning to cling to her skin, chilling her more than she cared for. Looking around, she could see people rushing to set up tents and canopies. She could have called out to any one of them and pleaded to them that she was cold and wet, but she refused to allow herself to do that.

Instead, she sat on the ground and drew her knees up to her chest. Her arms had to remain above her head, which was incredibly uncomfortable, but she still refused to call out to any of those people. Her anger flared wildly, and it was enough to keep her mind off the increasing cold and discomfort. She watched as Mark pushed through the increasing rain and entered the medical tent without even a glance in her direction. Her arms, which had burned with pain earlier, were going numb now. The problem she saw at this point was her body temperature. If she stayed out for too much longer, she'd develop hypothermia.

She heard voices in the tent but couldn't make out more than a word or two at a time. From the tone, however, Mark seemed to be checking on not a fellow soldier, but a close friend. The two of them actually laughed a couple of times. That, she heard clearly through the rain, and it filled her with an unfocused anger. She wanted to yell out and ask them how they could laugh in times like this.

When Mark left the tent, he did see Alison, and he made a face she couldn't quite read. He stared at her, apparently weighing his options, then made a decision and disappeared out of sight again.

After a few minutes, her mohawk man walked out from around the corner. "I knew I'd forgotten something out here," he said with a smile. He walked over to her and cut the restraint holding her arms above her head. They fell limply into her lap. She was unable to move them, and the ache in her shoulders was immense.

"Come on, get up," the man said. He gripped her arm and hauled her to her feet. "Move it. Get inside. I'm tired of standing out in the rain."

He lifted the flap of the tent and pushed her roughly inside. He motioned for her to take her usual seat near the entrance of the tent. Once she successfully made it to the ground, she began to shake and couldn't seem to stop. With effort, she made her fingers move, picking at the dirt floor in a way that had become second nature to her.

Mohawk man, she still didn't know his name and didn't really care to, sat on the dirt floor across from her and leaned back against a crate. Her eyes flitted across the crate itself, and she determined it wasn't the one that contained her belongings. Looking around the tent, she saw a number of other plastic crates and determined none of them were the right one either. As she was scanning the room, her eyes settled on Zak's face as he laid back on his cot, staring at the canvas roof.

Beyond him, she was finally able to spot the crate she was looking for, stacked at the top of a pile of others in a far corner. She looked back toward Zak as he shut his eyes and screwed up his face in what looked like a concentrated effort not to scream. Maybe it was the pain at the back of his head, but Alison thought it looked like something deeper. Something more personal.

After a while, the mohawk man fell asleep, and Zak continued whatever mental game he was playing with himself. She thought about trying for an escape but remembered that she wasn't outfitted to survive for long in the desert. However it would happen, hypothermia today, or heat exhaustion tomorrow, she'd die if she tried to run. But she could try to sabotage something important, or try for the mohawk man's rifle. She might even get off a couple of shots before someone else caught wind of the situation.

She imagined scenario after scenario where she left the world in a blaze of gunfire to join Eva and her parents in some great afterlife. It occurred to her, of course, that she didn't actually believe in an afterlife, and that was what stopped her from doing something irrational. Dying there and taking out a few soldiers would do nothing to help the Harbingers, and it wouldn't bring Eva back.

No, unless some opportunity to sabotage a large piece of machinery like their precious command mech presented itself, she would hold out. There was also an outside chance that she could make it back to the Harbingers somehow. If they approached within a reasonable distance and she could get her hands on a radio, she could even relay some information to them on an open channel.

Zak finally surfaced from whatever waking nightmare he'd been living and turned his head to see Alison looking at him. They stared at each other for a long moment, and Alison believed she succeeded in maintaining a flat expression.

"I'm fine," he said. "Just dealing with the pain."

In response, she raised her eyebrows, asking if he really expected her to believe that. She watched as his eyes welled up with tears, and he turned away from her again.

After a few moments, he looked back. "Why didn't you run away while you had the chance?" he asked quietly, glancing at the mohawk man.

Alison shrugged, and her shoulders flared with renewed pain. She thought about answering him but changed her mind. He pushed himself up into a sitting position on his cot with what appeared to be some effort.

"Did they give you dinner?" he asked.

She set her face and refused to answer. Did she get dinner. Was he joking? They'd left her tied up in a rainstorm, and she'd likely have developed hypothermia if she had been out there any longer. Fuck, no, they hadn't given her dinner.

Zak turned toward a plate of food she'd seen Mark bring him earlier. He swung his legs off the cot and picked up the plate. With another effort, he made as if to stand up, but he didn't succeed. Instead, he set the plate on the ground in front of him, then nudged it closer to Alison with his foot.

"I'm still pretty nauseous from my fall." He reached behind his head and felt the bandages there. "I'm not going to eat it, if you want it."

With a grimace, he laid back down and turned his head toward her. Alison was sure he was trying to establish some sort of good will, maybe in an attempt to extract some information from her.

He fumbled on the table next to him for the silverware and separated the knife from the fork. Apparently, his trust of her extended only to forks. He tossed it the short distance to the plate, and it landed next to a piece of rehydrated chicken with a sharp clang. They both looked at the mohawk man, expecting him to wake, but he didn't.

Alison decided a good meal was worth whatever shame she felt in taking it. It wasn't as if eating it obligated her in any way. Zak turned away as she scooted across the floor to the plate near the cot, and she was grateful for this small deference to her dignity.

She ate slowly, not wanting to let him know just how hungry she was, and also wanting to make sure all of it stayed down. For the duration of her captivity, her rations had consisted of not more than water, bread, and a few scraps of some awful potato dish clearly no one had wanted to eat. She'd even made sure to secret away some of the bread in one of her pockets, more to exert some control over her situation than any real fear of starvation. She knew what she was feeling was merely hunger and that real starvation took more than the time she'd been captive.

After she finished every scrap of food, she crawled forward and slid the plate quietly back onto the table beside Zak's bed. His eyes opened when he heard it, and he turned his face toward her. Startled, Alison moved back a bit. She had believed he was asleep.

Their faces were close. She looked into his eyes, and what she saw there was disquieting. A deep sadness came through that she didn't understand. For too long, she tried to read the source of his pain, and she began to register another emotion there. Guilt, or perhaps regret. He seemed to be willing her to understand something.

Just as Alison was about to look away, he opened his mouth to speak.

“I was there,” he said. The words fell out of his mouth quickly and without warning.

Alison felt her entire body seize as if she’d been struck. Her hand, still touching the plate, slipped off and to the dirt floor. A sudden and violent range of emotions surged through her. A whiplash urge to strangle him right there had her tensing her muscles, ready to spring at him.

She didn’t. Instead, she stared at him, scanning his face with her eyes. He’d said only three words, but they were all she needed to know. He was there. He was one of the bastards that had killed her family. Not someone loosely affiliated with the event, but actually there that night. Had he been the one at the gun in the truck? Had he thought about what he was doing when he tore her life to pieces?

Tears began to spill out from his eyes as he lay there, completely vulnerable before her. What right did he have to shed tears? What good would they do now?

CHAPTER 20

John stood in the front yard of what remained of Alison's home. He'd walked around the perimeter of the clearing but hadn't located the bodies of the rest of Alison's family. He had come across the remains of two of his rebel soldiers. One had been expertly shot with a rifle, and the other less so, with what must have been the larger gun mounted to the vehicle they'd escaped in.

All that remained was to check the structure in front of him. The fire had raged so intensely that parts of it had been rendered into little more than charcoal briquettes. Some parts of the house, while blackened and singed, remained standing. Half of the living room and even the front door were intact.

He put one hand on the dark, partially burned door, expecting it to be hot like the wood at the back of the house; but this part, while warm and smoldering in many places, had cooled enough to enter.

John pushed on the door, and it swung open unevenly. Due to some warp in the frame of the home, it gathered speed as it opened and banged heavily into the wall. The collision was enough to dislodge a substantial amount of soot from the holes in the ceiling above. John heard something groan and snap in what was left of the roof.

Everywhere, heat radiated from smoldering areas of exposed timber. The furniture in the living room had been largely reduced to cinders, and what was left of a coffee table lay in ruins. When John walked into the room, the smell of burned things filled his sinuses. He made his way down a twisted hallway that felt like something out of a funhouse. The heat caused him to sweat as if he'd stepped directly into the desert at high noon. As he neared the back of the house, the hallway opened into what used to be a kitchen. Cabinets, a table, and the accumulated things of lives lived in close proximity were now mere sketches of themselves. Along one wall, a pantry door leaned heavily in its frame. He tried to open the door, and it came apart, collapsing in a cloud of boards and ash. What food remained on the nearly bare shelves in the pantry was as damaged as anything else in the house. John turned to leave, then noticed a partially burned rug on the floor. Using his boot, he nudged it aside. Something glinted back at him in the low light.

Set into the wood floor of the pantry was a large metal ring. He leaned down and pulled on it. A trapdoor shifted upward, but only by an inch. It had been locked from the inside, of course. His pulse quickened with the implication. John got both his hands into the narrow space and pulled on the door with all his might. He felt it come up a half inch more than it did the first time.

He took a break and allowed the door to settle back down. Then, gathering everything he had, he heaved at it again. Suddenly, he was flailing back into the kitchen. He landed with a heavy thud on the floor, bringing up another cloud of soot from his surroundings. The house groaned in protest.

John looked back toward the trapdoor. It was open. He got back up slowly, walked over to it, and peered down into cool darkness. The air pushing itself out of the room beneath the floor was smoky. Not a good sign.

John hoisted himself down into the darkness. His boots touched the floor after only five feet or so, and he had to crouch in order to make his way further into the room. As his eyes adjusted, any remaining hope he'd held of finding anyone alive dissipated like the choking smoke that filled the space. He began to feel lightheaded, but the open trapdoor was allowing in enough fresh air that he thought he could continue. In one corner, he found the body of a woman with a soot-dusted bandanna wrapped around her face. He took one of the woman's hands in his, felt where a pulse should be on her wrist, but didn't find one.

John placed what must have been Alison's mother's hand back in her lap and scanned the room again. He still hadn't found Alison's daughter yet, and was beginning to think he'd rather not, when he noticed something. His heart began to beat furiously in his chest, and he wondered if the smoke might still be too thick down here. But no, it was a surge of adrenaline.

At the point where one cold earthen wall met the wood floorboards above his head, he saw a hole. It had probably been dug purely for ventilation purposes when the room was being built. He rushed across the room, his leg protesting the speed he was demanding from it. When he got to the wall, he reached up into the hole above. He felt something there and pushed at it hard.

An avalanche of dirt and embers fell on him, burning parts of his hand in stinging points. To his relief, after the cascade stopped, he saw what he was hoping for.

A bright red bandanna was among the things that had fallen in. Above him, at ground level, a part of the house must have collapsed onto the hole. But the bright red bandanna, unburned, was an indication that someone, someone small, may have escaped this room through the hole before the house had collapsed.

He dashed back to the trapdoor and hoisted himself up into the pantry. The hallway and living room were nothing more than a blur as he sprinted through the house and out the front door. He worked his way over to where the hole was. When he found it, he saw that he'd been right. A half-burned sheet of plywood from the roof covered the hole. He got his fingers underneath it and heaved it away. Underneath was a patch of undamaged grass, protected by the weight of the wood that had been on top of it.

John got down on his knees, looking for any further sign that someone made it through here before the hole had been sealed. He found something. A small footprint in the dark earth near the base of the house. It was perfectly defined. An impression of the sole of one tiny shoe had been perfectly preserved. Eva, despite the odds, must have survived at least the gunfire and the ensuing flames.

John looked in the direction the footprint pointed and saw only the tree line. Looking more closely, however, he managed to discern a path. It was a barely visible thing, but the more he looked, the clearer it became. He was looking at a path that led into the woods.

~

The radio clipped to mohawk man's jacket crackled behind Alison. A voice came through, telling everyone in camp to ready themselves for immediate departure. She slid back across the dirt floor to where she'd been before. She kept her eyes on Zak the whole time, as thoughts of putting all her hate into one vicious lunge at him began to take shape. Instead, she curled into a ball and listened as the sounds of commotion rose outside. The roar of the command mech cycling up its engines boomed though the camp. Something big was happening. Alison tried to remain calm. If there was enough chaos, this might be the moment she'd been waiting for.

Mohawk man opened his eyes and looked at her with disgust. He picked Alison up by her arm the same way he had earlier and pushed her back out into the rain. All around them, people were putting together their campsites in a hurried and haphazard way. The large tarps that had been spread out between each of the broad legs of the command mech had been detached and whipped away into the desert.

Soldiers all around them took down the medical tent and threw the canvas haphazardly into the back of the truck. Zak got off the cot slowly and attempted to help fold it up. He was brushed aside, and someone led him over to near where Alison was standing. She couldn't handle being near him, couldn't stand the thought of him even breathing. It felt like an intentional punishment when they were both led to the truck and loaded up together inside the back. When they were out of the rain, she pushed herself as far back into the cargo space as possible. Zak sat near the tailgate, seeming to understand that he should keep his distance.

"Here, Zak," a voice from calls from outside the truck. A soldier leaned over the tailgate and handed Zak a pistol. "Take this. You're on watch while we get the rest of this crap packed up. Turner and his crew are four hours out and under fire." He left to continue packing up the campsite.

Alison watched as Zak looked at the gun in his hands with disgust. Eventually, he wedged it securely between two plastic water jugs near him.

"You should get out of here," Zak said, catching Alison's eyes. "Now is the only time. I'm so sorry. Please, you have to go."

He scooted to one side and used a latch inside the truck to drop the tailgate down. Outside, the command mech began taking long lumbering steps out of the camp and into the storm. Every time one of the eight legs came down, a tremor could be felt in the truck as if massive stones were being dropped from the sky, one after another with increasing frequency.

"Where do you think I would go?" she asked, hoping the bitterness she felt spanned the gap between them.

"Listen, I don't even know your name," Zak said. "I think they're going to kill you or send you out there with nothing, unless you start giving us information. I don't need a lot, but I need something."

"Why would I..." She stopped, reconsidering her direction. "You killed my entire family, you son of a bitch. What makes you think that threatening me will get you anything? I have nothing left to lose."

Even as she said this, some part of it didn't feel entirely true. She thought back, and the queer feeling that she was missing something returned again. Her mind threatened to bring her back to the farmhouse, but she shook it off. She needed to stay here and figure out her next move. Nothing at the house mattered now. All she had left was vengeance against these people.

"It seems like that now," Zak said with a note of pleading in his voice. "But I swear the pain fades. Eventually, it does."

"Does it?" she asked, watching as his face betrayed the truth. His silence was enough for her. She lowered her head, curling into herself. She noted, before closing her eyes, that the plastic bin containing her possessions was in the back of the truck with them. It was near the tailgate, mid-stack, with a scratch that looked like a seven.

Alison heard the tailgate slam closed, and the truck's engine came to life. Anything not tied down in the back of the truck shifted a few inches as they lurched into motion. The sound of Zak's boots on the metal of the truck bed got her curious, and she opened her eyes. Zak was sitting on the narrow top of the raised tailgate with his torso out the open window. He was out in the storm looking around as mechs and trucks flew across the desert together, pulling up a massive cloud of dust despite the constant driving rain.

The driver of the truck was pushing the limits of a safe speed on this terrain in bad weather, but it provided cover for her as she inched toward where Zak had stowed his pistol. Each time the truck bumped or turned to avoid an obstacle, she shifted forward. She didn't think Zak was paying any attention but covering the sounds of her movement offered her the best chance of success.

She reached the gun, and her pulse quickened as she extended her bound hands to grab it. She wondered if this was a trick. Maybe he would slide back in as soon as she had the weapon and tell her it wasn't loaded. No, there wouldn't have been a point to that. She reached between the two jugs of water and grasped the gun with both hands. The molded plastic grip felt foreign and cold in her palm, but she pulled it out and worked her way back into the spot she'd wedged herself into when they'd boarded the truck. She watched as Zak continued to look around outside. Eventually, he slid back into the truck. Alison was relieved when he didn't glance to where his gun should have been.

Zak rubbed his eyes, dislodging the sand kicked up from all the vehicles around them. Once his eyes were clear enough, he closed them and seemed to rest. Alison could have killed him right then if she wanted to, and she did want to.

She looked down at the gun in her hands. It was a foreign-looking thing. It had very few moving parts, but the basic mechanics of using it appeared to be the same as any other handgun; aim and pull the trigger. It was one of the more common designs of the day. There would be a magazine of bullets, with no gunpowder or other accelerant. Just like the one Jim had shown her, this one relied on electromagnetic energy from a battery to propel bullets instead. From the digital readout on the back of the weapon, there were twelve shots in the magazine and a full charge on the battery.

Her wrists were still bound together, but she could hold the gun well enough that her aim wouldn't be too affected. She watched as Zak slept, and the truck continued on its course. They were headed toward a scout group that was evidently under fire. They had probably been discovered and set upon by members of her own group. Good, she thought. She hoped that Zak and his friends would be too late to help.

CHAPTER 21

She lowered her knees a little and drew the gun up. She levelled it in front of her and filled the sights with Zak's head. It would have been so easy. It was possible the others in the front of the truck might not even hear the shot over all the sounds around them. Alison felt her finger move, the one her father had always told her to keep alongside the firearm unless she wanted to kill what was in front of her. It slipped in front of the trigger and rested there. She stared at the man, one of the sons of bitches who'd blown her family home, her family, out of her life and into the wind like so much useless dust. Why couldn't she pull the trigger? This should have been easy. She tightened her grip and took in a deep breath, meaning to steady her aim. As she did, her mind raced back to another moment with her father she'd nearly forgotten.

She had been with him after returning home from one of their shooting trips. A folded paper target with her best shots from the day had been in her pocket. They'd always driven far out into what was technically restricted government land to practice because her father hadn't wanted anyone to hear the sound of the old-style weapons fire. This time, after they'd returned and brought the guns back inside, her father had taken her aside and looked at her seriously.

"Can you keep a secret, Allie?" he'd asked. "I really important secret?"

She'd been little more than a child, but, of course, she'd said she could. Her mother had smiled as she'd shucked corn cobs at the kitchen table and nodded her approval to Jack.

Her father had then picked up one of the rifles and walked over to the pantry and opened the door. Once inside, he'd knelt down, lifted a well-worn rug she had never paid any attention to, and moved it aside. A shiny metal ring inset into the wood floor was revealed. Alison remembered her complete surprise when he'd lifted the ring and pulled open a trapdoor.

This, he'd explained, was where he kept all the things they needed to survive. Here was where they kept extra food, and where he kept the food he grew for their neighbors. Then he'd asked her to look at him, and she had. His eyes had held hers in a way that made her feel both scared and safe. He was trying to convey something of importance to her.

"No one can know about this, Allie," he'd said. "This is where I want you to go if things ever get scary. If men ever arrive to take us away. This place is safe, and there will always be enough food for you to stay down here until things are quiet."

The truck hit a large bump, and it jolted her out of the memory. She was lucky she hadn't accidentally fired the gun. She quickly drew her knees back up to her chest and concealed it behind them again. The safe room, her mind was on fire with the memory of it. Why hadn't she remembered it until now? It was possible...no, it was even likely that her father had given the same speech to Eva at some point. Even if he hadn't, her mother would have dragged Eva there at the first sign of trouble. Alison felt hope for the first time since the fire, and tears began rolling from her eyes unabated. She had to get back to the house; she had to go home.

The bump of the truck had awoken Zak, and he rubbed sleep from his eyes. He looked out at the sunrise as it bloomed across the sky. The truck crested a large dune, and both Alison and Zak, along with the loose contents in the back of the truck, were momentarily weightless. They came down hard as the truck landed, and Alison quickly developed a plan. It had been long enough, she was sure of it. They must be closing in on where they'd been headed, she thought. The soldier had said they were only four hours out. She closed her eyes and pictured a map of the area. There was a cache of supplies nearby. Not one of hers, but part of the network of waystations she and the other couriers had shared. It would be difficult, but she could make it.

"Shit. Ouch," Zak said, rubbing where he'd hit his back as they'd come down. "You all right?" he asked her.

He looked up, but too late, as Alison pounced on him. Her arms were still bound, but she caught him off guard and hit him hard with the pistol. She reached for the tailgate release, pulled it, and it dropped heavily.

Zak had been using the tailgate for support, and now that it was down, his upper body was dangling from the back of the truck precariously. The blow she'd dealt to his head seemed to have hurt him enough, and she was able to kick at the crates around him in an attempt to dislodge the one she wanted. As the truck crested another hill, she kicked at the plastic bins as the weightless sensation of the truck flying over the edge of the dune returned. She watched with exhilaration as they finally slid out over the tailgate and into the sand. The moment she saw this, she launched herself out of the truck, hoping the slope of the dune would be a safe enough place to land. She held her arms around her head to protect her face and neck as she rolled down the dune.

She felt the sand start to slow her down when, suddenly, one of her legs spun out on its own. It rolled beneath her awkwardly. The shock of pain was enough for her to cry out and attempt to reach down to grasp it. She was still rolling down the dune, and since her hands were away from her face, she saw in one flash that Zak had also fallen from the back of the truck.

After a few more tumbles, she slid to a stop. She looked down and saw that her knee was dislocated. When she grasped it, a surge of pain coursed through her. She realized the gun was no longer in her hands and turned to see it lying in the sand a few yards away. Scrambling as best she could, she reached it. Another spasm of pain radiated from her injured leg, accompanied by the sickening sensation of her knee popping back into place. The pain was still immense, so she wasn't sure if the dislocation was the only injury. She laid back on the dune with the gun in her hand and tried to focus on pushing the pain aside so she could get moving.

Alison felt the tremors of something in the ground before she saw the source. A mech that had been bringing up the rear of the pack was about to pass over them. As the vibrations grew more intense, she brought her arms up to protect her head, half expecting the mech to crush her into the sand. But, to her relief, the mech cleared the dune in much the same way the truck had. It arced through the air; the pilot even used its thrusters briefly to propel it further down the dune. As it passed overhead, she remarked on how graceful it appeared against the roiling sky above her. Vibrant hues of the sunrise were splashed across the underside of the clouds.

After the unit passed, Alison heard Zak yell frantically toward the receding pack of mechs and trucks. She rolled onto her side, facing away from him to conceal the gun from his view. Here was that choice to be made yet again. She could kill him out here with no repercussions. Except that wasn't true. Her leg might be badly injured. Perhaps it wasn't broken, but she might still need help if she was going to be able to reach the supply cache.

Zak's footsteps as he approached were sure and firm. He wasn't injured in the fall from the truck. Alison cursed under her breath and rolled back toward him with the gun held firmly in her hands.

A sound like thunder rushed past them, accompanied by a deep tremor in the ground. She watched as Zak instinctively turned to look for the source. She couldn't help but look herself. The sound had come from the convoy receding in the distance. Near the cluster of vehicles and mechs, a rising plume of black smoke indicated where mortar fire, or something like it, had hit near the forces. A flash of light, momentarily as bright as the rising sun, was replaced by a fireball that quickly faded into another dark cloud of rising smoke. The shots were seemingly random, missing the tight formation of mechs by a few hundred yards each time. The lobs could have been warnings, or perhaps an attempt to keep them from advancing.

Zak was so gripped by the scene unfolding below them that he seemed to forget Alison was behind him. She welcomed his lapse and used the time to work through her options as the eight-legged command mech took up a position in the center of a spreading formation. The cadets weren't completely inept, she thought. They'd scattered at the first sign of trouble, and now they were probably trying to power down to get off the scans of their enemies, her comrades. If she was lucky, these idiots would have run up against the main force in their mad dash across the desert. She squinted through the rain and the distance to see what was firing but couldn't resolve anything at first.

As she continued looking, a concentrated ordnance screamed out of the sky and nearly hit the command mech. Her eyes flitted back to the horizon to see if another volley would come. After a moment, it did, a slightly wider pattern of rounds. She could see roughly where it came from; the next ridge had at least four mechs on top.

Zak seemed to remember she was still behind him with a gun and turned back to her. She leveled the weapon at him in the silence between rumbling explosions. They stared at one another, and she began to fully process her predicament. She was injured, not fatally by any means, but anything that limited her movement out here essentially amounted to a fatal blow. As she turned the problem over in her mind, her concentration was broken once again by the ongoing battle ahead. Zak saw her reaction and reluctantly turned as well.

The soldiers she'd been captured by began making a coordinated advance. Their guns unleashed a wall of fire toward the ridge where her comrades were positioned. She watched as a distant explosion, too big to be a shell, marked where a rebel mech had been hit critically. Other mechs along the ridge became visible now as they continued to fire. Zak's friends circled up around something down below, the scout team they'd come to defend. Alison smiled. The Harbingers had disabled the scout mech and simply waited for the rest of the group to come to the rescue. She wondered if the idea had been John's or someone else's.

Zak turned away from the scene below, his face pale. He must have also read the situation himself. While things appeared to be going well for the rebels along the far ridge, it didn't change her difficult situation on the dune. She wanted to shoot but continued to find more reasons to spare him than her anger could overcome. Eva could be out there, and anything that extended the possibility of reuniting with her overrode all other desires.

She cast the gun out into the rain, a completely symbolic gesture. Her only hope, the only thread she had left to pull, was to see if the guilt this man felt was enough to keep her alive. He retrieved the gun from the sand where it landed and stared down at the scene below. The rebel forces were continuing to bombard his friends mercilessly as they descended the ridge to begin their own advance. She watched in dismay as the trained cadets finally got coordinated. They concentrated their fire on each of the advancing rebel mechs in turn, picking them off one by one. In a few short minutes, the small group of cadets had taken down all of the advancing units, only losing one of their own in the process.

Though this took place nearly a mile away, the sound was overwhelming. Zak continued watching what must feel like a great victory to him when Alison saw the glint of something else coming over the far ridge.

It was as if the horizon had caught fire as an overwhelming force of mechs and gun-mounted trucks opened fire. The sound was like the crescendo of a Unification Day firework show, vibrating in her ribcage. She watched as a round screamed toward the cadet-piloted mechs and connected with the one in the center of the formation, blowing it apart. Zak's friends hastily organized a frenzied retreat to escape the continuous barrage. Soon, most of the cadet mechs were safely fleeing at full speed toward a mountain range to the east.

Alison watched with interest as the command mech stayed behind and made a suicidal charge into the rebel barrage. Whether this action was taken out of rage or a tactical decision to draw their fire, she couldn't tell. The mech scrambled toward the ridge, taking critical hits as it unloaded everything it had on the rebel forces above. Once, she thought the mech was down for good, but it engaged thrusters to compensate for two now completely useless legs. This chaotic, lurching thing managed only a few more steps, and then the command mech lost all power and plowed heavily into the earth. The forces on the ridge began to recede, apparently content with this success. They knew what they were up against now, Alison thought, and that information would allow them to move ahead with more surety. Zak's friends had lost at least three of their units in the battle and were currently scurrying for cover. They weren't a threat.

Zak was still standing out where he had retrieved the pistol, watching the scene come to a close. He sank to his knees, the gun held limply held in his hand.

Alison allowed herself to lay back on the dune again, as smoke drifted by overhead. She laid there for nearly an hour as she waited to see what Zak would decide to do with her. She focused on trying to find a way out of this, but she couldn't. Not without help.

She rolled onto her side, and scanned the slope of the dune for the containers she'd kicked out of the truck. She could see a few of them but wasn't sure which contained her belongings. Zak was still there, facing the battlefield, so she tried to crawl along the sand toward the closest of the containers. The pain in her leg flared, and despite an immense effort to hold it back, a groan escaped her lips.

Zak stirred from the trance he'd been in and turned his eyes to meet hers across the sand. The sorrow and fury she saw in his face was terrifying. She held her leg as he approached her slowly. Rain slid down the smooth metal of the pistol in his hand and dripped off, mirroring the tears that began to spill from his eyes. She watched his grip tighten on the weapon.

"Fuck!" he screamed. "Why? I don't know—"

His voice broke off. Zak brought his hands up, and for a heart-stopping moment, she believed he was about to shoot her. Instead, he beat at the side of his head in a senseless rage. The barrel of the gun itself struck his head, drawing blood that flowed out in a red line down the side of his face. His arms dropped to his sides and he looked down at Alison. Breathing heavily, he seemed to focus his rage. She let her own fury show through and didn't look away as Zak stared into her eyes.

They looked at one another for a moment that seemed to stretch, independent of time. In his eyes, she saw a lifetime of hatred warring with his raw and recent guilt. In hers, she hoped he would see that she'd changed. Her own fury and fear would be apparent, but something new had taken a place inside her; she needed to survive.

"I needed to see if she's still there," Alison whispered, hating how helpless she felt. "Even if there's nothing left. I have to go back. I have to go back."

He looked up at the sky, his chin trembling, and he walked past her toward the crates higher up the dune. She took a sudden deep breath and looked down at her knee, which had begun to swell wildly. The pain there was a constant searing fire from within, and it took most of her concentration not to cry out. She watched as Zak sorted through the supplies in the bins. When he returned to her, he dropped a small packet of pills in the sand near her face.

"Take these," he said coldly. "I'm leaving in an hour, with or without you."

She looked at the packet in front of her suspiciously. He walked back to the crates and continued removing the contents, laying them out in the sand. She was able to concentrate long enough to read the words on the side of the paper packet. They were painkillers. Not strong ones, but they were painkillers at least. She tore the packet open and took one of the two pills inside, wondering as she did why he had bothered giving them to her at all.

Zak returned and, without a word, withdrew a knife from his belt. He cut her wrist restraints with a swift jerk of the blade. Instantly, her fingers began to tingle as normal blood flow returned.

He straightened her leg out on the sand. She felt a searing grinding in her knee, and she was unable to suppress a moan. He didn't look at her eyes as he worked, cutting her pant leg from the ankle all the way past her knee. She examined her injured leg and was relieved to see that no bone had pierced the skin. Zak ran his fingers along her leg, pressing in places occasionally, checking for breaks. She was relieved when he finished and none of his prods had produced pain that would indicate one. But, when he lifted her leg and worked the swollen knee joint, the pain bloomed anew.

Satisfied with his examination, he removed a loose plastic sleeve from a backpack he'd filled with supplies. He worked her leg through one end of the sleeve and slid it up until it was centered on her knee.

"This is going to…" He paused. "Well, you'll see."

Without warning, he pressed a button on the sleeve. It inflated immediately, applying an immobilizing pressure to the injured knee. This time, Alison cried out. She quickly cut the sound off, then took the second pill she had been saving for later.

"From what I can see, nothing is broken," Zak said. "You might have ligament tears or something, but I'm not a doctor. This should be enough to let you move. If we're going to make it down, we have to move now. I'll do what I can to keep you alive. But, if you don't do what I say, I'll leave you here."

"Why?" she asked, still reeling from the pain of the brace setting. "Why are you doing this?"

"I don't know," he said.

"I need to get back." She allowed the tears to flow now. Her future, and any chance of ever seeing Eva again, now depended on Zak. She wasn't used to depending on someone else, but she had to try. "I need to see if she's alive. I have to go back. Please."

"They're gone," Zak said, his voice flat and numb. "I saw it all. There was no one left."

"You don't know that." Alison felt her voice strain, almost breaking at the edges of each word. She needed him to understand. "Someone might have lived. Please, I need to know."

For a long time, Zak said nothing. Alison looked up at him, trying to read what he might be thinking. He looked away from her and stood facing the wreckage of the mechs below. After a few moments, Zak held out one hand and helped her into a standing position.

It was all she could do not to simply fall back down. She tried to take a step forward, and her hand found a place on Zak's shoulder. He flinched but allowed her to stabilize herself. After another step, her uninjured knee buckled. Zak reached out to catch her. He lifted her arm around his neck and placed one of his arms around her waist. She thought about pushing him away, but the image of Eva, possibly alone in the darkness beneath the house, flashed in her mind and she accepted the help. As they walked, Alison looked back at the containers and spotted the one containing her pack. If she was able, she would have to retrieve it. The gun, a useful tool, was also all she had left of her father.

Together, they walked slowly down the dune toward the battlefield. Eventually, the dune leveled out into more manageable terrain and Alison was able to support more of her own weight. Ahead of them, the massive wreckage of the command mech rested in the sand. A breeze carried smoke off as fires continued to burn inside it. They walked together, her stiff leg dragging a line in the sand. As they worked around a large piece of twisted and blackened metal, Alison saw the figure of a man sitting in front of a small campfire. The man put his hand on his sidearm and turned around to look at them as they emerged from behind the smoking vehicle.

Alison saw recognition dawn on the man's face. This was Mark, the one who she'd attacked in the city and been captured by. This was the man who had been leading a group of cadets on a nearly certain suicide scramble across the desert. He stood and drew his gun, the shattered mech still burning behind him. As fury and grief washed across his face in equal measure, he raised his weapon and aimed it at both of them.

"Why is she here?" Mark asked. "Zak, why the fuck is she here?"

Alison was momentarily terrified that Zak might throw her to the dirt between them. She even felt his grip on her loosen slightly. She refused to tighten hers, and the pain in her leg flared. If Zak decided to throw her at Mark's feet, she wouldn't plead for her life. They'd taken almost everything from her, but she would not give them that.

"I don't know," was all Zak said. "I don't know, Mark."

"Brooke is dead."

Mark kept his gun trained on them. Alison tried to search his eyes to discern what he would do. Moments passed, and then she felt Zak's grip on her shoulder tighten. The pain in her leg lessened a bit as she was able to take some of the weight off it again.

"She lost everything, Mark. Everything," Zak said. "If there is even a chance that someone is left alive back at that house, I need to go. Just let us go. I have to make it right."

"Make it right." Mark laughed. The empty sound sent chills through her. "Sure, go off and play hero."

"That's not—" Zak started to say.

"Go now," Mark said quietly. "Go, before I kill both of you."

"I'm so sorry," Zak said, and he began to back away, pulling Alison with him.

Mark screamed. It was a wordless, unnatural sound that echoed through the field of broken machines as they fled.

~

John ran across the open field, away from the smoldering house. When he reached the tree line, he could see why he had missed this path during his initial search. It was too small for an adult to pass through easily. It was almost a tunnel in the vegetation, in fact. He got on his hands and knees and crawled through the opening, feeling a little silly as he did. The path opened up gradually, and he could see that it must have been broken over the years mostly by wildlife use. Eventually, he was walking along a more open pathway through the trees.

As he walked, he heard the bugle of a bull elk calling to its harem. Large game was rare these days, but small pockets of wilderness did support it occasionally. He stopped out of instinct and listened to see where the call had come from. In more abundant times, he had hunted elk and other kinds of game in the west. He'd learned the skill from his father, and his father had learned from his, in a chain John remembered was broken now.

In the silence, he reached into his coat pocket and removed the photograph of his family. He ran his fingers across the faces of his wife and daughter. In the dappled sunlight filtering through the branches above, he could almost imagine he was out here teaching his daughter to hunt. His hand trembled. He hadn't had a drink in days, and it was beginning to work on him. Would they have understood the man he had become? He asked this question of himself again, and for the first time he could remember, the answer might have been yes. John folded the photograph and returned it to his coat pocket.

The path wound idly through the trees, diverging into two at points but always coming back together in the same direction. Ahead, he saw another barely visible path leading off in another direction. This one was less defined, almost completely obscured, in fact. He could tell someone had been through recently only by small broken branches near the ground and an area of turned earth near the fork in the trail. As he walked down this new path, he looked ahead and saw something foreign to the environment. In the shadows beneath the trees was an unnatural gathering of tree limbs that looked like a small dwelling.

He approached it quietly, taking in the details of the structure. It had been constructed well, he thought. The work looked like something a military survival manual would have described, and this set him on edge. He circled it, looking for an entrance. When he spotted it, his anxiety subsided. The door was small and made of an old piece of plywood. Nailed to the front was a wooden sign, aged by the elements but still readable.

"Allie's Hideout," it read. And below, in larger letters, "Keep Out!"

John walked toward the door and reached for the hole that may have once held a knob of some kind. The door opened with a soft creak as the ropes securing it to the building stretched and groaned quietly. Light spilled into the open space from the door, and in this light, he saw the unmistakable shape of a small girl curled up against one wall. His heart raced as if he was pushing his way into an enemy foxhole. Instead, sleeping there, in a clubhouse built by Alison, was Eva. She couldn't be more than five or six years old, and John doubted if she had the skills to survive out here for long.

He stepped back from the door and sat down on a fallen tree in front of the hut. He had watched countless families be torn apart during his time with police and government forces. He'd been present, and even responsible, for many of them. Zak's family had simply been the one that affected him the most, the one he'd been forced to deal with at close range. The path he'd taken here was littered from the start with the broken lives of others. He'd tried to right the scales and it had led him here, to yet another family torn apart by the grand ideals of men in darkened rooms.

No, he thought. His path hadn't destroyed this one entirely. Not yet. Alison was still out there somewhere, she had to be. Until now, his actions had built a pattern of loss that had felt inescapable, but he could end it here. He could bring this girl back to the only family she had left. If the world was burning, they deserved to be with each other as it did. John gathered wood to build a fire and waited for Eva to wake up.

EPILOGUE

Cheers erupted on the command deck around Katherine. She let go of the command mech's main controls and her arms went limp at her sides. It was done. They'd unleashed a barrage of intense ordnance down onto the small core of mechs that had been following them since they'd left Taycher in flames. She had lost all six units she'd had trailing their main group. Katherine stood up from her chair, suddenly feeling more exhausted than she could ever remember feeling before. The jovial atmosphere subsided as she strode through the room. She wanted to celebrate with them, but the cost of the battle weighed on her in places she hadn't expected. She needed to be alone.

"Carry on," She worked up a smile and aimed it around the room in a way she hoped was convincing. "I'm just tired. Get our core moving to the coordinates I've marked. We'll stop there and reassess our situation. You all did well, but we lost people today."

She descended the steps at the back of the command deck and hadn't gotten to the bottom of the first flight before celebrations resumed above. This was the first victory many of her crew would have seen. She would let them revel in it for a while.

Later, when they were more seasoned, they might look back and understand why she'd reacted as she had.

She made it down to the crew deck and stopped, unsure of where to go next. There was a general mess hall further inside the guts of the mech, but she didn't want to go there. As she stood in the semidarkness, lit only by overhead strips and occasional wall mounted dome lights, she heard footsteps on the stairs behind her. Before she was able to duck into one of the bunk rooms or find another suitably hidden crevice in the mech, someone was beside her.

"Kids don't know what a victory really is yet, do they?" To her relief, it was Jim who'd followed her down. "Come with me."

He walked past her and continued down the next flight of stairs, headed to the cargo deck below the crew deck. She followed him down and he directed her to one of the more disorganized loading bays. He opened a small door almost completely obscured by supply crates and slipped inside. The room was a small forgotten office with a desk and a dusty chair. Nothing about the space would have been particularly interesting, except for the fact that it was the first time she'd felt any semblance of privacy for days. Since they'd fled across the desert with their small fleet of metal war machines, she had been under constant scrutiny. She sank into the old chair in front of the desk.

Jim opened a supply crate and took out a glass bottle of amber liquid. "We lost some good people down there today." He opened the bottle, took a swig and put it down on the desk in front of Katherine. The invitation to drink was there, but not forced.

"I don't even think I know any of their names." She picked up the bottle and swirled it, letting some of the aroma escape. It was a whiskey of some kind, and not bad from the smell of it. She took a drink. "I sent them out there and now they're just gone. I've lost people before, but it never gets easy."

"It shouldn't," Jim said, holding his hand out for the bottle. "The minute losing a soldier becomes easy for you is the minute I stop trusting you. I don't see that happening any time soon."

"Is that why you're here?" Katherine asked. "You always struck me as a military type."

Jim took a small swig and looked at Katherine in a tired way. "I don't usually like to talk about it. I haven't been that person for a long time, but yeah. I spent a good part of my youth fighting for the United Entities on the ground."

"Saw too many of your buddies fed into the machine?" Katherine asked.

When Jim didn't immediately answer, she looked over at him. His eyes were closed, and his face was pinched like he was fighting off tears. She realized she'd asked the wrong question.

"I fed too many of my buddies to the machine," he corrected her. "I was a lieutenant, and I routinely sent people out that I knew I'd never see again. All in service to the fucking idea of Stability Over Self."

"I'm sorry," she said. "I know how you feel."

"I'm sure you do. I know what you're feeling well enough to know that you're not just mourning the loss of our own people. Those were cadets from the Academy back there, weren't they?"

Katherine momentarily pushed back on what he was saying, but quickly gave in to it. He was right. "Yes, those were cadet mechs down there. I didn't even think about the possibility that they might take the training units and come after us. They were just doing what I helped train them to do."

"The entire time, I was wondering if I knew any of them." Jim leaned his head back against the metal bulkhead and ran his hand through his short hair. "They used to come out for the parties I'd throw in the desert to let off steam. I even liked some of them."

"What's done is done," she said. She needed to find a way to turn this around. She couldn't allow emotions to change how she felt about her choices. "We can't focus in close like this or we'll never get the job done right. I knew what I was signing up for, probably more than most. John wrote in one of his essays once that in order to destroy a sufficiently complex structure, you must only focus on the load-bearing pillars. The pieces that make up those pillars are irrelevant. If we spend too much time deciding which pieces deserve to be severed or saved, the enemy will have adapted its architecture."

"I wish John was here to say that himself," Jim said. "Dude has a real way of making sense of all of this."

"Yeah, and he deserted us," Katherine smiled wryly. "What does that say about us?"

"It doesn't say anything about us, Katherine." Jim was suddenly serious. "It says a lot about him, but nothing about us."

Katherine heard cheering coming from somewhere new in the mech. Word must have gotten down to the lower decks about the victory. She felt sick.

"Listen, you get some rest down here." Jim put the stopper back into the whiskey bottle but left it on the desk. He rested a hand on her shoulder. Normally she'd have shrugged off another person's attempt to comfort her, but it felt nice to have someone who seemed to understand her. "I'll stay on the command deck and make sure we keep a straight heading. Just come rescue me from the celebrations in a couple of hours, alright?"

She nodded. Some rest would be nice. They had been on edge for so long, not knowing who had been following them. That pressure was gone now, but in its place, she felt a deep tiredness. Their current state of security had come at a great cost, and their path forward was clear. They still had their precious cargo to deliver. Soon, they would reach the Hollows.

ACKNOWLEDGEMENTS

Thank you to everyone who reassured me that this was a story worth telling. In dimly lit bars, on phone calls from across the country, late at night when you could have been sleeping, trapped in a car with me as we drove across the desert, and in various other places over the years, your contributions to this story are significant. I tend to overstate how much I talk about my writing. I'll often joke about how everyone in my life has put up with my rambling about this series for years. In truth, the list of people I've had deep conversations about this story with is quite small. So, if you're wondering if I'm talking about you, I am. I'm a naturally introverted person when it comes to my writing, and your support made this possible.

Another incredibly important facet of my creative process has been those unexpected moments when people have shown support. This project lives, lived, inside of me for so long that I often thought of it solely as a personal project. Whenever I'd mention it offhand in a conversation, or someone else would bring it up in the presence of other people, I've been astonished to receive overwhelming and universal support. People genuinely root for others to succeed, and when I'm all wrapped up in my own thoughts it's wonderful to be reminded of that fact.

I wrote acknowledgements to some specific people in book one, and I wanted to thank those people again. Thank you so much for all of your help. I used to think of writing this series as a solitary act, completely removed from outside influence. That sounds absurd now, standing on the other side of this process. This story is nothing without people.

Daniel James Clark was born on a U.S. Navy base in Naples, Italy, and after a number of brief stops across the world early in life, settled in Henderson, Nevada, a suburb of Las Vegas. He began writing early but didn't begin seeking publication until 2019. His first short story, *A Sky Made Black*, was published in the Bell Press anthology *Futures* in November of 2021 and received a nomination for a Pushcart Prize. His first major publication is the *From Rust* trilogy of military science fiction mech novels from Vulpine Press. When not writing, he divides his time between professional photojournalism, nonprofit website management and design, and homemaking for his wife and two children.

Find him on Twitter @DClarkWords

www.ingramcontent.com/pod-product-compliance
Lightning Source LLC
LaVergne TN
LVHW041115080826
845145LV00007B/1819

* 9 7 8 1 8 3 9 1 9 5 7 7 8 *